W9-BVQ-408

PRAISE FOR *ANIMALS*

"A savage, heartbreaking, and breathtakingly beautiful work that is as thrilling as it is important. Deeply researched and masterfully crafted...This is a book that will sweep you up and hold you within its pages until it is done with you."
     PETER HOULAHAN, author of *Norco '80*

"Screenwriter Staples...makes the tragedy of animal trafficking vivid in his impressive debut...Staples skillfully weaves multiple plot strands, including CIA efforts to combat terrorism, with well-developed characters. His extensive research pays off in this moving, multifaceted tale."
     PUBLISHERS WEEKLY (starred review)

"Screenwriter Staples's first novel provides a kaleidoscopic view of the horrors of African poaching...From the beginning...he excels in creating scene after scene of uncompromising cruelty and sadness. Above all, Staples brings out the beasts in his human cast."
     KIRKUS REVIEWS

ANIMALS

ANIMALS

WILL STAPLES

**BLACK
STONE**
PUBLISHING

Printed in the United States of America

First edition: 2021
ISBN 978-1-09-406588-5
Fiction / Thrillers / General

1 3 5 7 9 10 8 6 4 2

CIP data for this book is available
from the Library of Congress

Blackstone Publishing
31 Mistletoe Rd.
Ashland, OR 97520

www.BlackstonePublishing.com

This is a story about animals,
some of which happen to be human.

PREFACE

Although wildlife trafficking is one of the largest illicit markets in the world (alongside narcotics, arms dealing, and human trafficking), very few law enforcement dollars are dedicated to investigating wildlife crimes. Thus, very little is actually known about how animals are trafficked. And most of the news stories about wildlife crimes center on poaching in sub-Saharan Africa or on the ivory markets of East Asia, with virtually no attention given to the dark underworld of corruption and organized crime that is driving the end of wildlife as we know it. It would be like knowing nothing about the drug war except that cocaine is produced in the jungles of South America and consumed in nightclubs in Los Angeles.

While the story you are about to read is fictional, the characters, locations, and story points are almost entirely rooted in fact. They are the products of hundreds of conversations with everyone from Dr. Jane Goodall to rangers in Africa, CIA officers, epidemiologists, and detectives in Hong Kong.

To experience the issue firsthand, I journeyed to seven countries on three continents. During the Southeast Asia section of the trip, where I was aided by Swiss environmentalist Karl Ammann, I purchased rhino horn and tiger parts in the black markets of Myanmar, was offered sautéed tiger meat (later confirmed by DNA tests) in a casino in Laos, infiltrated tiger and bear bile farms, went undercover as a buyer in the largest illegal rhino carving operation in Hanoi, visited doctors prescribing tiger and rhino as a cure for cancer, and was detained by a warlord's security force in Special Region 4 of Myanmar for documenting wealthy tourists sneaking over the border to eat endangered animals.

I then traveled to Hong Kong and Macau, where I met with officers from the Organized Crime and Triad Bureau and the Hong Kong Narcotics Bureau to learn how the cartels traffic animals and how they use casinos to launder the money from those transactions.

The final leg of the trip took me to South Africa and Mozambique, where I spent a week living out of a pickup truck with Damien Mander, founder of the International Anti-Poaching Foundation, after whom my son is named. Damien introduced me to rangers in Kruger Park and took me to a court trial for a corrupt ranger who was colluding with poachers. We joined rangers as they intercepted a group of three teenage poachers with a massive suppressed rifle and an ax, who were searching for a rhino. We then headed to private hunting reserves catering to Russian and American billionaires, and finally, deep into the poaching towns of Mozambique, where kingpins operate with impunity.

Though I admittedly knew little about the world of animal

trafficking when I began this project, I ended up having what amounted to a front-row seat for the Sixth Extinction. My goal with this novel is to expose as many people as possible to this issue. To that end, all my income from this book will be donated to nonprofit organizations dedicated to protecting wildlife.

Will Staples

Los Angeles, 2021

CHAPTER 1
COBUS

KRUGER NATIONAL PARK, SOUTH AFRICA

Cobus Venter knelt before the six-foot-long mound of freshly turned dirt. In his hand was a flower. The thirty-five-year-old South African planted the stem, gingerly forming a small pile of soil to support it. The sun had burned his tattooed arms the color of the earth and left his face as cracked as the mud around a drying water hole. Though Cobus hadn't touched a barbell in years, he still carried the musculature of a silverback under his olive-drab uniform.

The priest had just finished saying some words, but Cobus heard only the bleak narrative running circles in his mind, digging a deeper and deeper rut with each revolution. He had thought he left the war, but war had followed him. He didn't regret the things he had done—he could justify his every action—but he had nonetheless been infected by a darkness. He wondered whether he was the host who had brought the disease here and infected the land and people around him. Soon, they would all be dead, man and beast alike.

Other rangers stepped forward to lay their flowers on the grave, hoping this small act of beauty might somehow offset the ugliness of their friend's murder.

———

Kruger was a wilderness of souls where one could easily get lost. It was a place of absolute truth and a place of absolute lies. A place of godliness and godlessness.

Every year nearly two million tourists came to Kruger to experience the "Africa" they had watched in nature documentaries and explored in the glossy pages of *National Geographic* magazines. If Walt Disney had created Africa-Land, it would be Kruger. Its golden plains were dotted with mushroom-shaped acacia trees and boulder piles where magnificent predators lazed between meals and where elephants and rhinos lumbered about in plain view with their offspring in tow. Many visitors to Kruger left with a false sense that the Edenic landscape was Africa's rule, not the exception. But beyond the electrified gates wreathed with concertina wire was a different Africa—an undefended land where man's insatiable appetites had stripped away everything that could be eaten or burned, reducing the land to red dust. And this ever-growing void was metastasizing throughout sub-Saharan Africa, Asia, and Latin America.

No, Kruger was not the norm, but rather a cross between an ark and a fortress. It was one of the few outposts where nature was waging its final stand. It was, as soldiers like Cobus knew all too well, the front line in a war where the stakes were not just life and death, but the death of life itself. And the fortress walls were now being breached daily by marauders looking to cash in on the end of the wild.

Basani stood off to one side of the rangers, quivering as she wept. She had grown up in Malelane, just outside the park. She met Oupa when they were both training to be field rangers, and they had fallen in love while fighting together on the front lines of the poaching wars. Oupa and Basani made plans that at the end of the dry season, she would put down her rifle and they would try to start a family. Now those dreams were shattered.

Cobus wrapped his heavy arms around her shoulders. Basani was a physically strong woman, able to hold a five-kilo rifle in the low ready position for hours on end. But today she felt frail, her bones shifting loosely in his embrace.

"Oupa was family to all of us," he said to her. Basani sank into his arms, unable to bear her own weight. She heaved with grief, wetting his uniform with her tears.

Cobus was surprised, and concerned, at how quickly Basani returned to her work as a field ranger. He suggested she take more time to grieve, but Basani told him she didn't want to be alone. Although Cobus was one of Kruger's twenty-two section rangers, which meant he was technically her boss, that hierarchical construct had not survived the intimate realities of living and fighting side by side on the front lines in the bush. Cobus and Lawrence and the other rangers at Kruger were her family—her only family now.

In the weeks after Oupa's death, Cobus and Basani spent several late nights at the dive bars in White River, knocking back Carling Black Labels as she tried to make sense of her pain. Cobus could see she had been ground down by the futility of the poaching war. It affected every ranger in the park. No matter what they did to reinforce the border—fences, drones, motion-sensor cameras, crime scene DNA analysis—nothing seemed to stem the tide of death. Every year, more rangers and animals were being gunned down by shoot-and-scoot poachers who came from Mozambique to try their luck in the "Big Smoke," as Kruger had come to be known. Making matters worse, Cobus and several of his colleagues were beginning to suspect that the poachers had moles inside the park, who would tip them off to the locations. How else could the marauders locate, in a matter of hours, animals that even trained park guides might not find for days at a time?

———

Cobus felt the grass sweeping against his bare legs as he flowed silently through the savanna. He was one of a few Afrikaners who wore shorts instead of the standard-issue pants. It was an old Rhodesian bush warfare trick that let you *feel* the environment. To stay alive in the bush, you needed all your senses switched on.

The coffee was helping, but he was still hungover. The night before, he and Basani had shut down the local watering hole. As one drink led to two, then eight, he told her how he had signed up for the South African National Defense Force because he was looking for adventure, and then became a security contractor in Iraq because he wanted to do some good with his training. But Iraq was the jungle, and there is no good and evil in the jungle—or so he had willed himself to believe in order to justify the things he had seen and done there. In Fallujah, killing was a way of life. It was natural selection on a geopolitical scale. Though Cobus believed those statements to be true, the real truth was that over there, you could either emotionally process your experiences or be a good soldier, but you couldn't do both. And it wasn't until he returned to South Africa that the walls he had built to protect himself began to crumble.

"I feel like the war followed me here," he told her. He feared that in some way, he had brought death to Kruger and it had found Oupa.

"Perhaps it is not war that is following you," she said, "but the other way around."

Her words caught Cobus off guard. He took a pull of his beer to buy a moment to think. "Maybe," she continued, "you don't think you deserve peace."

"I just want to do some good," he countered. "And the only skill I've got is doing evil."

"You are a good man, Cobus." Now it was Basani willing him to have hope. "You deserve peace. And love."

Basani placed her hand on top of Cobus's and stroked it gently. Cobus froze, uncertain how to react to the tender gesture.

As the bartender informed them it was last call, Basani had given him a look—*the* look. Her eyes lingered as she took him by the hand and led him to the door. Cobus's heart pounded against his rib cage as they drove in silence down the inky black back roads.

He pulled to a stop at her home. She got out and stood beside the open door for a moment to see if he would be joining her. Cobus wanted desperately to go with her and share her bed, but he would wait. If it happened tonight on a drunken impulse, the morning would only bring her more turmoil. He would wait until her wounds healed, and then, perhaps, he might have the courage to act on his feelings for this unbreakable woman who saw hope for him—that is, if she would still have a cursed, violent man like him after the alcohol left her system.

———

Basani and Lawrence trailed Cobus as they patrolled the savanna with their black FN FAL assault rifles slung over their shoulders. The poachers were armed with weapons suited to hunting animals, and the rangers were armed with weapons for hunting poachers.

Unlike Basani and the other field rangers, Lawrence was raised on the Mozambique side of the border. Though the border town he grew up in was only a few kilometers away, he hadn't been home in five years—ever since the local poaching syndicate put a bounty on his head. It was as much retribution for betraying his tribe as a deterrent for any others who might choose the wrong side in the poaching war.

The thin green line of rangers stalked through the bush. The Lower Sabie region of the park was home to all the Big Five, and Cobus and his team had already spotted cape buffalo, elephants, lions, and a leopard this morning. Though their mission was merely to patrol, seeing all five in one day was always a little morale victory for the rangers. Only the rhino remained on the list to find, though the hulking gray beasts had grown harder to locate after being hunted to the brink.

Basani stepped ahead of Cobus as they approached a popular grazing area for rhinos and elephants. One of the greatest threats to the rangers was the very animals they were sworn to protect. Hundreds of thousands of years of hunting and evolution had trained the animals to fear men and protect themselves from the deadly apes by any means. But women had historically not been involved in the hunts. Thus, while nearly every male ranger had a repertoire of stories about being charged by giant deadly creatures, there were almost no instances of female rangers being attacked. Cobus therefore had Basani lead their patrols whenever they approached areas more densely populated with big animals, so that neither he nor Lawrence would end up as a red stain in an elephant's track.

As they moved east through the bush, Basani raised her fist. Cobus and Lawrence halted, scanning the grass for threats.

Basani pointed to a patch of ground where there were several cigarette butts and a Twizza soda bottle. "Poachers camped here."

Cobus evaluated the concentration of insects that had gathered at the plastic bottle. Though he had studied the art of reading spoor during his time at Kruger, he was nowhere nearly as skilled as Basani and Lawrence. "This is from last night?" he guessed.

Lawrence nodded as he studied the debris.

"The cigarettes are from this morning," Basani added with a note of concern.

Cobus instinctively toggled the selector on his assault rifle from "safe" to "fire," then pressed past Basani to lead the patrol. Basani and Lawrence heard the click of his selector, which sent a rush of adrenaline through their bodies as they mentally prepared for the possibility of a firefight. Though Basani and Lawrence were proficient with small arms and had ample training, they didn't have Cobus's combat experience and lacked his instincts when it came to hunting men. Cobus was a killer by nature and trade, and they were especially thankful to have him on their side in moments like this.

As Cobus advanced, he heard a heavy exhalation from the brush nearby. He paused and glanced out the corner of his eye to see a leopard on a head-high rock five meters away. It crouched as it watched Cobus. The cat issued a low, guttural snarl, eyes pinned to its human prey.

Cobus slowly shouldered his rifle, cautious not to make any sudden moves that might trigger the leopard's predatory instinct. Just last month, a leopard this size had mauled a ranger in a nearby section of the park. Cobus continued forward, rolling from heel to toe with each step to minimize his sound signature as he tried put distance between himself and the predator. Cobus had never shot anything with more than two legs, but he was willing to drop the hammer on one of the animals in his care if his life hung in the balance. He was far too young, with a lifetime of conservation work in front of him, to go out as a big cat's afternoon meal.

Behind Cobus, Basani also had her rifle trained on the regal creature, ready to end its life if it decided to attack Cobus.

Lawrence pulled rear security as they moved past, keeping his rifle sights glued to the leopard. But just when it seemed ready to let them pass without incident, it rose and began to follow. Lawrence tried to back away, but the leopard kept pace with him.

Cobus watched over his shoulder. His friend had sacrificed much for the animals at Kruger: his home, his family, his safety. And he worried that Lawrence might not put his own safety first if it came down to a kill-or-be-killed situation.

Lawrence stopped, then raised both arms in the air, making himself as big as possible. It was what the rangers told the tourists to do to discourage wild cats if they should encounter one, but by taking his weapon off the target, Lawrence was also betting his own life on a tactic that had a mixed track record. The survival protocol also called for people to shout and make as much noise as possible, but whoever had left the cigarette butts in the dirt was somewhere nearby. Giving up their position by shouting could get his whole team killed by poachers.

Lawrence stood, silently waving his arms like an excited airport groundcrew member as the leopard watched him. Snarling, it recoiled onto its hind legs, then turned its back and slunk off into the bush.

Cobus nodded to Lawrence, impressed by his deft handling of the situation.

———

The temperature rose as the rangers made their way toward the Mozambique border. It was the peak of the dry season in Mozambique, which meant it was also peak poaching season. When it rained in Mozambique, much of the population took to farming, but when the rains dried up, the Mozambicans were compelled to find other sources of income. Meanwhile, the lack of water in Kruger forced the larger animals to gather around the few remaining water holes in much greater density, making them easier to locate and kill. All the rangers were aware of this grim fact and carried extra magazines for their rifles.

Cobus knew the terrain well. Soon, he and his team would reach the tall chain link fence at the park's edge. And as they had done dozens of times before, they would trace the fence for several kilometers, checking to make sure no new holes had been cut in it. If there were, they would radio it in and search for the intruders, but the intruders would be long gone. The older-model walkie-talkies the rangers used weren't encrypted, and Cobus suspected that the poachers eavesdropped on their channels, just as he had listened in on ISIS communications in Iraq.

Several hundred meters from the fence, the rangers heard a loud, shrill bleating that sounded like a steam engine overheating.

Cobus shouldered his rifle and took off with Basani and Lawrence, crouch-running silently through the chest-high grass. Though Cobus couldn't place the source of the bleating, it sounded like an animal crying out for help. His muscles tightened in anticipation of a gunfight with the poachers whose spoor they were following.

Cobus and his team arrived just in time to see the small gray body drop to the earth with a thud. He immediately slung his rifle back down at his side. The rangers lowered to one knee, disappearing into the camouflage of the nearby brush. They watched in silent awe as the body lay wet and motionless. Then the glistening mass stirred.

Its mother, a two-ton white rhino, turned to her newborn calf and began cleaning him. Cobus stared in wide-eyed reverence as she used her giant horn to lever her son to his feet for the first time. The baby rhino faltered, then regained his footing. He wobbled, struggling to keep his balance as he stood beneath his mother's snout.

Cobus heard a sniffle and turned to see tears streaming down Basani's cheeks. He put his arm around her shoulder, drawing her body close.

"We'll name it Oupa," he told her, hoping that having this new baby boy to carry on her husband's legacy might bring her some consolation.

Basani turned to Cobus, her eyes red and voice bitter. "Someday, they will kill him too."

Cobus felt the darkness infecting her. He couldn't let that happen. If her light was extinguished, he feared he would have no path out of the darkness.

"Not this one," he said, willing her to believe it. "We will protect him."

Basani looked at the baby. She knew that a rhino that close to the border of Mozambique had a short life expectancy, and if it wandered over the border, its life would be measured in hours.

CHAPTER 2
KNIGHT

By the time Randall Knight made it to gate 5 at the racetrack, most of the crowd had found their way to the stands. Santa Anita didn't have the scope and pageantry of Churchill Downs, but the Colonial Revival features and the explosions of flowers reminded him of the track where he spent his childhood in upstate New York. And just like Saratoga, for several days a year Santa Anita became the center of the racing universe. A crackling electricity permeated the air as tens of thousands bet their hopes and dollars on animals they knew only by their statistics and odds.

Knight's fondest memories from his youth were his days off from school, when he got to work with his father, a trainer at the stables. It was his only time with the old man when he wasn't marinating himself in Wild Turkey. His father spent most of the year ankle-deep in mud and manure as he cared for the possessions of the international elites who stabled their horses in Saratoga. But on race days, little Randy

Knight and his father got to be the ultimate insiders in a rich man's game. His annual brush with wealth had given him a glimpse into a world he desperately longed to be a part of. And now he was.

Knight moved toward the lower-level betting booth, looking slightly out of place in his blue Armani suit among the hoi polloi double-fisting Budweisers in their jeans and T-shirts.

Withdrawing $10,000 in cash from a bank envelope, he approached the betting window. As he placed all the money on a single horse, Knight recalled his favorite teaching from Sun Tzu: *All battles are won before either side sets foot on the field.*

Moments later, Knight entered a clubhouse suite, where the blue bloods gobbled up shrimp cocktail and clinked champagne flutes in their garish pastel attire and costumey hats. He glanced up at the television to see the thoroughbreds approaching the starting gates. He had been down with the horses in that moment many times in his youth. Even now he could feel their huffing and pulsing, and he could picture their veiny masses of muscle bunching and releasing in anticipation.

Harlen Richards approached, giddy with excitement. His horse, Gladiator, had already won the Kentucky Derby and was the odds-on favorite to take home the $5 million prize at the Breeders Cup today.

Richards shouted to a server, "Get this man a drink!" Then he paused, second-guessing Knight's inscrutable expression. "Or are you on the clock?"

Knight ordered a mint julep. "Old Forester," he instructed the waiter. "Easy on the sugar."

With so much riding on the race, Richards was desperate to know whether the expert in front of him had personally placed a bet. Knight replied that he had put ten grand on a single horse. "I like to bet on a sure thing," he added, forcing a smile.

Assuming that Knight was talking about Gladiator, Richards slapped him on the shoulder. "Good man!"

As Richards and Knight clinked glasses, Knight let go of his smile. "We need to talk about the eight-million-dollar claim you filed on Midway." Midway was Gladiator's only son and Richards's future hope, and he had died spontaneously of kidney failure in practice earlier in the month.

Richards's elevated blood alcohol enhanced his irritation at the comment. "For Christ's sake, Knight! You insurance people are insufferable. Can't this wait until Monday? The race is starting in less than a minute!"

Indignant, Richards turned his attention to the track.

"I dropped by your stable this morning," Knight announced.

Earlier in the day, knowing that all hands would be on deck preparing Gladiator, Knight had gone to Richards's luxury compound in the Pacific Palisades to follow up on a theory he had developed about the colt's demise. His intuition rarely steered him in the wrong direction, nor had it that morning when he opened the trainer's freezer to find a Tupperware container filled with small toothy blobs of pink flesh.

"I found frozen mice in your trainer's refrigerator," he revealed.

Richards turned back. "*Frozen mice?*"

Knight recognized the look on his face. First, he would play dumb. Then he would lie. In Knight's line of work, you had to assume they were always lying, and they almost always were. Everyone was on the make, and every claim was a con.

Early in his insurance career, Knight had begun to take great pleasure in proving that people were lying to him about claims. It started with his professional life. Then the joy of proving people are full of shit began to bleed into his personal life. It was both toxic and intoxicating and had reinforced his isolated existence. Now, in his early forties, his greatest source of joy was proving that people were lying not only to him but to themselves as well. *Everyone is full of shit, and if they say they're not, they're full of shit for saying it.*

Knight explained that the frozen mice indicated the trainer was raising snakes.

"The man is eccentric. So what?" Richards countered.

Knight had also seen the darker side of the sport when he was young. Doping was as rampant in horse racing as in professional cycling. Typically, it resulted in a green curtain coming out on the track before the offending racer was injected with a lethal dose of barbiturates or else got a pneumatic bolt to the forehead—a task that always fell to his father back in Saratoga.

"He's doping your horses with cobra venom." Cobra venom had been used for years in horse racing, as a nerve blocker. It made the horses run like hell for a few years before they collapsed from organ failure. "Aside from being against the rules, it also violates a number of criminal laws."

Richards deflected as the horses took their positions. "I had no idea. That shouldn't affect my claim. Your company still owes me eight million dollars to replace him."

Perhaps Richards didn't know. Perhaps he was just like those pinstriped conquerors in Saratoga who had merely paid for an outcome without bothering to ask any questions about how the sausage was made.

The starting bell rang, and the horses blasted from the gates. As the luxury suite burst into cheers, Knight leaned into Richards. "Whether or not you knew doesn't matter. This isn't about the legal technicalities of insurance fraud."

"If I didn't know, you still owe me money," Richards interrupted.

"True, but do you think your trainer was only doping that one horse?" Knight continued. "You really think it's just diligent training that has Gladiator on the path to a Triple Crown? If word gets out, you'll be the Lance Armstrong of racing." Knight suspected that Richards valued his reputation at much more than $8 million and also would not take kindly to a lifetime ban from horse racing.

Richards bristled at the absurd insinuation that his prized horse was also cheating. The system had already been gamed by his genetics. "Gladiator is the offspring of two champion horses. He can win fair and square."

"Your horse has arthritis in his knees. I've seen his gait in practice. Without snake venom, he'll run out of gas on turn two and be lucky to finish in the middle of the pack."

Knight sat back and waited for reality to soak in. He hadn't specified which "sure thing" he was betting on. And if he had known about the snake venom for a week, he might have interfered with Gladiator's doping regimen. He watched Richards piece it together, noting the exact moment his Adam's apple rose with a nervous swallow. Yes, Richards was now keenly aware that the race wouldn't be decided by the horses or their jockeys, but by whether Knight had decided to halt the doping.

"Which horse did you bet on?" Richards forced out weakly.

Knight betrayed nothing as the horses approached the second turn, with Gladiator going strong. "Nobody wants to see this thing go to court," he said. "Walk away from your claim and fire your trainer."

Suddenly, Gladiator began to pull away, his poison-fueled body unwittingly pushing beyond its limits. Richards watched the horse's performance, looking like a man who had just been granted a stay of execution.

By the time Gladiator crossed the finish line two lengths ahead of the pack, Knight had already departed to collect his winnings.

Knight took no pleasure in working with men like Richards, but he did take pleasure in winning, both on and off the track. And he looked forward to using his payout to buy a new Montblanc watch next time he passed through the duty-free shop at the Dubai airport.

He returned to his high-rise hotel in downtown LA. He knew he should get some sleep. Instead he spent the next few hours playing pinball on his phone at the hotel bar as he drained their supply of Blanton's bourbon. Outside, the city lights blurred together, looking just like the cities he pinballed between: Riyadh, Buenos Aires, Moscow . . . For a moment, he forgot which one he was in . . . *Oh, right—Los Angeles.*

Knight could feel his belly dipping over his Yves Saint Laurent belt. It bothered him that he had let his body go to shit, but it beat depriving himself of his vices, and he could still get by well enough on his designer threads and cocksure attitude.

Out of the corner of his eye, he caught a waifish form mounting the stool two seats down from him. He could sense her anxious body language—the look she cast in his direction to take inventory before returning her attention to the bartender mixing her dry vodka martini with a lemon twist. Knight could sense the deep well of insecurity within her that would never be filled. He could use that.

"You're the face from those Gucci ads," Knight commented, as if offering some small bit of inconsequential trivia.

He watched her turn, uncertain what to make of him. At first glance, his tailored suit and neatly groomed generic haircut might lead her to suspect he was a consultant or investment banker. But the specific luxury brands he was wearing painted a different picture. More international. More curated.

"Let me guess." She paused for dramatic effect. "Private equity."

"Insurance," he replied.

She scoffed, as they always did. "That sounds boring."

Sun Tzu. Knight knew that the battle was already won before he launched into the next line in the familiar script.

"It is boring—until you lose something you care about." Her curiosity crept incrementally.

"What do you care about?" she asked reflexively, as they always did.

"Making enough money so I don't have to care," he quipped dismissively.

Knight turned, assessing the young woman.

"You should really insure your eyes."

The girl leaned in, intrigued. "How much are they worth?"

Now he was the one pausing for dramatic effect as she batted her eyelashes at him. "Three hundred thousand."

It was probably more than she had expected for just the eyes, and in truth, Knight always rounded up. The validation attracted her to Knight, who had now firmly established himself as the arbiter of her self-esteem.

"And the whole package—what's that worth?" she asked.

As Knight scanned her with clinical detachment, she mugged ever so slightly. He didn't enjoy the game as much as he enjoyed the total domination of his opponent, which it inevitably led to. The conquering.

"One-point-eight million. That would cover your 'total loss' based on your demographic and potential earnings." Knight paused, meeting the young woman's eyes. "But I'm guessing you dropped out of college to pursue modeling, and you're not getting any younger."

The girl recoiled. "What is that supposed to mean!"

Knight explained that her market value was in free fall. In five years, she'd be closer to a million. In ten years, half that.

"You can't put a price on everything," she said with a hint of desperation, as if her own self-worth was wrapped up in her objection. Her words reminded Knight of the bullfights he had attended in Catalonia. The bull was incapable of making any choice but to charge the flapping cape, only to end up with a sword between its shoulder blades. Knight drew his sword.

"Name one thing you can't put a price on, and I'll tell you how much we'd pay out if you lost it."

The model pursed her lips, silently searching for an answer that wouldn't come.

Knight's phone buzzed with an incoming text. If his boss was texting him at this hour, something very expensive had died. He winced as he read the word *Miami*.

The girl studied him, intrigued. "What is it?"

"Boring work stuff," Knight replied as he knocked back his drink and rose to leave, knowing he would be spending the rest of the night rushing to the airport and popping Ambien and scotch in first class on a red-eye.

The girl took him by the hand, longing in her $300,000 eyes. "Wait. What are *you* worth?"

Knight was briefly disappointed that he wouldn't get to enjoy the spoils of his conquest—she was top shelf, even by his standards—but he took pleasure in the fact that his departure would only enhance her feelings of desire for him.

"Me?" he said with a wry grin. "I'm priceless."

CHAPTER 3
DAVIS

CAMP FIVE ECHO, GUANTANAMO BAY

They were being treated like animals.

"Stay on the blue line and don't make eye contact."

Kevin Davis silently complied with the order being barked at him as he walked down the corridor lined with impenetrable red steel doors. The two military guards escorting him wore splash masks and blue rubber gloves. The conditions were beastly and unrelenting, but Davis swallowed his discomfort.

A germophobe by nature, he felt naked in his suit, which hung loosely off his whippet-thin frame. It had fit when he purchased it at Macy's five years ago, but he had lost twenty pounds since his anxiety had taken its toll on his appetite.

Davis knew that the interview was a long shot, but he was out of options. Camp Five Echo was notoriously the worst *known* place a prisoner of the Global War on Terrorism could find himself. As Davis passed the tiny cells, he glanced furtively through the windows to see prisoners pacing and pulling their hair. Davis had read reports that over a hundred prisoners in Gitmo suffered from psychosis, but to see it firsthand was deeply unnerving.

On a long enough timeline, any caged sentient being would internalize the psychologically fracturing fact that it had lost all free will and control over its environment. In animals, the resulting condition was known as *zoochosis*, and it affected everything from bears to monkeys to killer whales. The creatures began exhibiting repetitive stereotypic behavior ranging from walking in circles to rocking, to compulsive self-mutilation, caught in an infinite loop as unwavering as their surroundings.

Davis was also a prisoner. As his colleagues at the agency derisively put it, he was a *GS-13 bagman*. A series of unlucky choices had charted the course to his current professional doldrums. When he joined the CIA fifteen years ago, he had been eager to distance himself from the darker aspects of the War on Terror, so he became a money laundering specialist whose primary theater of operations was a cubicle at Langley. Through no fault of his own, he told himself, he had been involved in a bunch of dead-end investigations. They all had been thwarted by the murky Hawala banking systems that most Middle Eastern terror groups relied on. The most recent task group he'd been assigned to was a Gaddafi money laundering investigation that had also been fruitless. In a highly superstitious profession, Davis was now radioactive.

With no one willing to risk bringing his bad juju into their orbit, he now haunted the halls of Langley without being assigned to any new taskings. And because he wasn't taking any scalps, he was stuck indefinitely at GS-13 pay grade, which was proving insufficient to support his family's lifestyle. With his oldest about to matriculate at a private elementary school, money was tighter than ever.

_____

Davis paused as the guard directed him to the door where he would be meeting with the detainee. He had read about the enhanced interrogation Riduan had been subjected to, and he worried that the man might be too far gone to be of use. But Riduan was the only prisoner at Gitmo from Sumatra, which meant that he alone might hold the key to a GS-14 promotion.

As Davis sat down opposite Riduan, he inferred that the bearded, filthy detainee was beyond the point of being psychologically demolished. It angered Davis. Any student of interrogation knew that people are inherently positively motivated. Offer them a win, and they will give you one as well. But in the years after the Towers fell, the desire to hurt the people who hurt us won out over giving our enemies wins. So instead of relying on decades-old knowledge about the psychology of extracting information, America had indulged its more primal impulses and been left with mountains of garbage intelligence. And many detainees who had been potential vaults of actionable information were now sealed with their locks broken.

"_As-salamu alaykum,_" Davis muttered, his voice cracking unsteadily.

His greeting of respect fell on deaf ears.

"There is nothing left to take from me," Riduan proclaimed indignantly.

"I am not here to take anything. I am here to offer you something." Davis set his briefcase on the table.

Riduan slammed his palms on the table and lunged forward

against his bindings. Davis recoiled, a jolt of adrenaline spiking through his system.

"You have nothing to offer! No charges have even been filed against me! This is illegal! This is American soil. I have rights!"

Davis gathered himself, breathing a sigh of relief. The fact that Riduan was still angry, still fighting, was good. It meant he wasn't completely broken. His lock might just still work.

Davis responded coolly, as if informing a customer that an appliance warranty had expired. "There will be charges soon, and you will be convicted and executed. There is nothing I can do about that."

Riduan was speechless at the news. Davis continued, "What I can offer is this . . ."

Davis withdrew a single sheet of paper from his briefcase and laid it on the table.

Riduan studied the grid of numbers, some of them highlighted. Davis watched as the prisoner furrowed his brow, trying to make sense of it. There were a handful of dates, but none of them meant anything to the detainee.

"It's a bank account for a shell company in Jakarta," Davis explained.

Riduan's body language shifted. He was clearly shaken at the unwelcome revelation. As Davis laid all his aces on the table, he could almost see the detainee's options racing through his mind.

"The money was intended to finance a terror plot," David said. "One you were planning but that never happened, because you were captured. Now the money's just sitting there, two million dollars that nobody knows exists. Nobody except me . . . and your wife, who has been drawing down on it every month to raise your children."

Davis pulled out his phone and began scrolling through photos of Riduan's children, smiling and laughing. "Found these on Facebook. They look happy and healthy." He made sure Riduan got a good look at the photos. He wanted the knife set before he began to twist.

Davis put away his phone, returning his attention to the sheet with the bank account information. "That kind of money can last a long time."

Riduan took a deep breath as everything that still mattered to him in the world hung in the balance in this very moment. He touched the paper.

"What are you going to do with that?" he muttered weakly.

"I can give it to the Treasury Department, who will seize everything. Your family will be penniless and will do whatever people living on the streets of Jakarta do to scrape by. Beg. Steal. Maybe sex work. Or we can forget I ever found this."

Riduan looked up, and Davis could see the desperation in his eyes.

"What do you want?" The man's voice was barely a whisper now.

"I already know your organization is financed by drugs and kidnappings," Davis said. "What about animals?"

Riduan's eyes drifted as he began to formulate his answer.

CHAPTER 4
AUDREY LAM

HONG KONG

The Camry came around a bend on the mountain, offering Audrey Lam a panoramic view of Repulse Bay with its jade waters lapping at the amber sand. A thin white rope suspended on buoys formed a crescent a hundred meters out to sea, cordoning off the swimming area on the beach. It seemed a light-year from the frenzy of downtown Hong Kong, though it was only a twenty-minute hop away.

"Do you ever come here on the weekends?"

"Not since I was a boy," Stephen Hui replied, accelerating out of the curve. "Before they put in the shark net. You?"

"The last time I came here was when my son was eight. I brought him here to tell him his father wouldn't be coming home. I thought it would be good to give him a nice day before telling him the news." Audrey trailed off, reliving the painful day in her mind.

"Let me guess: he hasn't wanted to come back since."

She answered with a doleful look that said he was spot-on.

Stephen turned off into a row of condominiums at the edge of the beach. "Parenting is an impassable minefield. If you try to avoid one, you'll only step on another."

They arrived at their destination, a narrow metal-and-glass cube flanked by a row of identical boxes. Audrey stepped out of the car in her androgynous corporate attire and rang the door-bell. As they waited, she rubbed her eyes and squeezed them shut.

"Another long night?"

Audrey nodded.

Stephen cast her a concerned look. "You need to take care of yourself."

Before she could respond, the door opened. An American woman in her midforties peered at the credentials clipped on their jackets. "Are you following up on the noise complaint?" Before Audrey and Stephen could respond, she added, "The police already came and said the matter was resolved."

"May we come in?" Stephen asked.

The woman led them into her small two-bedroom unit, rambling nervously. "I told him and his friends to keep the video games down."

"Where is he?" Audrey asked.

"In his bedroom," the American replied. "I'll go get him."

Audrey stopped her. "We'll handle it from here. Which room is it?"

The woman directed them to a room at the end of the hall-way. Stephen went to the door while Audrey stayed with her.

"I'm sorry, why are you here?" the American asked.

"The officers who came to investigate the noise complaint thought they smelled cannabis in your apartment," said Audrey. "They referred the case to us."

"And what department are you from?"

"Narcotics."

Before the American woman could inquire further, Stephen emerged from the back room with her teenage son in handcuffs.

"Wait! What are you doing!"

Stephen lifted a small bag of marijuana and a glass pipe. "This was in his room."

Audrey took no pleasure in the matter, but her hands were as bound as the boy's. "We need to take him down to the station."

"You're taking him to *jail*?"

"He will have the opportunity to enter a rehabilitation program."

"Are you kidding me! He's going to get kicked out of school if this goes on his record!"

"We enforce the law," Stephen interjected, "and the letter of the law is not open to debate." He seemed to be enjoying this a lot more than Audrey, probably because of the woman's condescending attitude.

The woman followed as they marched her son outside. "I want both your badge numbers! I'm friends with the ambassador!"

Audrey maintained her composure. "We don't have badge numbers here. My name is Inspector Audrey Lam from the Narcotics Bureau. Here's my card."

The mother's tone shifted to desperation as Stephen put her son in the back of the inspectors' Camry and locked him inside.

"Come on!" she pleaded with Audrey. "All kids his age mess around a bit! You can't ruin his life over this!"

Audrey got in the car, taking one last look at the mother, empathizing with her pain before shutting the door.

––––––

The inspectors returned to police headquarters, where the young man was booked. Audrey spent the remainder of the shift summiting the mountain of paperwork on her desk before heading off to see her own son.

The past three months had been one long, never-ending day that oscillated between work and the hospital, with the occasional pit stop at her apartment for a change of clothes and a shower. It was a futile zero-sum game in which both lives demanded more than the twelve hours she had to offer. What kind of mother saw her sick child only a few hours of the waking day? What kind of narcotics detective didn't work nights?

Audrey entered the hospital room to find her twelve-year-old son, Joshua, watching an old Jackie Chan movie on television—old by the boy's standards, anyway.

"Turn it off," she told her son firmly. "You're too young to watch fighting movies." Soon, Joshua would get better, and she mustn't spoil the child during his convalescence.

Joshua propped himself up in bed, pointing excitedly at the TV. "But look, Mom! He's a detective, just like you."

On-screen, the hero cop vaulted over a car and kicked a criminal in the head.

"It's not like that in real life," Audrey told her son. "My job is to help make sick people better."

The boy winced. "I don't feel so good."

"You need to be patient. The medicine is working." In truth, she had no idea, but she hoped that was the case.

Audrey placed a folder brimming with papers on the bed beside her son. "I met with your teacher and got your new assignments." Though the boy had been in the hospital for two months with no end in sight, Audrey continued to maintain a constant line of communication with his teachers so he wouldn't fall behind in his absence.

The boy cast his mother a frustrated look. "Can't it wait until I feel better?"

Audrey glared at him.

"Fine." Joshua clicked off the TV and flopped back in bed, punctuating the display with a dramatic huff. Audrey opened the folder and pulled out the first sheaf of stapled pages, thus commencing her second twelve-hour shift of the never-ending day.

———

Audrey had known exhaustion. She had worked the night shifts in narcotics. She had nursed a crying baby through endless colicky nights. During those stages of her life, sleep deprivation had felt like an iron anchor, growing increasingly heavier until her body couldn't bear the weight, and she would nod off in her police car during a surveillance operation. But this was different. The fear and anxiety over her son's mortality had put her in a perpetual state of fight or flight, and she had resisted the pull of the anchor until it eventually broke free. She had crossed over to a point where she no longer experienced the sensation of sleepiness. Instead, her body and mind were starting to behave in strange ways. She felt an electricity in her body that caused her to sweat at all hours. Her memory recall no longer worked perfectly on demand, and though she maintained an even keel externally, she could feel her mood swinging dramatically. And as she bought two packets of peanut butter crackers from the vending machine in the waiting room, the empty calories reminded her that her impulse control had deteriorated.

Eyes dry and burning, Audrey retrieved her meager sodium-filled dinner from the machine. She leaned her forearm against the glass case and slouched forward, burying her brow in her sleeve, bracing herself to return to the antiseptic cancer ward with its punishing twenty-four-hour fluorescent lights.

"Is it your child?"

Audrey turned to find an elderly Chinese man standing by her. A worn suit dusted with dandruff clung to his frail frame.

"Son," Audrey replied.

"What kind of cancer?" the old man asked.

"Hodgkin's lymphoma."

"What stage?"

"Four." As Audrey said it, the guilt came flooding back. For months, her son had complained of night sweats and abdominal pain, but she had been too busy with work to take him to the doctor. She assumed it was just another of the many bugs that kids picked up at school and that it would eventually work itself out. By the time she had noticed the swollen nodes in his neck and armpits and taken him to the pediatrician, he was already at stage four—the worst stage—and the cancer had spread to his bone marrow and liver. The doctors had initially said there was a 60 percent chance of survival, but that hinged on the boy responding to the chemotherapy, which had not yet happened.

"I'm sorry," the man replied solemnly, his head hung low, exuding sympathy. "Sometimes, modern ways cannot solve our problems." The man fished in his pocket and handed her a business card.

Audrey looked at the man curiously as she took the card. It was for a "TRADITIONAL CHINESE MEDICINE" shop on Ko Shing Street. Audrey had been to Ko Shing Street many times as a young girl. It was the epicenter of traditional Chinese medicine—TCM, as it was called—and her parents often went there to buy red sage, ginseng, and other herbs to treat their minor ailments. Audrey hadn't been to Ko Shing herself in years, preferring the linear logic of Western medicine to the more abstract concepts, like *qi*, at the center of Eastern medicine.

Audrey was initially dismissive of the card, then noticed that it featured a clip-art image of a rhino head in the corner. Though wild animals had been used in TCM for millennia, China had banned trade in tiger and rhino parts in 1993 and officially barred them from use in TCM. But it was an open secret that many in China still believed in the old ways and maintained an underground trade in the endangered species for medicinal purposes. And though it was technically illegal, there was also the sense that the ban had been imposed because of American pressure as part of a Western agenda in a broader culture war between East and West.

Audrey inspected the card, uneasy at the implication. In her exhaustive research about her son's condition, she had read that rhino horn was considered an ancient cure for cancer. She hadn't put any more stock in the claims than in her parents treating ear infections with forsythia and coptis. But Western medicine was failing her son, and Audrey was growing desperate.

An angry nurse rushed over to interrupt the conversation. "Sir, you must leave the hospital at once!" she snapped. It was clear from her aggression that this wasn't the first time she'd had to kick the man out of the pediatric cancer ward.

"I just want to help her son before it's too late," the old man said. Then he turned and departed without further protest.

The nurse apologized to Audrey, explaining that the man was one of several rhino horn touts who lurked in the city's cancer wards, preying on families with sick loved ones and trying to exploit their grief.

Audrey thanked the nurse for the heads-up as she slid the old man's card into her pocket.

CHAPTER 5
SIMON

The T-shirt had been printed in late 2014, a good month before the Seahawks lost the Super Bowl. Over the coming months, it would find its way into a shipping container, which would find its way to Maputo, the capital of Mozambique. Eventually, the shirt found its way onto the bony shoulders of the fifteen-year-old sitting on an upside-down bucket outside his family's cinder block and thatch dwelling. "SEATTLE SEAHAWKS 2015 SUPER BOWL CHAMPIONS," the shirt declared erroneously.

"Happy birthday!" his father said in Swahili.

Simon turned to see his father standing in the dark doorway behind him, holding a brand-new pair of tan leather boots. Though Simon's feet were covered in calluses and dust from wearing the only rubber sandals he owned, he was uneasy knowing that the boots represented nearly a week's wages for his father at the petrol station. The father sensed his son's reluctance to accept them and didn't allow him an opportunity to protest.

"You deserve them. Besides, you'll need them at your new construction job."

Although Simon's family was poor, he was at least lucky enough to still have a father. His town, like many along the border, was full of widows whose husbands had tried their hand at poaching in the Big Smoke. It wasn't easy turning down the cash advances offered by the syndicate leaders, but Simon's father had a great deal to live for, namely his wife and his teenage son.

A horn honked, and an old Toyota pickup wobbled toward them on the lumpy road, carrying two gaunt African men in the back.

"I have to go, Papa."

Simon's father patted his son on the back of the neck. The boy proudly kicked off his sandals and hopped in the bed of the truck holding his boots.

He looked back at his father, who waved as he receded into a cloud of dust behind him. Simon felt a brief tinge of guilt that he had lied to his father about his job. But it passed. His family badly needed the money he hoped to bring home.

———

Twenty-five kilometers away, Thomas Mabunda pulled to a stop in a remote section of Kruger Park. In the back of his open-air truck, white tourists scrambled for their telephoto cameras and swapped out the lenses. It had a been a successful safari in the park today, and ever since they had to stop for a pride of lions sleeping in the road, Thomas suspected it would be a rich day for tipping.

His guests were drenched in sweat from the roasting midday sun, and Thomas had heard murmurings about their increasing thirst for ice-cold Castle lagers back at the lodge. He was about to take them back to their air-conditioned resorts for beers when he caught the flash of gray. To the untrained eye, it looked like any other boulder strewn about the grasslands, but Thomas recognized it instantly as Kruger's crown jewel.

As the young rhino named Oupa grazed with his mother, he looked up to see a half-dozen disembodied glass eyes staring at him. He moved closer to his mother, and Thomas fished out his cell phone and snapped a photo over the steering wheel. A white rhino and her calf! Yes, it would be a rich day indeed, he thought to himself as he sent a text with the image.

———

Back in Mozambique, Simon laced his new boots as the truck jounced through his small town in the miombo woodland. Plastic and paper trash lined the road.

The workers passed around a loaf of white bread and a two-liter bottle of Fanta. Simon politely declined when they came his way. The men were skinny, with jaundiced eyes. Simon suspected that like many of the adults in the region, they had contracted Henry the Fourth, or the "slow puncture," as HIV was now called.

They stopped at a small thatched hut about two kilometers outside the village. The driver waited in the truck as the two men in the back got out. Simon elected to stay in the truck, fearing what lay inside the eerie hovel. The two men told him to get out and follow them into the hut. Simon had passed the hut before but had never gone inside. It was the home of Inyanga, the local *sangoma*, or traditional healer.

Inside, the hut smelled strongly of marijuana from a large joint that was smoldering in a tray. On the wall, a leopard skin hung next to a crucifix. The shelves were filled with *muti*, traditional medicines, stored in repurposed plastic bottles and glass jars. The hut brimmed with an indiscriminate hodgepodge of Christian, Muslim, and African religious paraphernalia that had found their way into the sangoma's practice.

Inyanga sat cross-legged on the dirt in the center of the room. Her face was caked in some sort of magical brown powder, or perhaps it was simply dirt—Simon couldn't tell. Her large bare breasts hung pendulously at her waist, and her torso was crisscrossed by white and red strings and long beaded necklaces. In her hand, she held a staff decorated with paint and some long hair of unknown provenance. She reignited the marijuana as the leader of Simon's group told her of their plans and requested her protection.

When he had finished, Inyanga emptied a jar into her hands, revealing a mix of bone fragments, bolts, bottle caps, half a domino, and a red die. She cupped the odd collection in her hands then tossed it all on the mat before her.

Inyanga read the bones and sighed deeply at what they revealed. She informed the men that their journey could be fruitful, but they would need help from the spirits. "You will need to be invisible," she said, or they would surely perish.

She told the men that she needed to perform a ceremony and give them special strings that would cloak them on their journey so that they would go unnoticed by anti-poaching units. She assured the men that the particular strings she would provide had made numerous trips over the border and had always returned without incident. The power of invisibility would cost them the small fee of two hundred meticals up front, and when they returned, they would owe her 10 percent of their profits, as well as the tail of whatever creature they killed.

The leader picked up the joint from the tray and took a deep drag, then blew the smoke out his nose. "Okay," was all he grunted, then signaled for his colleague to provide the up-front funds.

The sangoma instructed Simon to stand and take off his shirt. She then took a small razor blade and made a tiny slice in the skin on his upper back. Simon winced in pain and turned to his colleagues. They glared at him coldly. *Don't be a coward,* their eyes said.

Inyanga continued to make a series of nicks down his upper back and legs. She then withdrew one of her jars of *muti* and rubbed a dark, gritty substance into the wounds, which added to the burning sensation Simon was experiencing all over his body.

Inyanga then blessed Simon and untied one of the red and one of the white strings that were draped like a bandolier over her shoulder. As she stepped forward and tied the strings around Simon's waist, he could feel Inyanga's bare breasts pressing against his stomach. It was the closest thing to a sexual encounter the adolescent had ever experienced, and he timidly averted his gaze.

Once the strings were tied, she stepped back. "You are now invisible to the *mlungas* until you return these to me."

Inyanga repeated the ceremony with the other two men. Then, with the spirits now on their side, they stepped back out into the light and remounted the pickup truck.

———

The truck rolled to a stop in the middle of the savanna, and the three men silently piled out. The leader opened the tailgate, revealing a secret compartment. Inside were an old AK-47 with a folding wire stock, a rusty hand axe, and a .303 hunting rifle with a makeshift silencer fashioned from an oil filter.

The second in command tied the empty Fanta bottle to a tree

on the side of the road to mark their drop-off point, and the hunting party headed out into the veld. The leader carried the AK-47 while the other man carried the hunting rifle. Simon trailed the gunmen, awkwardly lugging a large plastic jug of water.

An hour later, as their knees parted the tall adrenaline grass, a mobile phone vibrated, and the man carrying the silenced rifle stopped and checked the incoming text, which included a geo-tagged photo. Over his shoulder, Simon saw the image of a white rhino and her calf. Aside from a couple of private reserves, they had been extinct in Mozambique for some time now. Simon felt a quiver of excitement at the possibility of seeing one in the wild.

CHAPTER 6
THE RHINO

KRUGER PARK, SOUTH AFRICA

It was Cobus's favorite time of day, when the breeze picked up and the shadows grew long. Flanked by Basani and Lawrence, he marched along the mud at the edge of the meandering Letaba River. Crocodiles lazed in the shallows, and lions perched on the rocks, preening and licking their chops. It was a strange thing, Cobus mused, dedicating your life to protecting creatures that were naturally inclined to kill you.

Basani had been in an increasingly dark mood since her husband, Oupa, died. The futility that had surrounded her now lived within her. Her job was protecting animals, and she was beginning to feel like a caretaker at an abattoir.

"We save as many as we can," Cobus offered. "That's all we can do."

"The only way these animals will ever be safe is if people stop buying them," she muttered as the rangers plodded forward.

Lawrence had never left southern Africa, and he had never met an African with the slightest interest in possessing, let alone ingesting, rhino horn. "How can a horn be worth so much blood?" he asked.

Cobus had done some research on the horn trade. "By the time rhino horn hits the streets in Asia," he informed them, "it's worth more than gold."

Basani was infuriated at the absurdity of all the death. "Do these people know the horn is just a giant fingernail?"

"It's not just fingernail," Cobus informed her. "To some, it's a status symbol with mythic powers."

"We should poison their horn," Lawrence seethed. "Maybe they would stop killing rhinos if the rhinos killed them."

Cobus considered the elegant simplicity of Lawrence's proposal. Basani, on the other hand, was less keen on the idea of waging an offensive campaign to harm the end users. "All life is sacred. All life is worth protecting."

"Someday, I want to meet these people," she added as she withdrew a photo of her dead husband from her pocket. "I will show them this photo of my Oupa, and I will ask them why they killed him."

Lawrence suddenly raised his fist, eyeing something on the ground. "Fresh spoor."

Basani knelt, inspecting a boot print in the mud. A millimeter of water had gathered in the depression.

"It is still filling with water. Maybe five minutes old."

Lawrence knelt beside her, studying the creases forged by the boot's tread as they slowly drowned in the rising water. "New boots."

Basani gave Lawrence a conspiratorial look, knowing what he was thinking. "Your size."

"I'd rather like some new boots," Lawrence said as he rose.

Cobus inspected the boot print and felt the adrenaline taking hold. "They were heading south."

Basani looked at the pattern of the water filling the print and shook her head at Cobus's assessment. "The toe struck the ground first. They were walking backward to throw us off. They are headed north."

"Are you sure?" Cobus asked.

"You read books; I read tracks," she told the white man.

As they inspected the boot print, they heard a distant thump. A flock of birds took flight north of their position.

Cobus recognized the sound instantly. He shouldered his rifle and raised his fist to get his team's attention. Once he had their eyes, he gave the thumbs down: enemy. Then he pointed toward the birds.

Lawrence reached for his radio. "Should I call it in?" he whispered.

Cobus shook his head. "They might be monitoring our channels."

Alone and on foot, the three rangers took off in pursuit. The crocodiles sunning themselves on the banks paid them little mind as the humans splashed through the river toward the origin of the gunshot.

———

Simon felt sick to his stomach as he watched the large mother lying on the ground, snorting blood out of her nostrils. The creature had stumbled for a good ten seconds before it lost its footing. It now flailed hopelessly, only accelerating its own demise as impossible amounts of blood pooled in the dry, cracked dirt beneath it.

Simon had killed chickens and rodents for his family since he was a little boy. He hadn't thought this would be different. But there was something much more complex and emotional about the death of this creature—something almost human about the sadness and desperation in its eyes.

Nearby, the baby rhino watched his mother with horror. At each failed attempt by the mother to rise, the baby wailed. The whole affair had gone on for minutes and showed no sign of ending anytime soon.

Simon implored the poachers, "Please, kill it."

One of the men raised his silenced hunting rifle, but the leader—the man with the AK-47—stopped him. "No. Save the bullet."

He slung the assault rifle behind him and approached the rhino with a small ax. Gripping the mother's horn in one hand, he cocked his arm to swing down.

"Wait." The poacher with the hunting rifle shushed the others, then pointed southwest. All three men scanned the brush near the river. Simon sensed the danger, even without knowing what form it took.

The poacher with the rifle flattened out in the grass, shouldering his weapon. The leader put his handheld radio to his ear and shook his head. Keying off their movements, Simon lowered himself on his belly until all he could see was the grass directly in front of his eyes.

———

Cobus, Basani, and Lawrence slithered up the berm at the river's edge. The top grew thick with vegetation that hadn't been swept away by the big rains earlier in the year.

Lawrence squinted at the grass beyond the trees. Then he saw the unmistakable glint of a rifle scope. *THUMP!* Lawrence ducked as bark exploded from the tree beside him, showering him with splinters.

Cobus's instincts and training took over. He hand signaled for

Basani and Lawrence to drop back down the berm and maneuver to flank the enemy.

Cobus moved with military decisiveness, crouch-sprinting from cover to cover, feeling the adrenaline ratchet up his heart rate.

THUMP! A round struck a tree next to Cobus as he darted past. He dropped to one knee and traded fire with the poachers, less concerned with hitting someone than with providing suppressive fire for his comrades.

———

Lawrence and Basani keyed off Cobus's movements, leapfrogging in perfect synchronicity as he sent lead in the direction of the threat. The AK-47 cracked, the suppressed hunting rifle thumped, and the rangers' assault rifles boomed.

Amid the cacophony, Lawrence maneuvered undetected alongside the poacher with the AK-47, who was firing high-velocity 7.62 mm rounds at Cobus. Lawrence lifted his FN-FAL assault rifle. He would have only one shot before his position was known.

Suddenly, the poacher spotted him. He turned his rifle onto Lawrence. A shot rang out. The poacher dropped to the ground, clutching his throat, which Lawrence's bullet had torn in half.

His position compromised, Lawrence darted for his next cover position.

———

Simon had been hiding in the thick bush when the leader of the crew collapsed beside him, writhing as he bled out from the gaping wound in his neck. As the rivulets of blood snaked through the grass toward Simon, he spotted the AK-47, lying in the dirt two meters away.

He poked his head up, searching for the reapers who had just felled his colleague. He didn't know where the reapers were, but they were out there, and soon they would come for him.

Before they entered Kruger that morning, the leader had warned Simon that the rangers made a sport of executing poachers in cold blood rather than arresting them. With that warning in mind, the boy scuttled across the dirt like a lizard and reached for the AK-47.

———

Across the field, Basani sighted the teenage boy. He was young, and she rightly suspected that he was just one of the many local kids the poachers recruited to carry their provisions. If they took him alive, he would have to serve the mandatory twelve-year sentence, but there was still hope for this one. *Please don't*, she thought to herself as she held her finger on the trigger. *Don't make me kill you, child.*

The second he touched the rifle, the kid was thrown back as if it were an exposed power line. He rolled onto his back and touched his chest, then lay still.

"One left," Basani called to Cobus as she watched the boy fall, anguished that he had forced her hand.

———

"Cover me," Cobus said. He turned to her for confirmation. As she nodded, pink mist burst from her back when a bullet the size of a finger blew through her torso.

Cobus rushed to her. He tried to apply pressure to the wound as she hyperventilated. The fear in her eyes was palpable. Seeing the scope of her injury, Cobus knew at once that he could do nothing for her. The closest medical help was at least twenty minutes out, and there would be nothing they could do either. Death would come any second now.

"It's okay. I'm here." Basani looked up at Cobus in silent understanding. Then she stopped breathing, and her body relaxed in his hands.

Cobus held her and kissed her on the forehead as an avalanche of rage gained momentum within him, finally pouring out in a primal roar.

Hands slick with Basani's blood, he snatched up his FN-FAL, amped up on vengeance, some beast inside him unleashed. With no regard for his own safety, Cobus broke from cover, charging as the poacher reloaded his bolt-action rifle. His eyes bulged at the sight of the crazed *mlunga* bearing down on him.

Cobus dropped the poacher with his first two rounds, then continued firing as he advanced on the motionless body. A final shot to the head from point-blank range split the crown of the poacher's head in a small explosion of brain and blood and bone.

Then all was silent.

———

Lawrence approached the body of the lead poacher. The man still clutched his throat, though his body was still. Lawrence flicked his eyeball to make sure he was dead. No response.

He keyed his radio. "This is Lawrence Tukela in Lower Sabie. A rhino has been hit—horn still intact. We have one ranger KIA. Two poachers dead."

Lawrence moved to Simon, who was sprawled on his back, chest heaving as he wheezed out blood. "One poacher appears to still be alive, over," Lawrence added as he solemnly eyed the dying boy.

Lawrence lowered to one knee, keeping the boy company as he passed to the other side. Blood welled from the boy's chest and ran from his mouth and nose, soaking the cracked dirt where he lay. Within a minute, there wasn't enough blood to continue his vital functions.

"He's dead," Lawrence uttered. His eyes wandered to the boy's feet and the brand-new boots Lawrence had coveted during the pursuit. The expensive boots were at odds with the boy's threadbare clothes. If they had taken the boy alive, he would have had no qualms about confiscating the young poacher's property, but Lawrence was not one to rob the dead.

———

Across the field, Cobus placed Basani's hands across her chest. He took one last look at her peaceful face, still warm and full of color. Reaching in her pocket, he withdrew the photo of her deceased husband, Oupa. As he rose, he folded it and placed it in the pocket nearest his heart.

A wail from the fallen mother rhino pulled Cobus back into the moment. Her breath had slowed, but she was clearly still in excruciating pain. Rhinos were stubborn beasts and could often take a full day to die. Fortunately, her son, Oupa, had been scared off by the thunder of the gunfight and disappeared into the brush. Cobus squatted and placed his hand on the rhino's face. The anguish in her giant damp eyes drove the knife through Cobus's already broken heart. Tears rolled down his cheeks. He rose, wiping his face with his sleeve as a dark resolve gripped him.

Cobus pulled back the bolt on the hunters' .303 rifle and chambered a round.

Lawrence rushed to his friend. "Cobus, no! You need to wait for the vet to assess her. This is a crime scene."

"I won't watch her suffer."

He leveled the rifle at the rhino's concave forehead, pained but knowing he had no choice. He had never shot an animal before. He swallowed, hesitating. Knowing that if he pulled the trigger, it would destroy them both.

He forced himself to keep his eyes open and not cower from what must be done as he squeezed the trigger past its breaking point.

CHAPTER 7
THE TIGER

For the past year, Knight had experienced a recurring dream. He was a Mongol warrior clad in animal skins, living as a single being with his immense black mare. It began this time as it always did, with him standing beside his horse, scanning the horizon, feeling the emptiness of knowing he was the only human for thousands of miles. Desperately thirsty, he made a small incision in a vein in the mare's neck. The blood trickled down her skin and into a horn that already contained her viscous milk, creating a red and white eddy. He drew the horn to his lips, drinking down the acrid pink slurry until it streamed down his cheeks. Covered in the skin and milk and blood of horses, he mounted the mare and ventured out onto the endless grassy plateau of the Mongolian steppe—an abyss to be conquered.

———

The flight attendant woke him with a gentle hand on his shoulder. "Sir, time to put your seat up. We're about to land." His eyes fluttered open, staring at her for a disoriented moment. He was still dizzy from the sleeping pill, head aching from the scotch. Where was he landing, and why was he headed there? He raised the window shade and gazed out: coastline, white sand, golf resorts, lagoons. *That's right*, he remembered. *Miami.*

———

Knight had a diverse array of clients, but his bread and butter was private zoos. There were thousands of them throughout the country, with especially high concentrations in Florida and Texas. They ranged from personal collections of the rich and famous to low-rent roadside attractions where lions, tigers, and bears rotted in chain-link pens. And then there were the big corporate players, like SafariWorld outside Miami, that sold the safari experience to the masses.

Knight entered the theme park's main gate, where a cartoon giraffe held a sign noting that the park was temporarily closed. He followed the signs, making his way through an elephant habitat, then past a lone rhino whose horn had been cut off to deter thieves, per Knight's advice.

Knight finally arrived at his destination: the great cats exhibit. The veterinarians looked like spacemen as they wandered about in their biohazard suits. Several stooped to examine the carcasses of dead tigers littering all the pens and communal yards. There were a least two dozen, gaunt and collapsed like punctured tires. Even by Knight's jaded standards, the scope of the devastation was terrible to behold.

Knight approached one of the tigers with clinical curiosity. Wearing only a paper mask for protection, he squatted before the dead animal. Blood seeped from its pink nostrils. With his pen, he pried open the creature's black lips, exposing bloody gums and teeth. Just as he had expected.

A high-pitched noise caught Knight's attention. He scanned across the exhibit to find a cuddly little tiger cub, squeaking with glee as it wrestled with a large ball. The cub was seemingly unaffected by the outbreak or the fact that all his fellow inmates had succumbed to some horrible withering disease.

A theory began to form in Knight's head. He pulled down his sweltering mask, exposing his face as he took a deep breath of fresh air.

Knight entered the cub's pen and opened his briefcase. Taking out a baby bottle, he filled it with water and powdered milk. He shook the mixture together, then swept the baby tiger up in his arms and began feeding it like a father nursing his newborn. Knight ran his fingers through the soft fur on the nape of its neck, soothing it. The tiger squinted in a silent purr, leaning into Knight's touch.

"I've got some questions for you, buddy."

Knight withdrew a small syringe from the briefcase and took a blood sample as the oblivious cub sucked down the milk.

A zoo vet in a clean suit approached. "Sir, it's not safe here."

"It isn't airborne," Knight said.

The vet didn't share his confidence. "We don't even know what killed these cats yet."

Knight didn't need lab analysis to know. The symptoms allowed for only one possibility. "Feline leukemia virus," he called back over his shoulder. "Transmitted in the blood when the cats nip each other. It doesn't affect people."

"Neither did bird flu, until it made the jump to humans and killed a bunch of folks in Southeast Asia," said a voice behind him.

Knight turned to see a woman with graying blond hair standing at the edge of the exhibit. She wore a safari shirt that seemed as much a costume as a uniform. "You must be the insurance guy," she said. "I'm Kate Henley, the mammal curator."

Knight made his way over to her. "I didn't see anything about a new cat listed on your policy."

"We just got it last week. Hadn't gotten around to adding him to the policy yet. Fortunately, he seems okay."

"Where'd this new cub come from?"

"A dealer in Macau."

"I'll run the DNA, but it looks like a purebred Sumatran."

"It is," she assured him.

"That's a tough cat for a private zoo to get. You went through a non-AZA supplier?"

Kate grew defensive. "He said it was a rescue tiger."

Her tone told Knight he was correct to assume that the seller wasn't a member of the well-regulated Association of Zoos and Aquariums. "Can you give me the dealer's contact info?"

"I'll have my assistant get it for you." Kate glanced at the cub, concerned. "Do you think the new cat was the host?"

"That's the smart money," Knight said.

"Then why didn't it die?"

"In any outbreak, a small percentage are genetically immune. Their immune system can control the disease, but they are still infected and still carriers." Knight had read somewhere that 1 percent of all northern Europeans were even immune to AIDS. Interesting, certainly, though he still wouldn't be rolling the dice on any unprotected one-night stands.

"How on earth are we going to replace all these cats?" Kate asked him.

The curator seemed much more concerned about potential lost revenue than about the animals under her care.

"I know suppliers," he said. "You'll be fine."

"How soon can your company pay out the claim?"

"You're asking for two hundred thousand per lost cat. That's five million total, and another five for lost revenue. Before we can cover the losses, we need to confirm the origin of the infected tiger."

The curator bristled. "I've got all the paperwork! What else is there to know?"

Knight was used to this sort of aggressive attitude, especially when so much money was on the line. "These creatures are like fine art," he said. "Sellers say they come through official channels, and buyers want to believe them. But there are no real official channels."

Knight's phone rang. It was Neil Perkins, the British boss of his London-based firm. He stepped away from the curator and lowered his voice.

"There's no way this little tiger developed feline leukemia in the wild," he told Perkins. "Until now, the virus never affected anything bigger than a civet cat. This strain could only emerge with multiple species in close proximity."

"You smell fraud?"

"Sumatran tigers have been hunted to the brink of extinction. There are only a few hundred in the wild, if that. Anyone who sells you a Sumatran 'rescue tiger' is selling a unicorn. And any decent mammal curator would know that." And if the zoo knowingly purchased a black-market tiger that then killed the rest of their population, the claim would be invalid."

"This is an important client, Randall. We can't appear to be dragging our heels."

"I need you to trust me on this one."

"Where do you think it came from?"

"I don't know." Knight gazed at the bloody carcasses strewn around the field. "But wherever it came from, there are going to be a lot more dead tigers."

CHAPTER 8
THE AGENCY

The rain was coming down in buckets. Davis set his travel mug full of coffee on the roof of his Taurus, where it diluted and cooled with each drop of water that fell in. He hurried to buckle his daughter into the car seat. His umbrella was resting on his passenger seat, and the rain was beginning to soak into his suit. His daughter pushed his hands away, forcing him to wait as she insisted on doing the last buckle herself. Davis felt the water seeping through his shirt as he waited in impotent frustration.

She finally clicked the buckle, and he shut her door. Of all days to start out soaking wet, this wasn't the one.

Davis's giant Newfoundland canine approached him from behind, panting. Davis shooed the dog away, annoyed. "Go back inside, Buddy." Buddy shook himself dry, flinging smelly water all over Davis's pants. *Fucking piece of shit dog*, he thought to himself as he tabulated the vet bills they had racked up over Buddy's irritable bowels.

Next to him, Marion wore a long raincoat as she loaded into the family minivan with their eight-year-old son. "Any word yet on whether that promotion is going through?"

Davis deflected. "I'm not getting paneled until next quarter."

She didn't force the issue, but time was running out to get the deposit in. "It's just that Grayson's tuition is going up, and with Devin starting preschool, I need to know if we should be exploring other—"

Davis cut her off. "I'm going to be late. We'll be fine." He hopped in his car, eager to end the conversation.

He threw the car in reverse. Marion shouted something and waved both hands for his attention. *Whatever it is she wants, I don't have time to talk about it. Not today.* Then he heard a hard thud on the roof, followed by sixteen ounces of coffee and milk cascading down his windshield. *Fuck me.*

———

Thirty minutes later, Davis was walking down the hall of the CIA's Counterterrorism Center, his baggy suit now heavy with a sticky mix of rain and sweat. CTC was the big show, the Super Bowl of the human race, and it bustled with well-groomed men and women who moved with purpose. Davis envied them. They had places to go and were going places.

At Davis's side was Ken Peterson, one of his last allies at the agency. Peterson had seen Davis's reach exceed his grasp before and seen Davis's career stall out because of it. For whatever reason, Peterson liked him, which was why he immediately guffawed when Davis insisted on a meeting with Peterson's bosses in CTC to pitch them his new idea.

"Are you sure you want to bet the farm on this? There's an opening at the Juba station. It would mean a guaranteed pay bump to GS-14."

"Move my family to South Sudan!" It was an outrageous proposal and one that Peterson would never accept for himself.

"Yeah, you speak French, right?"

Davis appreciated the effort. His friend was trying to sell him on the idea for his own good—anything to keep him from self-immolating in front of the who's who of the agency. "Juba could be a great short-term solution for you guys."

"My family can barely handle the thought of leaving private school," Davis said, dismissing the idea. "There's no way I'm dragging them to the desert in North Africa."

"You were a Gaddafi specialist who hasn't been assigned in five years. What do you *think* is going to happen in there?" Peterson nodded toward the conference room at the end of the hall.

As they approached the large double doors, Peterson stopped his friend, pleading with him once more not to dig his own grave.

"Listen to me, Kev. The next wave of cuts is coming any day, and you don't want to be looking for a chair when the music stops. You need a plan—a real one."

But Davis did have a real plan, and he was about to put it into effect. He braced himself for battle, then pushed through the doors.

———

Davis felt that it was going well. He had never delivered a presentation to a director-level meeting, let alone at the CIA's Counterterrorism Center, which was Mount Olympus for case officers. He tried to project confidence, and thanks to the mercy of optical physics, he couldn't see the anxious boredom on the faces of the attendees through the wall of light cast by the projector beaming his PowerPoint deck. The officers checked messages, tapped pens, all of them having a million places to be besides here.

Davis's years on Wall Street before joining the agency had honed his graphic design skills, and he was confident that at the very least, his charts looked professional and sold the magnitude of the threat.

"Animal trafficking is a ten-billion-dollar industry, making it the second-largest illicit market after drugs, just ahead of arms dealing—"

A voice cut him off. "Look, we can all agree that it's real sad for these furry little animals. But we're the agency, not the park rangers."

Davis found the source of the objection: Ron Nelson. *Shit.* Nelson was a throat-slitter, a political animal within the agency who had hitched himself to the right star early on. And that star was Director Wilkes, the avuncular CTC chief, reclining in his seat at the head of the table.

Davis dug in, having rehearsed his answer should objections arise concerning the CIA's mission. "We've all seen terrorists benefiting from commodities under their control, whether it's oil in Syria or heroin in Kashmir. Where do you think all that money from animal trafficking goes? It finances terror attacks like the Westgate Mall in Nairobi."

Davis pulled up a grainy CCTV video of African men with AK-47s slaughtering shoppers. He continued, hitting the audience with more images: Janjaweed death squads on horseback in Sudan, Joseph Kony's child soldiers in Congo, Maoist rebels in Nepal. He presented the theory du jour in the conservation community: that many of the worst terrorists in the world had tentacles into the illicit animal trade. Even Hillary Clinton had publicly drawn the connection. Davis stammered as he tried to defend himself before Nelson cut him off again.

"Bad people do bad things in bad places. This doesn't establish a causal relationship or even signify that the two are related."

Director Wilkes finally weighed in for the first time, and Davis stood at attention, trying to project confidence he didn't have. Wilkes knew that good leads could come from unlikely places. Hell, Saddam had been apprehended through tracking fish sandwiches. But even by the "fish-sandwich standard," Davis's case seemed thin.

"Do you have any substantive leads?"

"I have a Gitmo detainee on the record that an Indonesian terror group is trafficking wild tigers from Sumatra to fund attacks."

For a split second, Davis seemed to have the room's attention.

Nelson guffawed. "You're talking about Riduan Dwikarna. The guy's crazy as a bag of squirrels."

Davis ignored him, turning his attention to Wilkes so he could jam through his punch line. "This is a direct threat to national security, which is why I propose we create an animal-trafficking section to address this new threat."

"And I imagine you would nominate yourself to lead this new initiative?" Nelson said, to quiet chuckles from other officers in the room.

Davis nodded, suddenly feeling naked as the room waited for Director Wilkes to decide his fate.

"We'd all love to see the CIA help out on this issue," Wilkes declared, his voice heavy with compassion. "But we need to make sure every dollar spent here saves lives. Unless you can prove a direct link to terrorism, we simply can't justify the resources."

Davis swallowed, his throat completely dry. "Sir, we all know that threats proliferate and change. This is real."

Wilkes studied Davis for what felt like an eternity, then exhaled deeply. "The Sumatra connection is interesting. I'm willing to fund a small expedition to see if there's a durable intelligence interest."

Davis breathed a brief sigh of relief as Wilkes adjourned the meeting.

"We'll reconvene in a month and see if this thing has wheels."

CHAPTER 9
THE ELDERS

The village elders—the *induna*, as they were called—had plenty of reason to be upset. The *mlungas* had come and set up canned hunting concessions all along Mozambique's border with South Africa. In exchange for leasing the land to the white foreigners, the locals were promised schools and medical clinics. The schools and clinics turned out to be cinder-block sheds that were abandoned immediately after their construction. Now the locals found themselves in a situation where the white men could make hundreds of thousands of dollars hunting the people's birthright for trophies, whereas, if the indigenous people hunted the same animals they had hunted for millennia, they would end up in prison—assuming they weren't shot on sight, as was the policy throughout the region.

Cobus and Lawrence stood before the induna, who were seated at a picnic table in a clearing, under a gangly guarri tree.

Though these men were from the lower mud-hut class, they dressed in slacks and shirts as if they were headed to church. One of the induna hung his head in his hands, unable to speak through his grief.

"His son was only there to carry water!" a man shouted at Cobus. "Why did you shoot him?"

Cobus let their grief and anger wash over him. He couldn't blame the men for their pain. In fact, he shared it.

Another elder protested the legality of the kill. "If you don't have a rifle, you don't get shot! That is the law! The boy never touched a gun—they should send you to jail!"

Cobus remembered what his boss, a British former SAS officer, had told him in Iraq about dealing with people in an emotional state: *calm is contagious.* Cobus did his best to keep his words measured. "He reached for a gun. I saw it with my own eyes."

Simon's father looked up from his hands, eyes wet and red. "Who shot him? Was it you?"

Calm is contagious. "Her name was Basani," Cobus replied in a measured tone.

"She was killed in the firefight," Lawrence added.

The news of the female ranger's death silenced the induna.

Cobus continued. "As long as your sons keep bringing guns over the border to hunt rhino, we will keep killing them until all your sons are dead."

The men were taken aback by Cobus's blunt ultimatum. He softened, addressing the father of the deceased.

"This poaching war is a tragedy for both sides. I am truly sorry for your loss."

"What do you want, *mlungu*?" Simon's father bitterly spat through his tears.

"Please, just tell me who supplies the guns. No more of your boys have to die. Let us end this war."

Cobus knew it was a long shot asking them to rat out one of their own, especially after he and his team had just slaughtered three of their tribe on the other side of the border. He hoped their love of family superseded their tribal loyalty.

The induna turned to each other, searching their souls. Forced to choose a side.

———

Cobus drove straight from the meeting with the elders to ranger headquarters at Kruger. The induna had weighed their tribal loyalties against the lives of their children and had opted for protecting the next generation over the criminals in their midst. For as long as Cobus had been at Kruger, he had gone to war with men from Mozambique whose guns could be traced back to thefts in South Africa (where lax firearm laws meant that the country of fifty million people had a staggering six million guns). Cobus suspected that someone was stealing the guns, then supplying them to the desperate and willing who would try their luck in the Big Smoke. But the source of the guns had never been uncovered. Now Cobus had a name.

"The poachers are supplied their guns by a syndicate leader named Nimpini. The Hawks have a warrant out for his arrest for a farmhouse murder three years ago."

The Hawks were an elite police unit in South Africa who were known for taking scalps. Nimpini had been a thorn in their side ever since he raped and murdered the farmer's wife before stealing the guns from their home and ghosting back across the Mozambique border. The farmer's missing hunting rifle, which he had used for hunting bushpigs on his property, was subsequently used to kill five rhinos and a ranger.

The man Cobus was so urgently pleading his case to was Willem van Wyck, the managing ranger at Kruger, who oversaw Cobus's region. He sat heavily behind his desk, absorbing Cobus's findings. Willem had a thin mustache and close-cropped silver hair. The walls in his office at park headquarters were papered with maps of the park, dotted with colored pushpins denoting the sites where poachers had slaughtered the animals under his care.

"We don't even know where he is." Cobus was struck by the disinterest in Willem's voice.

"He's in Massingir, forty kilometers from the park. The bastard is living out in the open like Robin Hood. If we can arrange a transborder operation, we can have him extradited and find out who he's supplying. Maybe we can even flip them and see how high up the chain we can go."

"A transborder operation? Impossible."

Cobus boiled. "We're never going to stop the bleeding if we only fight them inside the fence. There's always another poacher willing to try his luck in the Big Smoke, and Nimpini and the other syndicate bosses will just keep throwing bodies at us. How many more of our rangers are you willing to lose?"

"Stopping one man won't make a difference, Cobus. You think there aren't dozens—*hundreds*—of other Nimpinis out there?"

"It's a start. You've seen the ballistic reports. Nearly all the hunters in our region are using the same guns, which means they're coming from the same kingpin."

Willem gave a weary sigh. "There's no way we are ever going to coordinate an operation in Moz. Do you have any idea how many corrupt officials on both sides of the border have skin in this game? If Nimpini really is their golden goose, do you think they'll just let us snatch him?"

Cobus exploded. "If we're not trying to win this fight, what's the point!"

Cobus's thoughts immediately went to Oupa, the young rhino he had sworn to protect. He pointed to a giant steel vault in the corner of Willem's office. "You have a safe with one hundred kilos of confiscated horn, and every day we add more when another rhino is slaughtered. We have to draw a line somewhere, boss."

Willem shot up out of his seat, poking his finger at Cobus. His face was red, and the engorged veins looked like vines criss-crossing his forehead. "Goddamn it, boy! I am trying to protect the last viable rhino population on earth. We do what we can, but that's all we can do."

Cobus stood defiantly before his boss, his heart racing as adrenaline pumped through his veins. Willem's aggression had set off something primal in Cobus. He didn't move, fighting the overwhelming instinct to visit great violence on this ambassador of futility.

"Fuck this. I quit."

CHAPTER 10
THE DOCTOR'S ADVICE

HONG KONG

Joshua was working through some division problems on his worksheet. Audrey had turned away for barely a second when she heard the pencil clatter to the floor. She turned to see her son's empty hand dangling off the edge of the bed.

"Joshua . . . ?" she gasped in alarm.

For a moment, her chest locked up as her mind leaped to the worst-case scenario, but the boy's faint snoring brought her back. Watching the rise and fall of his chest, she breathed a sigh of relief.

Audrey set aside the thick stack of homework for her son, swapping it for a brick of paperwork from her briefcase. Her partner, Stephen Hui, had encouraged her to pass off some of her workload to other inspectors while her son was in the hospital, but Audrey was not one to be guided by any sense of proportionality. It didn't matter if the sky was falling—every detail would be attended to, every guideline followed. Every time.

The oncologist tapped her on the shoulder. Audrey didn't remember falling asleep, but she must have, given that she hadn't heard him enter. He spoke quietly to avoid waking Joshua. "Is his father here?"

The subject was a painful one for Audrey. "He lives in Guangzhou. It is just my son and me now." She had done her best to juggle her career and her marriage, but in the end, her efforts weren't enough to keep the family intact. Though it was her husband who had left her for a younger woman, she blamed herself for the divorce.

Audrey turned her attention to her son. "How is he?"

"So far, the chemotherapy isn't working. I'm sorry I don't have better news for you."

Audrey could sense the concern in his tone. The doctor had always maintained a stony facade, but now the cracks were evident. "What does that mean?"

"We'll try one more round, but if he doesn't respond . . ." The doctor trailed off, then corrected course. "We don't want to do him any unnecessary harm with additional radiation. We're doing everything we can, but we're running out of treatment options. We'll increase the dosage in the next round and hope we get the results we're looking for." He nodded silently, as if to keep hope alive, but it didn't take a skilled detective to read his doubts.

Audrey leaned toward her sleeping son and stroked his head tenderly. A clump of hair came loose in her hand. She tried to fight back the tears.

As the oncologist departed Joshua's room and ventured down the hallway with his chart, Audrey chased after him. "Doctor." He stopped. "Are there any new experimental drugs or studies he could participate in if this doesn't work?"

"If there were anything else we could do for your son that might increase his chances of a positive outcome, I assure you we'd already be doing it. The treatment he's getting is the best in the world, but science has only gotten so far with curing cancer."

Audrey started to speak, then hesitated. The doctor could sense there was something she needed to get out, and waited for her to gather herself. She glanced about her. Seeing no one within earshot, she spoke quietly, knowing that the question she was about to ask was filled with peril. "Are there any *alternative* medicines we can try?"

"Alternatives?" the doctor asked skeptically, clearly suspecting where the conversation was headed.

"Traditional medicine." Audrey paused, then forced the words out. "I heard that rhino horn is sometimes used to treat cancer."

The doctor was visibly upset by the suggestion. "As well as being *illegal*"—he stressed the word in case the detective could somehow not know what she was suggesting—"it has no proven medicinal properties."

In all her years, Audrey had never ventured anywhere near the line separating the lawful from the lawless, and now here she was, speaking in hushed tones about committing a premeditated crime. The lines between sleep and wakefulness, right and wrong—all the dichotomies in her life, for that matter—were beginning to blur.

Audrey hung her head and nodded at the doctor's dismissal of the idea, feeling ashamed that she ever suggested it.

CHAPTER 11
WILLMORE

FALLS CHURCH, VIRGINIA

Ben Willmore twisted in his seat to stretch his lower back. Pinned on the wall of his cubicle was the quote "All good things are wild and free," by Henry David Thoreau. It was ironic that Willmore, who had always loved the outdoors, now found himself chained to a desk. Nonetheless, he still wore the faded cargo pants and tucked-in polo shirt he had worn in the field, and still carried a Benchmade folding knife clipped in his pocket.

On this particular morning, he had been sitting at his desk for three hours straight, perusing dark-web marketplaces with endangered animals for sale. The anonymity of the dark web had made shopping for the rarest, most critically endangered, most illegal animals as easy as shopping on eBay. All you had to do was download Tor Browser, and within minutes you had a direct line into the kingpins and cartel leaders moving wildlife on an industrial scale. The technology was so impenetrable, none of the criminals even bothered with middlemen or code words for their products.

Early in his career, Willmore would have been shocked to come across a pangolin for sale, but now it all seemed so humdrum. The big challenge was tricking the sellers into giving up their identity. This meant baiting the hook correctly and reeling in the fish without scaring it off his line.

His first day on the job, now over a decade ago, Willmore's boss had warned him of the number one rule of animal enforcement: Get out before the commercialization of wildlife hardens you so much that you accept it. The fish in the oceans and rivers were being depleted, but the fish Willmore was targeting seemed to be in endless supply. Though he was proud of the work he did in Special Operations at the US Fish and Wildlife Service, deep down, Willmore could feel himself inching closer to the precipice of apathy.

The phone rang. He checked his caller ID and recognized Knight's number. He had known men like Knight when he worked as a fly-fishing guide on the Snake River, outside Jackson Hole. *Situational conservationists*, he called them. Willmore always kept his defenses up when Knight called. He suspected that Knight thought himself smarter than he, and also suspected that Knight probably was. But both men trafficked in information, so there could be symbiosis.

"What can you tell me about Pei Exotic Pets in Macau?" Knight asked.

"Pei, huh?" Willmore rubbed his weathered baseball cap against his weathered brow, the name striking a chord. "Can't tell you much."

Two hundred miles away, Knight rocked back in his leather office chair, looking out at Central Park from his metal-and-glass perch. "What if I told you they procured a Sumatran rescue tiger for a US zoo?"

"Ha!" Willmore laughed. "Pei Exotics selling a rescue tiger—that would be something."

"Talk to me."

"No way. Pei Exotics is off the menu."

"I've got a ten-million-dollar claim riding on this. I'll make it worth your while."

"Can't do it. There's an ongoing investigation." Willmore would let the fly dance on the water and draw in the cutthroat trout.

"Even if I told you I have a client who tried to insure a red-tailed boa?" Knight countered, baiting a hook of his own.

"Give me a break. Boas are Appendix Two." A listing on CITES Appendix Two meant that trade in a species was legal but regulated. The Convention on International Trade in Endangered Species of Wild Fauna and Flora was the international treaty governing animal trade. Animals listed on CITES Appendix One were the real action—the so-called big-game hunting of conservation. These were creatures on the brink of extinction, and where Fish and Wildlife agents like Willmore made their bones.

"You'll have to do better than that, my man," Willmore scoffed.

"What if I told you the boa had heroin stitched inside it? Came through a dealer in Orlando."

Willmore grinned in spite of himself. Knight knew his audience. He also knew that federal prosecutors hated wasting precious resources on cases involving animals. Even prosecuting Appendix One cases entailed a lot of arm-twisting in the US Attorney's Office. This meant that the one thing better than a case involving Appendix One animals was a case that overlapped with narcotics or some other crime that prosecutors actually *did* care about.

"Who's the dealer?"

"You'd have to leave my client out of the investigation."

"This better be legit."

"Have I ever given you a bad lead?"

Willmore checked to make sure no one was listening, then spoke softly. "Deal. Pei Exotic Pets is a front company run by a guy named Wan Koi. He's the Red Pole of the Sun Yee On triad."

"Red Pole?" Knight asked.

Willmore didn't need to pull up Wan Koi's file. He'd been tracking the bastard for years. "It means he's the head muscle of the most powerful crime syndicate in Asia. The dude is a grade-A dirtbag. DEA and Interpol both want a piece of him. He's into everything from amphetamines to sex trafficking. We'd love to nail his ass, but we've got no extradition treaty with China, and he would never set foot outside Macau."

"Do you know if they're in the tiger game?"

"They're into anything you can put on a cargo ship. Animals, drugs, people—you name it."

"Thanks for the intel, brother. I'll text you the name of that snake dealer."

As the call drew to a close, Willmore began to have second thoughts about the thread he had offered Knight. He leaned forward on his elbows, lowering his voice. "Randall, be careful. People who interfere with the triads' operation have a tendency to get dismembered."

Willmore waited for a response.

"Randall, you still there?"

CHAPTER 12
LEE

Henry Lee looked sharp in his slim-fitting suit, which moved flawlessly with his runner's body as he ushered the American executives into the sitting area of his palatial modern suite. Out the window and across the water, the vaulting high-rises of Kowloon framed Victoria Harbor.

Ever since his internships working for Wall Street's masters of the universe while at Harvard Business School, Lee had developed a taste for Patek Philippe watches, Prada shoes, and $500 haircuts. The two junior associates flanking him, acolytes of their capitalist messiah, cut similarly refined figures.

"Please, have a seat." Bill Carlson, the guest of honor, settled into a large armchair opposite Lee.

"Did you review my proposal?" Lee continued in his perfect American accent.

"The numbers are impressive." Carlson casually adjusted his

tie as he spoke. "But our lawyers say tigers are a CITES Appendix One protected animal. How can this possibly be legal?"

Lee projected confidence bordering on aggression. "It isn't yet, but it will be by the time this venture would launch. Legalized trade in wildlife will be one of the top issues at the next international CITES convention. We're currently working on securing the necessary votes to downlist tigers to Appendix Two and create a legal trade in tiger parts."

"'Securing the necessary votes?' I assume you don't mean bribing."

"Lobbying."

Carlson shifted uncomfortably at the gray of it all. He was eager to break into the Asian market. Emerging markets were where the action was, but there were also risks associated with venturing into uncharted territory. Western corporations operating in Asia had a history of getting themselves into trouble because Asian markets were "nontransparent business environments." Deals could evaporate or be nullified, and the boundaries of the law could be difficult to triangulate.

Carlson had no interest in dancing anywhere near the fringe of the law and jeopardizing their $2 billion pharmaceutical empire. Moreover, according to the United States' Lacey Act, any involvement in the trafficking of protected animals could land Carlson personally in federal prison. At least, that was what his associate's due diligence had told him.

Carlson all but dismissed Lee. "The CITES convention is right around the corner. You better work fast if you're going to have the slightest prayer of getting those votes."

If Lee felt the urge to lash out at the impudent American, he hid it well. "As soon as the legislation goes through—and it will— we'll be looking at a billion-dollar industry emerging overnight."

Carlson's associate, Beth, looked up from her portfolio brimming with due-diligence questions. "Official traditional Chinese medicine stopped advocating use of tigers in 1993. Are you sure there's demand for this tiger wine?"

"People's beliefs don't change overnight. For a thousand years, my people have believed in the sacred power of the tiger."

Beth glanced at her notes. "That's *jinbu*, right? The idea that you are what you eat?"

"It is more than that," Lee told her confidently. "The new rich are looking to spend their money. We are offering them both a status symbol and a health tonic."

Carlson got it. "You are selling exclusivity."

"Many Chinese are already spending their money on tiger wine—just on the black market," Lee informed him. "When it becomes legal, demand is going to explode."

"In a country that killed its last tiger thirty years ago. Which brings us to the supply issue. Even if you can, um, *acquire* the votes you need at CITES—and that's a rather large *if*—how are you going to meet the demand? You're talking about sourcing thousands of tigers."

"Tens of thousands," Lee corrected.

Both Carlson and Beth stared at him. "Tens of thousands of tigers?" It sounded impossible. Beth's research had informed Carlson that only two thousand tigers remained in the wild, with maybe a few thousand more scattered around the world in zoos and private collections.

The silence persisted, and Lee cast his eyes across Carlson and his team, projecting power.

"Gentlemen, there are plenty of pharmaceutical companies that want to tap into the Chinese health tonic market. But only we can provide the ingredients at scale. We need a partner, but that partner does not need to be you."

Carlson glanced at Beth, intrigued but not sold. "We could set it up as a new company, with a new board, to wall it off from the KR Pharmaceutical brand," Beth offered. "On paper, KR could just be an investor and strategic partner. There'd be some exposure, but it would be limited."

Carlson nodded, considering, then returned his attention to Lee. "There's just one other issue."

Lee had to know the question that was coming, though he betrayed no hint of discomfort. "My father . . ."

Lee's father had fled China fifteen years earlier, during the crackdown on organized crime, and he was still listed near the top of their most-wanted list. Heroin trafficking. Racketeering. Human smuggling. Trading in endangered-animal parts. The allegations painted a picture of a vast underworld empire, with Lee senior running the show.

Carlson nodded grimly. "His background is concerning, to say the least. You have to understand that KR Pharmaceutical is wary of any ventures that could tarnish our brand. We simply cannot be linked to anyone engaging in criminal activities. And I suspect that none of your other suitors would want that either."

"No one has heard from my father in fifteen years. He will not be a problem."

Carlson patted his knees and turned to his colleagues. "I'm willing to continue the conversation. If everything you say checks out, we'll launch in the spring."

He rose and gave Lee a forceful handshake. "In the meantime, you better find yourself some tigers."

A grin crept up the corner of Lee's mouth. "I already have."

CHAPTER 13
NIMPINI

MOZAMBIQUE

"What is the reason for your visit to Mozambique?" the immigration official had asked him at the chaotic border crossing just east of Komatipoort.

"I'm going on safari," Cobus replied.

The official gave him a disapproving look, then stamped his passport. Moments later, Cobus was back in his matte-black Mitsubishi Triton pickup, heading east into Moz.

It was late morning on a desolate section of road between Moamba and Magude when a police vehicle shot past, heading in the opposite direction. Cobus saw the officer's eyes lock on to him as he sped by.

Don't turn around. Don't turn around. Cobus tracked the police car receding in his rearview mirror, continuing to glance back every few seconds.

A minute later, the cop appeared in his rearview mirror.

The officer flashed his lights, and Cobus pulled over, annoyed but not surprised. It happened nearly every time he came to Mozambique. His white face was a billboard advertising free cash.

"Howaya, mate?" Cobus asked as the officer approached his window. Like all of Africa, Mozambique had a troubled history of colonization and slavery. Though the European overlords had long been expelled, the wounds were still raw, and Cobus was scrupulous about not projecting any sense of entitlement or authority that would put off a man with the power to incarcerate him.

"Do you know how fast you were going?"

"About seventy, mate." Cobus knew that the speed limit was eighty kilometers per hour, and he had been cautious to leave a buffer in case he encountered any opportunistic officers like the one now leaning on his window. All that mattered to Cobus at this point was separating himself from the policeman before he decided to search the car.

"You were going one hundred." The accusation was nothing new to Cobus. It happened all the time throughout Africa. This was the moment the typical tourist would grow indignant, implicitly daring the official to exercise his authority. Then came the fatal mistake: they would say they were in hurry. They were important! They had places to be: a safari, a fancy lodge—anywhere but on the side of a remote stretch of road with a greedy cop. At that point, they would be offered the opportunity to pay the "on-the-spot fine," a.k.a. bribe.

Cobus had long since learned that the currency of detention was time. As the locals said, "You may have a watch, but we have the time." Whoever had more time would win this battle of wills.

"Huh! That's strange. My meter said I was going seventy, but you say I was going one hundred." Cobus paused, feigning befuddlement. "Where was that, exactly?"

"I followed you for five kilometers."

Bullshit, Cobus thought, but he knew that this trial wouldn't be won on the facts.

Cobus swallowed as the officer angled for a view of the back seat. *Please don't ask to look under the blanket.* If he did, the officer might discover something that could land Cobus in a Mozambican prison, and Cobus had no intention of being taken alive. He began formulating how best to kill the officer with his bare hands, if it started to break that way.

The alternative was paying the on-the-spot fine to get the officer to fuck off, but Cobus knew that would only lead to word spreading of an easy mark in their territory, and more cops would come swarming, with more curious eyes. No, that wasn't an option.

"Who's in charge of this region?" Cobus asked with polite curiosity, cautious not to come off as threatening.

"Chief Chongo."

Cobus lit up. "I know Chief Chongo! He's a big man!" *Big man* meant Chongo was important—a man worthy of respect and fear. "Where is he?"

"He is gone."

Probably a lie, but so was Cobus's claim that he knew this Mr. Chongo. He was gambling that no officer would want to hassle his boss to get his back on a shakedown for a few meticals.

"When will he be back?"

"Not until tomorrow."

"No worries, mate. I'll wait until we can get this all sorted. I don't want to disrespect the big man on his home turf."

The cop no doubt figured that Cobus was fucking with him, but didn't want to risk the outside chance that this annoying

Afrikaner actually knew his boss. Instead, he sent Cobus on his way with a stern warning.

———

Three hours later, the Triton rolled into a village of ramshackle mud huts assembled with crooked vertical posts. Twenty-five kilometers from the South African border, it looked like a cross between an indigenous village and a modern ghetto. It seemed not so much a casualty of globalization and more as if the developed world had turned its back on these people and defecated its decaying car batteries and rusted soft drink advertisements in their yards. All the old-growth forest in the region had long since been cut down, leaving an apocalyptic landscape of red dirt, devoid of any wildlife bigger than a cane rat or a puff adder. The animals were gone not as a result of poaching, but because of an expanding human population hunting for the pot to feed their families.

The pickup slowed, prowling past boys with water jugs on bikes, who took note of the unfamiliar vehicle and the white face in dark Oakleys behind the wheel.

At the edge of town, Cobus passed a petrol station. He instantly recognized the man working the pump as the father of the boy Basani had killed. Cobus hoped the man wouldn't recognize him through the tinted windows of his truck. Even if he did, he likely wouldn't say anything, for fear of exposing the fact that he had ratted out the local kingpin to Cobus and Lawrence when they met with the village elders.

As the Triton moved down the lone strip of pavement in the center of town, the mud huts gave way to large new cinder-block houses with satellite dishes and shiny SUVs. Cobus knew immediately that he had come to the right place, for there was only one way to generate that kind of wealth in a region that was ground zero for rhino poaching. The cinder-block mansions reinforced Cobus's opinion that for the kingpins, poaching wasn't about poverty. It was about insatiable greed. And the poor were just another vulnerable species they preyed on.

The Triton pulled up to a large building papered with "VOTE FRELIMO" posters. The dirt lot out front featured a statue of Jesus, surrounded by high-end superbikes, Range Rover Evoques, and Audi Q7s. Cobus spotted a police car at the end. Maybe he would be seeing the big man Mr. Chongo after all.

Cobus sat in the truck, knocking back a can of Castle Lager. On his head was a garment that looked like a brown ski cap. He tossed the empty can next to several other dead soldiers on the floor. He had bought a twelve-pack of liquid courage when he stopped for petrol in Magude, and had worked halfway through it by the time he reached his destination.

Steeling himself, Cobus pulled down his cap, a ranger-issue woodland camo balaclava that concealed his entire face. He then pulled out the shotgun he had concealed under a blanket on the floor behind him.

———

Cobus tugged open the metal door and entered the building, which looked like a cross between a mansion and a clubhouse. Men in flashy clothes were day drinking after a hard morning hunting endangered animals. A Mozambican police officer was shooting pool with his shirt unbuttoned and hanging open.

The room fell silent, all eyes on the masked intruder with a shotgun leveled at them.

"Nimpini," Cobus demanded.

The men traded nervous glances. Cobus spotted the police officer sliding his hand toward his holstered pistol. He whipped the shotgun muzzle toward the officer's face. Stepping forward, he took the officer's pistol, then ejected the magazine and put the empty weapon in a duffel bag slung over his shoulder. "I'm only here for Nimpini," he assured his wide-eyed hostage.

The officer's self-preservation instinct won out, and he surreptitiously nodded in the direction of the bar. *No honor among thieves*, Cobus mused.

Holding the shotgun with one hand, he withdrew a folded piece of paper from his pocket. He flapped it open, revealing a printout of a wanted poster for Nimpini. Cobus compared the man behind the bar to the man on the paper. Same scar bisecting his chin and lower lip. Same motherfucker.

Cobus turned back to the police officer and instructed him to lie facedown on the floor, arms and legs spread. He then had all the other men starfish on top of him. This way, only the top man had the option of daring to make a run for it—a decision that would inevitably prove fatal.

Cobus shrugged the empty duffel bag from his shoulder and dropped it on the bar. "Where are your guns?"

Cobus followed Nimpini into a back room, posting up at the doorway so he could keep eyes on both Nimpini and his pile of henchmen. Inside the room, Cobus saw a rack filled with high-powered hunting rifles and Kalashnikov variants. These were the guns that had killed both the humans and the rhinos Cobus had held so dear. "All of them in the bag. Now."

———

As he headed for the door, Cobus warned Nimpini's men that if anyone followed, the first bullet Cobus fired would be into their leader's head. He then bound his prisoner's wrists and shoved him into the back seat of the Triton.

Several kilometers outside town, Cobus pulled off on a dirt road leading into the dusty woodlands of Mozambique. He dragged Nimpini out of the pickup and tossed him in the dirt. Nimpini landed face-first, the sharp stones on the ground lacerating his chin. He looked back to see Cobus approaching, clutching his shotgun. Before he could question what was about to happen, Cobus lifted Nimpini's hips off the ground so he was on his knees and shoulders, face planted in the dust. Then Cobus reached under him and unbuckled his pants, tugging them down around his ankles. Nimpini was familiar with the use of rape as a weapon, but he had never been on this end of it. "No, please," he whimpered.

"Don't flatter yourself. You're not my type."

Cobus rose and pointed the shotgun at Nimpini's face. "Get up and take a piss and a shit. Now." Nimpini stared at him, confused. "Take a piss and a shit, or I'm leaving your body here for the vultures. And don't get any on your clothes."

Cobus would have to get through at least one border checkpoint with Nimpini in his truck, and there was always the possibility of being stopped by the cops on some bullshit traffic violation. It would be a long drive—a half day at least—and should Nimpini soil himself on the journey, the odor could lead to suspicion, which in turn could lead to inspection and subsequent incarceration for Cobus. Hell, if the tables were turned, Cobus would have shat himself in a heartbeat to tip off the South African border agents that he was being smuggled into their country.

Nimpini squatted and whimpered as he tried to force himself to defecate—surely no easy feat under the current circumstances. With his life hanging in the balance, he ultimately succeeded, which got him a brief stay of execution back on the floor in the back of Cobus's pickup.

Cobus then dug in the glove compartment and took out a syringe he had stolen from the veterinary offices at Kruger. He stuck Nimpini with the needle, which was loaded with the same barbiturates the rangers used to sedate big game for transport. It was a long journey ahead, and Cobus didn't want his captive mustering the courage to try to flee along the way. Since Cobus was just guessing the appropriate dosage for a human, he knew there was the possibility the drug could make Nimpini stop breathing altogether. Nimpini's survival, however, was low on Cobus's list of concerns right now.

Cobus reached his hometown of White River shortly after 10:00 p.m. and continued west out of town on the road to Pretoria. The road between the park and the administrative capital of South Africa was sparsely populated, and Cobus easily found a quiet place to turn off right after the 30 km marker. He could hear Nimpini groaning behind him.

Cobus circled to the back of his pickup and opened the sack full of guns, withdrawing one of the suppressed high-powered hunting rifles. He then removed the blanket covering Nimpini and led his blindfolded prisoner to an open patch of dirt behind the Triton. Nimpini stumbled, still lethargic from the remaining barbiturate in his system.

Cobus withdrew a small shovel from the back of his truck. The tool had served him well over the years and gotten him out of more than one ditch on South Africa's rutty back roads. Now it would be used to *make* a ditch. Cobus tossed the shovel at Nimpini's feet and cut his bindings. "Dig," he ordered his prisoner.

Nimpini hesitated, looking into the makeshift suppressor mounted on the hunting rifle. Out here, no one would hear him scream, and no one would hear him killed. He picked up the shovel. His life was now being measured in minutes.

As Nimpini dug the hole, Cobus crossed to one of the trees at the edge of the small clearing and carved a hash mark in it with his knife. Between the km marker and the tree, he would be able to find this place again if he needed to.

An hour later, Nimpini was drenched in sweat, standing waist-deep in the grave he had dug for himself. Cobus noted that Nimpini had taken particular care with the excavation, clearing away any rocks or roots that might make eternity in this final resting place any less comfortable.

"That's enough," Cobus informed him.

Earlier in the evening, while Nimpini was unconscious, Cobus had traversed the road over the Massinger Dam in his pickup. The sun was low in the sky, casting a blood-orange glow on the black water. Cobus considered pulling over and tossing the large bag with Nimpini's guns into the lake. It was a bulky cache of nearly a dozen weapons, with a combined weight of over fifty kilos. The contents had probably been responsible for the deaths of over a hundred rhinos and a handful of rangers at Kruger and the surrounding properties. No good could come of having weapons like these in the world.

Cobus also knew, however, that his actions could potentially kick off a war between the syndicate and the rangers, and in that event, he and his colleagues would need these types of untraceable high-powered weapons to do bad things to bad people. If there was one thing his military training had taught him, it was to always have a contingency plan.

Cobus kept Nimpini's suppressed rifle aimed at his prisoner and instructed him to remove the bag of weapons from the truck. Nimpini struggled to drag the sack from the truck to the hole, where he had to get on all fours to shove the formless dead weight over the lip of the grave. It landed with a thud.

Nimpini turned and raised his hands at Cobus, his eyes filled with terror as he stared at the rifle he had sent on so many raids into Kruger.

Cobus swept the rifle to the shovel resting on the ground, where Nimpini had dropped it.

"Get to it. They're not going to bury themselves."

––––––

The one piece of evidence Cobus kept from his encounter with Nimpini was the kingpin's mobile phone. Cobus had seen shocking reports by a fly-by-night Swiss environmentalist who had proved through DNA analysis that horn from Kruger's rhinos often appeared in Asian markets within five days of the kill. This indicated that there was a streamlined, highly efficient distribution channel that flowed north.

Cobus hoped the call log on Nimpini's phone would reveal his Asian buyer, but all he had found were dozens of numbers in both South Africa and Mozambique, with no associated names. Cobus knew that if anyone could help him interpret the data he had seized, it was Jan Snyman.

Jan and he had grown up playing rugby together in the small farming town of White River. Though it was a seemingly idyllic community nestled in the rolling hills outside Kruger, it also had the highest violent crime rate in all South Africa. Like Cobus, most of the younger generation escaped as soon as they reached adulthood. But Jan had chosen to stay and become a police officer.

During Cobus's adventure in the Middle East, Jan had developed a sizable cocaine habit, which eventually cost him his badge. Now the perpetually paranoid Afrikaner worked as a private investigator in Mpumalanga, the province that was home to both White River and Kruger. Jan was ostensibly a truth seeker by trade, but many viewed him as a serial liar and an opportunist. Cobus saw Jan for what he was: a scavenger in a wilderness of lies. And such a creature could be a useful ally.

Cobus met with Jan on the deck of a roadhouse bar on the outskirts of White River. True to form, Jan had arrived twenty minutes early and was tapping his foot anxiously as he drank his beer. Cobus pulled out Nimpini's phone and put it on the table between them.

"How did you get Nimpini's phone? I thought he was rolled up by the Hawks."

"I was the one who dumped him on their doorstep," Cobus replied. After burying Nimpini's weapons in the forest, he had driven three hours to Pretoria, where he deposited Nimpini on the sidewalk outside the elite police unit's headquarters. He tied and gagged his prisoner, then duct-taped the wanted poster to his chest lest there be any confusion about the package he had delivered. Cobus had then parked down the street, waiting until he could photograph the officers taking him inside. He was short on trust these days and wanted insurance against some crooked cop releasing Nimpini for a price.

"You're a crazy son of a bitch, Cobus. Always have been." Jan got out his laptop and plugged in Nimpini's phone.

"Do you think you can figure out who his supplier is?" Cobus asked.

"We'll see." Jan began importing the data from the phone into his computer.

"Are you still under contract with SANParks?" South African National Parks was the organization responsible for all the national parks in the country, and the last Cobus had heard, Jan was working for them, investigating poaching networks.

Jan scowled. "Don't even get me started on that shit-fight. Those bastards accused me of being in on the game."

"*You?*" Cobus inquired with appropriate shock, but he knew Jan well enough to suspect he had an unreliable streak.

Jan looked around and lowered his voice. "I got too close to something. It's a fucking hall of mirrors here, mate. You can't trust anyone."

Cobus circled behind Jan to see what was on his screen: a map of Southern Africa, with pins and lines forming a complex web.

"What's this?"

"A map of the poaching syndicates in South Africa and Moz. Every time SANParks busted someone, I ripped all the call logs on their phones, then had this software do link analysis to build a geospatial model of their communication structure. Turns out all the kingpins report to the same number."

Cobus could see a constellation of data points all gravitationally bound to a single star in Mozambique's capital. "This number in Maputo?"

Jan nodded. As the new data from Nimpini's phone continued to populate the map, it, too, orbited the Maputo number. "Looks like he was Nimpini's buyer as well," Jan added.

"Where does the horn go after this number in Maputo?"

Jan shook his head. "That's the big question. After that, it goes down a black hole. No one has ever figured out what happens between this phone number and when it hits the streets in Asia."

The revelation instantly triggered Cobus's predatory instincts. "Why not? Who does the number belong to?"

Jan let the waitress pass before answering in a hushed tone, "A consular officer from Vietnam."

"Why has no one exposed him?"

"He's politically connected. The guy's untouchable. There's no legal way to get at him."

"I'm not looking for a legal way."

CHAPTER 14
THE SUMATRA CONNECTION

Davis knew that his best—and only—shot at connecting animal trafficking to terrorism and thereby getting promoted was to prove that Jemaah Islamiyah was selling wild tigers captured near its base of operations. J.I., as it was known, was the same Southeast Asian extremist Islamic rebel group that Riduan Dwikarna had belonged to. At Guantanamo, Riduan had confirmed the rumors about J.I. being funded by animal trafficking, and now it was on Davis to track down just who in J.I. was sourcing the tigers. The traditional approach of working his way up the supply chain would be laborious and take time he didn't have. Fortunately, Davis's research indicated that only a few places in Sumatra still had tigers. Rather than follow the bread crumbs, he decided he would go straight to the bakery.

Davis began by sifting through stacks of CIA reports about all the known J.I. operations in Sumatra. He marked the group's locations on a map while simultaneously gathering everything he could find out about wild tiger populations in Sumatra, hoping to identify areas where the two might overlap.

Because Indonesia in general, let alone a few tigers on one of its islands, was not a top priority for US intelligence resources, there were no human intelligence resources he could call on in the region, and what little signals intel the agency had was limited to dated satellite imagery. Instead, Davis would have to rely almost exclusively on open-source intelligence, or OSINT. In layman's terms, this meant surfing Wikipedia pages and perusing articles by self-proclaimed experts whose credibility could not be verified.

In the early hours of his Internet browsing on the topic, a simple search for "Sumatran tigers" had turned up an interview with a slick-looking man in a suit discussing the state of the world's wild tiger populations. Davis played it in the background as he worked.

The interviewer introduced his guest. "We're here with Randall Knight, an insurance agent who's spent his entire life in the business of animals."

"I'm in the business of keeping animals alive," Knight clarified.

"So you consider yourself an animal lover?" the host inquired.

"Animal protector."

"Do you have any pets yourself?"

"I'm on the road too much to have anything counting on me back home. Properly taking care of animals is harder work than people think."

Davis's secretary poked her head into his office. Dropping a small stack of printouts on his desk, she said, "This is everything I could find on Sumatran tiger populations."

Thumbing through the documents, he saw that because the tigers were such elusive animals, most of the recent sightings were from at least seven years ago, and that many researchers questioned how up-to-date the population estimates really were.

"India, Siberia, Sumatra," Knight continued on the video clip. "These are the last places tigers can be found in their natural habitat. At this point, there are more tigers in private collections in the US than in the wild in the entire world. That makes these animals extremely valuable. And that's where my company comes in. We protect this precious investment."

"What about breeding programs to reintroduce the captive tigers back into the wild?"

Knight shook his head. "It would be great if it worked, but no big cat has ever been successfully reintroduced in the wild."

"Literally? Not *one*?"

"Other animals, yes, but not cats. That means once tigers are gone from the wild, they're never coming back."

"And how soon will that be?"

"Maybe a decade."

"I went to Princeton," the interviewer noted. "So you're predicting that our mascot, which has always been a symbol of strength and power, will exist only in cages."

"Princeton won't be alone. Most of the exotic wild animal mascots are on their way out the door: panthers, bears, wolves."

Even Davis, a city creature who never thought much about wild animals, was shocked. It seemed that every few years, he would read something about how the tigers and polar bears and elephants were in dire straits, yet, somehow, they were still in the wild. He had grown numb to the environmentalists' cries that the sky was falling. Now, it seemed, it finally was.

As he worked his way through the Internet articles about Sumatran tigers, he plotted the various populations on his map of J.I. operations, searching for places of intersection. One area of overlap emerged as the only plausible lead: a small section of forest in the remote southern tip of Sumatra. Reports as recent as five years ago estimated close to fifty tigers remaining. Aside from having the island's most credible surviving tiger population, the national park where they lived was a short drive from where Riduan Dwikarna had operated his terror cell. Finally, Davis had a lead with some legs—that is, if the OSINT was reliable.

He fired off a message to his point of contact at Guantanamo, asking her to confirm his findings with the prisoner. By the next morning, Riduan had assured the officer that yes, indeed, the tigers they were sourcing came from Bukit Barisan Selatan National Park.

Davis had his secretary book him a one-way flight to Palembang, Indonesia.

CHAPTER 15
THIEVES

KRUGER PARK, SOUTH AFRICA

The dark silhouette flew through the night. On the Honda motorcycle were two figures, their faces blacked out by their helmets. The headlight was off, but the riders could easily navigate the pale-blue strip of asphalt lit up by a poacher's moon that had just reached its apex. The man on the rear seat had a large hunting rifle strapped to his back.

The motorcycle throttled down to a purr as it passed the sign for Kruger Ranger Headquarters. Tonight, dozens of rangers would be staking out the most vulnerable regions of the park, without a thought for the security of their own command post.

The motorcycle pulled up at an angle to the front door, and the pillion rider fired his suppressed .303. The massive slug obliterated the front door lock with a dull thud.

The motorcycle burst through the door, and the two men rode down the narrow hallway, setting off motion sensors as they passed. They knew there was no beating the sensors, meaning their only option was to outrun the rangers' response and keep their helmets on so the cameras wouldn't capture their faces.

Skidding around a corner, the Honda pulled up at one of the offices. The riders dismounted and shined their small red flashlights along the walls, illuminating various maps of the park. The beams ultimately fell on the mission's objective: a giant safe.

The driver opened a duffel bag and took out an angle grinder. Holding the zirconia-infused aluminum-oxide disk to the safe, he began cutting.

As the burning steel splinters flew in a bright fan, the other rider tuned a radio to the rangers' channel and listened to the chatter of the guards responding to reports of the break-in at Ranger Headquarters. "Three minutes," he told the breacher, whose work was slow going but progressing on schedule.

The little blizzard of sparks subsided. The breacher stepped back, and the door of the safe yawned open. Inside, their flashlights found dozens of horns confiscated from slain rhinos. The men filled their bags with the gray gold.

By the time the raiders mounted up to depart, the first responders to the incident were already running down the hallways, with guns out and flashlights on.

The rangers spotted the Honda as it pulled out of the office and screeched off down the concrete floor in the opposite direction. They aimed their guns at the infiltrators but couldn't get a shot off before the motorcycle zoomed out the back door.

———

The Honda veered off the edge of the parking lot and headed down into the forest, its off-road tires and heavy-duty shocks eating up the rocky terrain. The men knew this land well, having stalked poachers here on many occasions before. They made their way to the main road outside the park, where a black pickup truck was parked on the side of the road.

The men dismounted from the Honda and rolled it deep into a thicket, then covered it with a green tarp. The bike likely wouldn't be found for several days, and even if it turned up sooner, it wouldn't matter, since it had been purchased for cash across the border and sterilized of its plates and VIN number.

The riders removed their helmets as they got inside the black pickup.

"Do you think they know which direction we went?" Lawrence asked.

"We're clean," Cobus assured his accomplice.

They drove straight to the garage at Cobus's house in White River. Cobus emptied their bags on a table, and the two men lined up the horns in four long rows. Seen all together under a naked lightbulb, it was an astonishing amount of horn, worth millions. How many millions, they wouldn't know until it was all weighed, but it would be a nearly incomprehensible amount of money for two men of their station in life.

"Are you sure about this?" Lawrence asked the man who had convinced him to go along with his criminal endeavor.

Cobus stared at the horn, his resolve hardening. He was sure.

He would infect *them* with the darkness that he carried.

CHAPTER 16
TIGER COUNTRY

35,000 FEET ABOVE THE PACIFIC OCEAN

Davis slid his shoes off and balled his toes as he reclined the two inches his economy-class middle seat would allow. Over the previous eight hours, he had worked his way through a thick stack of OSINT research, and he needed a break. With no magazines of his own, he opened an in-flight shopping catalog, thumbing through the advertisements for replica swords and premium pool floats. It wasn't that Davis had forgotten to bring anything to read—it was that Davis was a man with no personal interests to read about. Several years back, his doctor had advised him to try taking up a hobby to help with stress reduction. Davis tried knitting, online ukulele lessons, and even painting but had failed to stick with any of them. Then he was told to get a dog—*that fucking dog with its financially crippling irritable bowels*. Davis was also a man without vices—not out of principle, but because he had failed at those too. He had sworn off alcohol in college after getting drunk and embarrassing himself at a rush party for a fraternity that later rejected him, and the smell of tobacco smoke always triggered his sensory issues. And as a young boy, Nancy Reagan had instilled in him a fear of drugs that stayed with him until he joined the agency, at which point he wouldn't have been able to experiment with cannabis even if he wanted to.

Most recently, Davis had decided to take up mindfulness meditation after seeing a news piece about it on TV. He finished munching his snack pack of airline pretzels, then chased it with the last of his ginger ale. He popped in his earbuds and booted up a ten-minute meditation, hoping it might quiet his mind and allow him to drift off to sleep like the large Eastern European snoring on his shoulder.

Davis closed his eyes, and the voice in his ear began to guide him on a body scan, focusing his attention on various parts of his anatomy. The stiller and clearer Davis tried to be, the more he became obsessed with the wet breath of the man next to him condensing on his neck. And then there was the maddening itch on the side of his nose. He tried to "let the sensation pass without judgment," but he couldn't. Davis feared he was at risk of failing at this too. Though he was supposed to be focusing on his knees, his lizard brain was skittering all over his body to places where his skin itched unbearably.

Finally, Davis pulled out the earbuds and began scratching all over like his goddamn fleabag rescue dog. When the sensation subsided, he deleted the app from his phone and allowed his anxious thoughts to dance like a dragonfly skipping from lily pad to lily pad.

———

Forty-eight hours and four layovers after leaving Washington, DC, Davis stepped outside Sultan Mahmud Badaruddin II International Airport in Southern Sumatra. The first snowfall of the year had hit the DC area only a week before, and now he was stepping off into ninety-degree heat with humidity that felt as if he had forgotten to turn on the bathroom fan during a hot shower. His pale skin immediately glistened with sweat, giving him the appearance of a man who had contracted some tropical flu. But Davis had never felt better. Victory—no, *vindication*—was within his grasp.

He immediately attracted a gaggle of drivers as he headed for the taxi stand. He chose the one with the cleanest-looking car—a Suzuki SUV—and unfolded his map on the hood. He pointed to the spot where the two circles denoting the terrorist and tiger locations overlapped.

"I need to go to this place. Bukit Barisan Selatan National Park." Davis suspected he was butchering the pronunciation. "I'm looking for tigers."

The driver nodded enthusiastically. "Yes. Come, come. I take you." He then seized Davis's wheelie bag and loaded it into the SUV before Davis could commence a negotiation. Whatever the cost, the money didn't matter anyway. What mattered was that Davis would soon be at the epicenter of J.I.'s trafficking operation. There, he would flash some cash posing as a buyer and see who came out of the woodwork offering Sumatran tigers. It was only a matter of time before he would generate some leads on who was running the animal side of the notorious terrorist organization.

———

It was a long and circuitous drive to the park—much longer than the satellite imagery would suggest. The SUV's air conditioner was broken, and though Davis had the windows open, he still felt like a steamed vegetable. As they got deeper into the mountains, the smooth pavement gave way to a dirt road that was pitted with a minefield of deep puddles that had been filled by a tropical downpour that passed through earlier in the day. The SUV bounced past a large trailer truck rumbling downhill in the opposite direction. Davis followed it with his eyes, curious why such a large vehicle would find itself in such a remote stretch of protected forest.

The Suzuki crested a hill, and the driver pulled to a stop. "This the place," he said.

Davis surveyed the surrounding mountain range, his shirt and pants soaked through with sweat. He turned to the driver. "*This* is the national park where the tigers live?"

The old-growth triple-canopy rain forest that once carpeted the hills had been clear-cut and burned, replaced with neat, serried rows of young palm trees.

"Yes. This the place. I show you." The driver seized the map dangling loosely in Davis's hand. "See, this is where we come."

Davis exploded. There must be some mistake. "There are no tigers here! These are palm trees!"

"Yes, palm oil."

"I don't give a shit about palm oil! I need to find the tigers." Davis withdrew a thick manila folder brimming with web print-outs. "All these reports say there are tigers in this park!"

"That wrong. No more tiger. Tiger gone."

"How long?"

"Last one. Five year."

"No one has seen a tiger here in five years?"

"Maybe more. Not since farmers burn the forest," the driver added nonchalantly, feigning a hint of remorse at the environmental devastation.

"You said you would take me to see the tigers!"

"You say you want to come to Bukit Barisan Selatan Park. I take you this place. I no say nothing about tiger."

Hopelessness setting in, Davis leaned back against the SUV and slid to the ground until he sat with his head leaning back against the white door panel. He pressed a sweaty, cold bottle of water to his forehead. As the reality of his failure sank in, his chest constricted, each breath seeming to deliver only half the oxygen his brain needed. Though Davis was sitting on terra firma, he could feel himself drowning. The visceral terror of suffocation was only minimally reduced by the knowledge that he had been through the experience of panic attacks before and came out the other side alive. Davis closed his eyes and stuck his tongue between his teeth, desperate to regain control of his breathing before he descended into a full-fledged attack.

CHAPTER 17
THE SMUGGLERS

MAPUTO, MOZAMBIQUE

Pham Kien spent the morning reviewing visa applications. Though the work was monotonous, and he rarely found cause to deny a request, on this particular day his body hummed with nervous tension, for he would soon be receiving a major delivery. He watched the clock tick down to noon, then left the building, passing through the reinforced steel gate and the guard post on the way to take his lunch break.

The message on his phone instructed him to drive three blocks east and park outside an abandoned construction site. As Pham waited in the car, he gripped the steering wheel, palms sweating, as they did whenever he received a text referencing *bamboo*.

Pham had grown up in privilege. His parents had been politically connected in Hanoi for decades. His father, a prominent construction magnate, had pulled some strings to get Pham the posting at the Vietnamese embassy in Maputo. It was a low-level job, but his father was optimistic. The job would allow his son to develop relationships that would aid them in the great land grab going on throughout Africa. All over the continent, foreign businessmen, primarily from Asia, were involved in expansive building and agricultural projects that would reshape the region.

The Africans had grown accustomed to their new Asian partners, who were masters of soft power. American and European investment came with a posturing of authority and strings attached, as well as the colonial baggage from centuries of subjugating the "dark continent," as the pale-faced marauders had derisively called their homeland. Not the Asians though—they came bearing gifts in the form of economic opportunity and bribes, both of which were welcomed by the kleptocratic politicians and warlords throughout sub-Saharan Africa. These Asian cowboy capitalists were here to enrich their new friends—at least, the ones in positions of influence who were willing to sell their homeland to the highest bidder. And as the Africans soon discovered, some of these outsiders were also willing to pay top dollar for very specific wild animal parts.

It was for this last reason that a year ago, a skinny Mozambican in a Vodafone soccer jersey had approached Pham on the street and muttered "rhino horn" under his breath. Pham had never seen rhino horn in person, but rumors of its power had led to its cult status in Vietnam. Pham bought that first ounce on a lark and sent it home in a diplomatic pouch to his friends, who immediately wanted more. And as more horn found its way to house parties in Hanoi, one of Pham's friends back home was introduced to a buyer from Macau, who was curious how much product these young Vietnamese upstarts could get their hands on.

With demand for his product exploding, Pham wangled an introduction to the regional poaching syndicate leader, Nimpini, who began providing him with horn by the kilo. The horn would then be loaded into the diplomatic pouches bound for the capital of Vietnam. From there, it would hop a boat out of Hai Phong Port and cross the South China Sea to Macau, where the buyer waited with an endless supply of cash and demand for horn.

It had been no small feat growing his business, and the heat it drew to him had necessitated the greasing of numerous palms within the embassy. This, in turn, had squeezed his bottom line and forced him to move more volume to make a profit. The business had burgeoned into a full-time side hustle, and Pham was now neglecting the family construction business he'd been sent here to develop.

It was at this apex of his criminal career that this young player from Hanoi received a text regarding a new harvest of "bamboo"—the code word Pham and Nimpini had established for rhino horn in their communications.

As Pham waited nervously, he spotted a white man built like a mountain gorilla approaching on the sidewalk. The unfamiliar, imposing man yanked open the passenger door and got in. Pham recoiled, startled at the intrusion.

"I have your *bamboo*," the man grunted.

———

Before Cobus turned Nimpini over to the Hawks, the syndicate leader had bargained for his life with everything he could cough up about his buyer in Maputo. Nimpini didn't know Pham's name or his day job, only that he was a middleman with bottomless pockets. And Cobus intended to find out who it was that he sat in between. But first he had to persuade Pham to talk.

"Where is Nimpini?" Pham asked, his voice trembling with fear.

Cobus placed a heavy bag in Pham's lap. Pham eyed it nervously, probably wondering whether it contained the head of his former supplier—the weight was about right, and the contents were hard and curved like a skull.

"Nimpini's in jail in South Africa," Cobus said. "I'm the new supplier."

The nervous young embassy official cracked the bag enough to glimpse a large single horn. The wide base of the cone still had dried blood and gristly pieces of nasal cartilage clinging to it from where the poachers had hacked it out of the rhino's snout.

"There's more," Cobus told Pham. "A lot more."

"How much?"

"Too much for you to smuggle in your dainty diplomatic pouches. I want to meet your buyer."

"I can't do that. The contact talks only to me."

"Not anymore. Your services are no longer needed."

Cobus watched the wheels turn in Pham's head as he tried to run the calculus between the carrot on offer, and the potentially lethal stick if he refused.

"This horn is for you," Cobus continued. "Two kilos—it's worth one hundred and fifty thousand US. Call it a finder's fee for making the introduction to your contact up north."

"How will you transport the horn without me?" Pham wondered.

"I'll deliver it personally."

"What happens if I refuse your offer?"

"My associates and I will torture you with drills and power saws as long as it takes for you to give up your buyer, which I'm guessing won't take long. Then we'll burn your corpse to ashes so there will be no way for your family to identify the body."

Pham's face drained of blood, his expression one of abject terror.

"Pull up the number," Cobus said. "I'll tell you what to say."

Pham picked up his phone from the cup holder, his hand trembling.

CHAPTER 18
WILD, WILD EAST

MACAU

Cobus stood at the window in the front of the hydrofoil ferry, peering through his own haggard reflection at the obsidian-black ocean stretched out before him. Surrounded by dozens of tourists dressed for a night out on the town, he was keenly aware that he looked sloppy and out of place in his faded jeans, flannel shirt, and loose-fitting green military-style jacket. In the distance, constellations of lights began to rise from the South China Sea, gradually resolving themselves into buildings and construction cranes.

Perhaps no city in the world had changed as much in the past twenty years. Macau had originally been built up as a trading post by the Portuguese. Though the Chinese and Portuguese cultures had been stirred together in Macau for centuries, the two were ultimately oil and water. The only area where the two worlds truly blended to create something new was the food—hot, greasy, and exploding with flavor.

On the eve of the millennium, the colonial port city had reverted to Chinese control, though it operated under a different system from most of mainland China. It became a special administrative region, making it the only place in all of China where gambling was legal. Overnight, it turned into the Vegas of the East. And just as the mob had used its illicit gambling expertise to build Vegas, the first homesteaders in Macau's emerging casino industry were the triads, or "black societies," as the ruthless gangsters were known. An entire ecosystem of prostitution, gambling, and narcotics blossomed overnight. Casinos like the towering pineapple-shaped Grand Lisboa offered the Chinese elite everything they couldn't get on the strictly regulated mainland. By 2006, the former Portuguese port town had surpassed Vegas by every metric.

Eventually, news stories began to proliferate in international newspapers about the "Wild Wild East" and its debaucherous nightlife. Troubled by the bad press, the Chinese government decided to crack down. In short order, nearly all the triad leaders either were arrested or fled the country, and the street-level corruption was replaced by multinational conglomerates, many of them American, that built casinos on a scale the world had never seen.

But some of the black societies that had initially fostered the culture of vice in Macau still operated on the city's fringes, maintaining a foothold in prostitution and smuggling rackets. And Cobus planned to make them an offer they couldn't refuse.

———

The ferry glided up to the dock, and Cobus stepped into the bright white glare of the Outer Harbor Ferry Terminal. He made his way to the pillar near the tourist information kiosk, where he had been told to wait for a liaison known simply as "Broken Tooth." Cobus thumbed through a Lonely Planet guide to blend in as well as he could, hoping to look like just another asshole Westerner as he periodically glanced up to look around. Ten minutes later, his connection came wending his way through the bustling terminal.

The man's face was a chronicle of street fights far worse than the one that got him his nom de guerre. Cobus noted that the triad foot soldier's long hair and wispy beard gave him the look of a pirate.

Though Broken Tooth didn't speak English, Cobus could draw some inferences about the type of man he was dealing with. And he could tell that Broken Tooth wasn't the type of guy who would have asked any questions even if he spoke Cobus's language. He was a man who followed orders and whose blind loyalty to his boss had rewarded him with influence and cash. He probably had no idea Cobus was put in touch with his boss through the triads' contact in Maputo, or that Cobus had strong-armed his boss into a meeting by brazenly threatening to cut off their rhino horn supply if the boss declined.

Cobus watched Broken Tooth silently fidget with his cigarette as the triad escorted him across town in a new Mercedes C-Class. Surveying the city, Cobus was struck by the strange inversion that had taken place in Macau. The colonial section, once the center, was now just a quaint vestigial appendage dangling from a mega-lopolis of casino complexes and modern commercial districts. And hidden away just behind the glowing palaces were block after block of bleak tenements that had been vomited up to house the labor force required to indulge the vices of the international elite.

Broken Tooth pulled to a stop in the red-light district, which brimmed with Macau's notorious "saunas"—thinly veiled broth-els where skinny teenage girls lingered in their shrink-wrapped cocktail dresses and ice pick heels. Cobus was surprised that the women lounging in the doorways made no effort to engage him, but then again, there was enough new money in China to fill their evening without their having to solicit foreigners whose language and culture they couldn't understand.

Broken Tooth led Cobus into the Emperor Sauna, where he was bathed in the pink neon glow of the lobby. A dozen teen girls stood in a line like mannequins, wearing color-coded schoolgirl outfits based on what services they offered. Cobus scanned the tableau in bewilderment, feeling as if he had just stepped into a science fiction story set on some alien planet.

Cobus's eyes fell on a booth in the corner, where a middle-aged john groped the buttocks of a girl straddling his lap. She couldn't be more than thirteen years old. Cobus tried to tamp down his disgust. He was in the jungle now. *And in the jungle, there is no right and wrong—only predators and prey.* He would need to hold on to that bit of wisdom if he planned to survive this game he was playing.

Cobus followed Broken Tooth up the stairs to the half-empty VIP floor, where his boss, Wan Koi, held court as three breathtakingly gorgeous young women pole-danced nearby. Wan was in his thirties, dressed thug-chic in brand-name attire. His arms were covered in tattoos of dragons and tigers. He had the look of a man who had no intention of ever engaging in civilized Chinese society.

Broken Tooth approached Wan and whispered in his ear. Cobus stood before Wan, each predator studying the other to see where he fit in nature's hierarchy.

"Pretty girls," Cobus uttered, nonchalantly evaluating the crown jewels of Wan's sex empire.

"When they get old, we sell them to the Middle East," Wan

informed Cobus matter-of-factly. "One man's trash is another man's treasure."

Cobus was surprised. It was the first English he had heard since he stepped off the ferry. His host spoke it perfectly, albeit with a light accent.

Wan stubbed out his cigarette. "So you are the man with the bamboo."

———

Wan's convoy snaked through the tight streets of Taipa. The South African had promised to deliver a sizable amount of horn, and Wan wished to inspect it in a secure location. He rode separately from Cobus, not yet trusting the white man who had come seeking access to his business.

The cars approached the security checkpoint for the container port, where they passed through without showing any credentials. It was a roundabout journey for Cobus to end up only a few hundred meters from the ferry terminal where he had landed earlier in the evening. Though they could have saved half a day if Wan had just met him at the terminal, Cobus wasn't surprised at all the back-and-forth. Wan wasn't the kind of guy who came to you—unless, of course, you were the Sky Dragon, the *capo dei capi* of the Sun Yee On triads.

Cobus followed Wan and his security detail through a warehouse, where a dozen men were sorting shipments of pills and bricks, which, based on his own history of substance abuse, he assumed were speed or cocaine. Cobus knew that being allowed to see the narcotics escalated the jeopardy he was in. It indicated that by the end of the meeting, Wan intended either to be in business with the South African or to make him disappear.

But what shocked Cobus wasn't the drugs. It was the animals.

The cages, stacked twenty feet high, contained a veritable ark of the world's endangered species: eagles and monkeys and bear cubs alongside leopards and turtles and all manner of snakes and lizards that had been transplanted from their natural habitat. They lurched and spun and squawked and snarled in their claustrophobic cells. The image of their suffering sent Cobus's blood pressure soaring.

"Where is it?" Wan asked, snapping him back to the moment.

Cobus was surprised by Wan's directness. He had read and heard that Chinese culture was hidebound with ritual, but this was the new China, and Wan was part of a voracious new breed that valued money over tradition.

Cobus peeled off his jacket and unbuttoned his shirt to reveal plastic packages of light-gray powder duct-taped to his torso.

"What is this?" Wan asked skeptically. Cobus had promised him a horn.

"I ground it up in Africa—easier to transport."

Schwack! Wan snapped open a long, narrow knife and stepped toward Cobus. Slicing the tape, he handed the packages to his men, to weigh on a nearby scale.

As Wan cut the packets from Cobus's body, Cobus spotted a baby clouded leopard, staring back at him from a small cage. Cobus's heart broke for the innocent young creature that would likely soon end up in the back of a Bugatti in the Middle East. The leopard cubs' downfall was that they were adorable, which made them attractive pets in their early years. But nearly all would be put down when they reached adolescence and became too much of a liability. Wan noticed Cobus staring at the animal.

"Some creatures are worth more alive. Others are worth more dead. We'll see which one you are."

Wan cut into one of Cobus's pouches and dug out a small mound of powder on the tip of his blade. He deposited the powder in a ceramic dish, where Broken Tooth carefully squeezed a drop of acid onto it. The mixture immediately bubbled.

Broken Tooth seemed impressed. "One hundred percent pure."

Wan said to Cobus, "Where's it coming from?"

"Rhinos. That's all you need to know. There's five kilos there."

Wan eyed the shipment. "I'll give you ten thousand per kilo—fifty thousand for the whole batch."

"The street value is half a million," Cobus protested.

"We're not on the street."

Cobus was in the jungle now. He couldn't show weakness. "And you are not the only buyer," he said brusquely. "Five hundred thousand for this shipment, and I can arrange for five to twenty more kilos every month for as long as we're in business—unless you know someone else who can move this much bamboo."

Wan considered.

"Do we have a deal, or do I need to interview other buyers?" Cobus demanded.

Wan extended his hand. As Cobus reached out to consummate the negotiation, Wan gripped his hand tightly and pulled him close. "If you sell to anyone else, I will chop off this arm."

CHAPTER 19
THE SALESMEN

NEW YORK CITY

Knight kicked his feet up on his desk as he delivered the soft sell on autopilot. "I know the policy is expensive, but it's nowhere near as expensive as a lawsuit."

He heard a knock on the frame of his open door. Looking up, he saw a slender man with slumped shoulders standing awkwardly in the doorway. He gestured for the new business prospect to have a seat as he wrapped up his call.

"Chimpanzees are unpredictable animals," Knight continued. "One guy I know has this chimp. His favorite thing in the world is watching Wimbledon and jerking off when the girls grunt in their little skirts. Another lady—not my client—got a chimp, and out of the blue it decided to rip off her neighbor's ears and face and hands. They're called wild animals for a reason."

As Knight listened to the phone with divided attention, he slid a bottle of Macallan eighteen-year and a lowball toward the man sitting opposite him in silence. Knight made sure everyone felt like royalty in his office. Anyone could sell you insurance, but when you went with Knight, you were buying him and his first-class service.

"I don't drink."

Knight sized the man up. By his body language and the way he had waited submissively in the doorway, Knight suspected he was middle management, which priced him out of the more exotic animal markets, such as apes or big cats. The man shifted in his ill-fitting suit, looking uncomfortable in his own skin. Though he didn't scream "Florida" and didn't have a ponytail, Knight thought he had a read on him.

Knight covered the phone, whispering to the man. "Let me guess. You're a reptile guy?"

Reptile guy? The man shook his head, looking uncertain whether to be offended by the assumption. Knight returned to his call. "Well, if you decide you want to dump little Curious George, I can put you in touch with interested buyers. Let me know."

Knight hung up and rose from his seat, packing up his brief-case. He had a lot of money riding on finding the true source of the baby tiger at SafariWorld, and almost no time. His flight to China left in just over an hour. *And who the hell was this guy in his office wearing an off-the-rack suit?*

"You'll have to pardon me. I'm heading out the door. I didn't think I had anything on the calendar. What can I help you with?"

Knight glanced at the man again, annoyed he had misread him as a reptile guy. His radar rarely let him down. Before the man could answer, Knight took another crack.

"Wait, wait, wait. Let me guess." The fact that he was wearing a suit, even an ill-fitting one, narrowed the possibilities. The meek man probably *worked* for someone important, someone rich. *That's it.* "Horses. Private collection." Yes, he must work for someone with a very expensive horse that people would pay a handsome price to breed. "You're here to insure bloodstock," Knight finally hazarded.

"I want to talk to you about illegal animal trafficking."

Knight bristled at the implication that he would know anything about such matters. There were dirty players in the animal game, no doubt, but he wasn't one of them.

Knight sealed his briefcase. "I only deal with reputable clients."

The man could sense that Knight was being defensive. In fact, he had wanted to put Knight off balance and had succeeded. He shifted gears, softening. "I'm just gathering information."

"And you are?"

"Kevin Davis. I'm with the CIA."

Knight looked up, more surprised than impressed.

"Jesus, you're allowed to just *tell* me that?" Knight had never encountered a CIA officer in the wild, and based on what he had seen in the movies, he expected them to be more . . . well, unlike Kevin Davis.

"We only use our pseudos overseas."

Knight was skeptical. "Since when did the CIA care about animal trafficking?"

"I'm trying to make them care so we can put some resources into it."

Resources. Ha! So that was it! Knight had always assumed people took low-paying government jobs out of some quaint, irrational sense of duty. But now he recognized who was really standing in front of him. This carpetbagger was little more than Willy Loman with a badge.

"Amazing! It doesn't matter who you are or who you work for—we're all just doing biz dev." Knight loved exposing people's bullshit and couldn't contain his amusement at his deduction. It wasn't about the smug satisfaction of knowing he was right, but more about the wilting expression they couldn't hide when he exposed the lies they'd been telling themselves about their own virtue.

"What do you think about the connection between animal trafficking and terrorism?" Davis pressed.

"I think it's a fairy tale to get people in flyover states to care about saving pandas." Knight withdrew his passport from his desk and pocketed it, double-checking that he had his phone.

"A detainee told us that Indonesian terrorists in Sumatra are trafficking tigers."

"Well, there's your connection." Knight tossed him a forced smile. "Looks like you don't need me."

"You're not convinced? That tiger cub at the SafariWorld Zoo was from a region in Sumatra where terrorists operate. It's hard to believe the two aren't connected."

Knight was impressed that Davis had at least done his homework, even if he had gotten the answers wrong.

"And I'm purebred Welsh, but it doesn't mean I fuck sheep. Look, when you've been in this line of work as long as I have, you get very cynical about people. Everyone is on the make, and every claim is a con. Half the fun of the job is proving people are full of shit." Knight glanced at Davis, the last bit directed at him and his misguided theory.

Davis persisted. "Is the curator lying?"

Knight didn't have time for this. His car was waiting outside. "Zoo curators want stuff their competitors don't have, so they don't ask a lot of questions. So then it becomes my job to ask those questions." He tried to convey finality with his tone.

"So you don't think the tiger came from Sumatra?"

"I assume you've been there. There are no tigers where there's no habitat."

"If the tiger didn't come from there, where did it come from?"

"That's what I'm trying to figure out."

Knight studied Davis, his curiosity nagging at him. He couldn't picture this mousy guy with a gun if he were shooting water balloons at a carnival. "What, exactly, do you do at the CIA?"

"I'm a money laundering analyst."

"You get a degree for that?"

"The agency recruited me from Wall Street after 9/11."

"Talk about a pay cut."

Knight hesitated as he moved toward the door. Maybe he had read Davis wrong. Maybe Davis really was one of those true believers who got all weepy when he heard the national anthem at baseball games.

"I have a plane to catch. You want my professional opinion? Stop wasting my hard-earned tax dollars. The next 9/11 won't be coming from a bunch of ponytailed herp fanatics at a reptile convention. It's bad for business."

Davis blocked Knight, desperation creeping into his voice. Knight had answers of great import to Davis, both professionally and personally. "I just need to show that dollars from animal trafficking are supporting known terror groups. Can you help me out? Please."

For a fleeting moment, Knight regretted the snarky tone he had used. This guy had given up a solid six-figure job with a promising future to fight injustice for low-to-mid five figures. Knight couldn't help but respect the nobility of it in spite of himself.

"Try ivory. Boko Haram is on your terror watch list, right?"

"Yeah."

Knight called back as he slipped into the hallway. "Leave your card with my assistant. I'll text you a guy in Cameroon. You might have some common enemies. Just tell him I sent you."

———

Davis reflected on his victory as he watched Knight depart. It was a successful interrogation. He had seen the glimmer of shame when he told Knight he had nobly quit his Wall Street job to join the agency. He then used that shame to create the conditions for Knight to want to help him. From the interviews he had watched online, he also suspected that Knight had a monumental ego, and by feigning desperation, Davis could offer Knight's ego a win. Knight, the master bullshit detector, had been swayed by a moment of earnest personal revelation about Davis's past, and decided against his selfish nature to grace Davis with the charity of knowledge and connections. Never mind that Davis had made the whole thing up. He would have to remember that approach if he crossed paths with Knight again.

———

As Knight tugged his wheelie bag toward a black town car idling on Columbus Circle, he received a call he had been expecting all day from Dr. Lara Klesser. Lara ran the Veterinary Genetics Laboratory in Pretoria, which was the leader in sequencing exotic animal DNA. And in a business where provenance was nine-tenths of the law, that kind of data was invaluable. While Knight's company relied on all sorts of private labs in its forensic investigations, Lara's animal DNA lab was the only one of its kind in the world.

"Dr. Klesser, did the university receive my earmarked donation?"

Knight knew that Lara didn't mind his requests. They were usually a fun puzzle to solve, and his donation would buy a cutting-edge PCR machine she had her eye on.

"Yes, we're very grateful, Randall."

"Any luck with that tiger?"

"Where did you say the tiger cub came from?" Knight could hear a loud whirring noise in the background—likely one of Lara's techs drilling a confiscated rhino horn or lion bone for a sample.

"Supposedly wild caught," Knight replied skeptically.

"Unless two of the rarest tigers in the world traveled thousands of miles to mate, that's impossible."

The tiger was a mixed breed—Sumatran and Indochinese DNA. In Knight's experience, hybrid and inbred tigers emerged only in captivity.

"How certain can you be of that finding?"

"We used twenty-three data points in the DNA. In a murder trial you'd need only fifteen data points for a conviction."

Knight thanked her for her time, then hung up, his mind racing with questions. Who the hell would mix tiger DNA when all zoos and collectors wanted only purebreds or designer cats? Moreover, how did some shady importer in Macau get his hands on it? Though Knight's job was to investigate the claim, the fact that the definitive answer to those questions could save his company a lot of money was now secondary to the thrill of hunting down the hidden truth.

CHAPTER 20
TRADITIONAL MEDICINE

HONG KONG

Audrey sat by her son's bed, listening to the beep and whir of the monitoring equipment as he slept. Joshua had lost ten kilos and was now the same weight as when he was only nine years old. The detective had tried to work, but she was too distracted. Her desperate fear for her son had forged an idea in her—one that she had assumed would pass, but it hadn't. It was an idea that forced her to weigh her principles against the life of her son. If he should die and she had failed to do everything in her power to save him, what kind of mother was she?

Audrey fished a card out of a zipped pouch in her purse. She turned it over to reveal the advertisement for the TCM shop. For thousands of years, her people had relied on the old ways. And now she had bet Joshua's life on Western practices only a few decades old. And the new ways were failing. She held the card delicately in her fingers as she pondered its Faustian proposition.

———

The next evening, as her shift was ending, Stephen invited Audrey to try a new noodle stall a friend in the Triad Bureau had recommended. Audrey politely declined, saying she had other plans. She then headed out on foot.

Her destination was only half a kilometer away. As she turned off Queen Street onto Ko Shing, she was immediately hit by a wave of smells that took her back to her youth: cinnamon, ginseng, goji berries, dried fish and other earthy aromas she couldn't quite place. She pressed deeper down the congested, narrow street, which glowed pink and red and green from the neon signs over the medicine shops. Their wares ranged from the standard herbs to grislier things. Many of the storefronts featured clear plastic sacks of shark fins that looked like giant tortilla chips, while others sold all manner of curious animal parts: deer tails for joint pain, dried seahorses to help the kidneys, geckos flayed and mounted on sticks like jumping jacks, to be eaten to cure disease. Audrey, however, was looking for something even more exotic.

She checked the address on the business card, surprised at the building it had led her to: a modern high-rise at the end of the little street. She entered the bottom floor, which featured an arcade of small shops. Passing vendors of beauty products and luxury goods, Audrey eventually arrived at a hole-in-the-wall medicine shop.

Skeptical, she double-checked the address before entering. At the counter was a single customer—a trendy young Chinese woman in a short designer dress, with jewelry that dazzled. The woman was in the midst of purchasing an ornate bottle of rice wine with a tiger on the label. The old woman behind the counter smiled as she handed the woman her change. "Your boyfriend will be very pleased with this," she assured her. "As will you," she added with a wink.

The wine went into a decorative gold and red display box, which in turn went discreetly into a brown paper bag. The stylish young woman took it under her arm and left.

Audrey approached the counter, nervously scanning her surroundings as she handed the old woman the business card.

"I was given this card in the hospital. My son is very sick."

The old woman's expression grew somber. "Cancer. I see."

"Can you help him?"

The old woman fetched an overcrowded key ring from a drawer, then crossed to a small, locked cabinet. The keys jangled as she searched for the right one and then unlocked the door. She returned to the counter with a carved wooden box. "I believe this is what you are looking for."

The old woman opened the box, revealing a small chunk of what looked like grayish wood, with furry fibers hanging off one end. "It filters out foreign substances in the body. Good for first- and second-stage cancer."

Audrey's stomach sank. "My son has stage four. Can it help him?"

"There have been many cases where it has been success-ful," the woman said with a hint of optimism. "One very important politician here in Hong Kong was diagnosed with stage four liver cancer. He took horn and now he is cancer free. I can't tell you who he is, because he is a very powerful and respected man."

Audrey hesitated, uncertain whether to cross the line that she was tiptoeing on. Doing a transaction with a criminal enterprise would fly in the face of everything she stood for as an enforcer of the law. "Where does it come from?"

The woman withdrew a small framed photo from a shelf. It featured a blindfolded rhino lying on the ground as its horn was sheared off by clean-cut white rangers in Africa using a small chainsaw. "The animals are sedated—it doesn't harm them, and they don't feel a thing. Even if they were awake, there are no nerves in the horn and it grows back very quickly, like hair. It is all very humane and legal."

"How does it work?" *It*, as if not saying the name of the contraband somehow diminished her crime.

The old woman pulled out a wide, green ceramic dish in the shape of a pie tin with a lip. Painted on the dish was a small blue rhinoceros. She fetched an electric teakettle and poured a splash of piping hot water into the dish. She proceeded to rub the chunk of rhino horn against the bottom of the dish, which had an abrasive surface that acted like a file. The horn slowly began to sand off. The horn dust mixed with the water, forming a milky mixture. The woman then poured the rhino-horn tea into a cup. "Would you like to try?"

Audrey waved her off. The woman could sense her concern at the transaction. "Don't worry. We don't have any problems with the police. Many powerful people come to my store."

The woman drank the tea as if to reinforce the legitimacy and safety of the whole affair.

"Do you have any that is already powder?" Audrey asked.

The old woman nodded. "Many people prefer fresh, but this is just as effective."

From under the counter, she pulled a plastic bag full of grayish powder. It featured a dragon stamp. "This will get you started. Just put a pinch in water or tea."

Audrey cradled the small baggie in her hand. "How much is it?"

"Five hundred for one gram."

Audrey was astounded. "That is more than the cost of cocaine."

"Cocaine cannot save your child."

———

Audrey didn't bother stopping to get food on the way to the hospital. She had lost her appetite, and anyway, she had only one thing on her mind: curing her son before it was too late. She entered Joshua's room to find him already asleep. Audrey crossed to the window facing the hallway and closed the blinds.

She stood beside the table where his uneaten food still waited, and opened the paper bag the old woman on Ko Shing Street had given her. She then withdrew the packet of powdered horn. Her son stirred awake in bed and watched quietly as she dropped a pinch of the horn into a Styrofoam cup of hot water she had brought from the waiting room.

"What is that?" he asked his mother.

Audrey tested the temperature with her finger. "Drink it. It will make you better." She held Joshua's head up as she brought the cup to his lips. Moments later, the mixture glided into his digestive tract and began interacting with his stomach acid.

———

The sun rose outside the waiting room where Audrey had relocated so that her typing would not interrupt the boy's sleep. She had done the right thing, she told herself. She was giving Joshua every possible chance at survival, and if the ultimate cost of her trespass was her career, it was a small price to pay for her son's life. Whatever the consequences, there would be no regrets. It was the last thought that crossed her mind as she drifted off into a deeper slumber than she'd had in months.

———

She was still asleep when a commotion woke her. "All medical staff report to room seventeen immediately!" the intercom blared.

Audrey stiffened in her chair as a herd of doctors and nurses stampeded down the hallway. "Room seventeen!" she heard them shout. *Joshua's room.*

Fearing the worst, Audrey rushed after the doctors, trailing them to her son's room, where it seemed the whole hospital was funneling in.

A nurse stopped her at the door to room 17, saying that she needed to wait outside until the doctors could stabilize her son. Audrey angled for a view through the window. She was horrified to see Joshua convulsing violently on his bed.

"What is going on!" she cried. "What happened?"

Before the nurse could respond, a doctor called out in a panicked voice, "Get me twenty cc's of phenobarbital!"

Audrey felt a sudden wave of nausea as the doctors rushed to save her son's life. What had she done?

"Ms. Lam, we need you to wait outside."

Audrey covered her mouth, feeling the sudden urge to vomit.

"Ms. Lam! Please! You can't be in here right now!"

But Audrey couldn't get her feet to move. A nurse placed his arm around her, sensing she might pass out. "I've got her." He escorted her out to the waiting room, where she sat catatonic in a chair, rocking forward and back with her hand still cupped in horror over her mouth.

The nurse lowered his face to hers, trying to get her attention.

"The doctors are doing everything they can in there. Is there anything I can get you? Are you going to throw up?"

But Audrey couldn't hear the words coming out of his mouth. All she could hear were the four words running over and over in her mind: *I killed my son. I killed my son. I killed my son. I killed my son. I killed my son. I killed my son. I killed my son.*

CHAPTER 21
THE TOURIST

MACAU

As Knight drove his luxury rental car across the bridge into Macau, he was struck by the scale of it all. He had been to Las Vegas many times to meet with clients who were interested in the most exotic and expensive pets one could decorate their homes, casinos, and magic shows with: giant designer mixed-breed cats like "ligers" and "tigons," large sharks that were accustomed to roaming thousands of miles in the open ocean, and all manner of albino serpents. But Knight had never had occasion to come to Macau. Up close, with its colossal high-rise casinos jammed together on a tiny swatch of land in the South China Sea, it made Vegas look quaint.

The insurance man had been eager to break into the Chinese market for some time. Since the explosion of China's middle class, thousands of private zoos and safari parks were popping up all over the country of 1.4 billion people. These market dynamics represented a tremendous opportunity for a man with Knight's skill set, but he had so far been unable to make any inroads into the insular Chinese market. Now seeing all that wealth up close in bright neon relief only made him hungrier to get in on the action in China once he wrapped up the SafariWorld case.

He pulled up to the Sands Casino, where he valeted his rental car, then proceeded to the taxi line, carrying an envelope addressed to a "MR. LAO" under his arm. The Sands seemed to fit the character he was playing—an American tourist in Macau—and the request he would be making to potential drivers would not seem unusual in this particular context.

Knight made his way to the front of the taxi line and ducked his head in the driver's window. "Hey, buddy, do you know any places where I can find young girls?" he asked. The first driver waved him off, so he proceeded down the line, and it wasn't long before Knight found himself in the back of an old Toyota Corolla pulling away from the casino.

In reality, Knight had no interest in young girls this evening. Rather, he was looking for someone to do an errand for him—someone who wouldn't ask questions if the price was right—and soliciting prostitutes was an effective moral litmus test. This cabbie would do just fine.

Shortly after they pulled away, Knight asked the driver if he could make a brief detour. "I need to deliver an envelope," he said.

After hanging up with Ben Willmore at US Fish and Wildlife, Knight had tracked down an address for Pei Exotic Pets in Macau. According to his online map, it was only five minutes away. Knight needed to find out everything he could about their operation.

———

Across the harbor, on the island of Taipa, Cobus had just arrived at Wan's warehouse. It had taken thirty hours to get there from Mpumalanga Airport in rural South Africa. He had made a point of taking a longer route that connected to Macau through Qatar and Malaysia, avoiding the tighter customs of the Beijing or Hong Kong ports of entry. He came straight from the Macau International Airport to the warehouse, where the Sun Yee On triads still insisted on frisking him. Though the boss was increasingly developing a bond with his fellow apex predator, he had instructed Broken Tooth and his security not to take any chances with Cobus. Cobus was also taking his own security precautions by insisting that he worked alone, never revealing that Lawrence was aiding him from the South Africa side. Cobus knew he had to be indispensable to Wan. Otherwise, the triad leader would circumvent Cobus and have him dispensed with.

Cobus set his suitcase on the table and removed the clothes and pair of shoes he'd packed inside. He then ripped open the false bottom he had painstakingly sewn shut the morning before.

Inside the secret compartment were bricks of powdered horn—the fifth shipment of its kind that Cobus had personally delivered. Broken Tooth took the bricks from Cobus and placed them on a scale. They weighed four kilos to the gram, just as Cobus had promised. Broken Tooth handed the bricks to Wan's foot soldiers, who immediately set to work cutting them into smaller packets and stamping them with his trademark dragon logo.

An argument in the back of the warehouse suddenly got Broken Tooth's attention. He turned to see one of the triad guards standing in the doorway, jamming his palm into the chest of a Chinese man. The man wore a Bluetooth earpiece and waved an envelope in the air as he tried to maneuver into the warehouse. "I have a delivery for Mr. Lao," the infiltrator said loudly.

"There is no Mr. Lao here. Go away," Broken Tooth said, but the deliveryman was insistent.

"Mr. Lao! Mr. Lao!" he cried out.

Triad soldiers covered in gang tattoos began circling the deliveryman, shielding his view of Broken Tooth and Cobus and the illicit activities happening behind them. The deliveryman froze. "Please, I know nothing. I will just leave," he pleaded.

He tried to step toward the door, but a triad blocked his path.

Cobus feared for the deliveryman's life as the triads turned to Broken Tooth, waiting for him to decide the man's fate.

Broken Tooth instructed his men to search their captive. They found only a wallet, which they handed to Broken Tooth.

Broken Tooth took out the frightened man's driver's license and photographed it before returning the wallet. "There's no Mr. Lao here," he grunted. "Now, go."

———

The deliveryman turned, still clutching the envelope, and departed. Walking back to the car, he resisted the urge to break into a sprint, for fear that it might get him shot in the back.

It seemed an eternity before he reached the end of the block and got back in the front seat of his taxi, ashen and trembling. Earlier that evening, just after he picked up the American at the Sands, his fare had asked if he wouldn't mind hand-delivering a package for him. The driver had suggested he could wait while the American dropped it off himself, but the man had insisted he didn't want Mr. Lao to know he was in town. He then sweetened the deal by offering an extra thousand Hong Kong dollars for the errand.

When the driver stopped at the warehouse on the docks as directed, the American had upsold him once again, insisting that he wear a Bluetooth earpiece with a hidden camera to confirm that Mr. Lao had received the package personally. The driver protested, but the American insisted that he provide proof if he wanted the reward for delivering the letter to the fictional Mr. Lao.

———

Knight sat behind the driver, letting him catch his breath. Disinterested in the driver's fragile emotional state, Knight asked him for the earpiece so he could review the footage of the delivery.

"Mr. Lao wasn't there," the driver muttered as he handed back the earpiece with the camera.

"That's okay." Knight plugged the camera into his laptop and began playing the POV footage from the warehouse. At first glance, he knew he had just what he needed. Images of wild cats and other endangered species flickered past. It was just the kind of place Knight would expect to find counterfeit Sumatran rescue tigers. "Did you see any tigers in there?"

"No, but I wasn't looking. Those are very dangerous men. I am not doing that again." Knight ignored the driver as he found several improbable seconds of footage of a sturdily built white man standing next to Broken Tooth and a scale loaded with powdery white bricks.

"There *was* no Mr. Lao, was there?" the driver finally realized. "You made the whole story up to use me."

"Must have been the wrong address," Knight said breezily.

The driver glowered at him in the rearview mirror. "You lie to me! You try to get me killed!"

"You did good." Knight tossed a Hong Kong $1,000 note forward between the seats. It fluttered onto the driver's lap.

The driver asked Knight to get out of his car, but Knight informed him that he had another task for him and that it would be financially worth his time. For now, he told the driver, they would park down the street and wait.

CHAPTER 22
SOLICITATION

Cobus made his way through the old town of Macau, toward the red-light district. He knew that the game he was playing couldn't last forever and that the walls would soon close in. He approached the Emperor Sauna, where he planned to tell Wan that he had a massive shipment of horn coming in from his contact in Mozambique. What he wouldn't be telling Wan was that it would be his last shipment. Nor would he mention that the entire shipment would be laced with strychnine.

Though Cobus had thus far limited his exposure by poisoning only a fraction of the horn he was bringing in, there was no getting around the fact that all the poisoned horn he had supplied could ultimately be traced to a single South African supplier. As soon as Wan connected those dots, he wouldn't settle for just an arm. He would want Cobus's head as well. But if Cobus could maintain the lie just a little bit longer, he could inflict maximum harm on the syndicate, and on the demand for rhino horn, without being harmed himself.

His ultimate act would be to adulterate the remaining forty kilos of horn he and Lawrence had taken from Kruger and flood the Chinese market with it—enough to poison thousands of people—then take the $2 million he had amassed and disappear.

Once he was safely back in Africa, Cobus intended to use the money to purchase a canned hunting reserve in Zimbabwe and convert it to a private game park. Perhaps, he could even entice his good friend Lawrence to come join him and run ranger operations.

A security guard in a suit unhooked the velvet rope and ushered Cobus to the VIP area without a word. Heading upstairs, Cobus prayed under his breath that no one had connected the initial wave of poisonings to him quite yet.

———

As Knight reviewed the footage the taxi driver had taken for him, he had been less interested in the evidence of international crimes and much more interested in the sole white face he had seen in the background. Knight knew that the Sun Yee On triad was all Chinese nationals, and putting pressure on the Chinese to arrest their own people would be an arduous task. Their Caucasian compatriot, however, likely came from a country with strong diplomatic ties to the States—one that US Fish and Wildlife could undoubtedly lean on to clean up an animal trafficker traveling under their flag. And the Chinese would have no problem deporting a vile foreigner who had come to their shores to commit crimes. Though Knight didn't plan to make good on any of these threats, he could use them as leverage on the white man, to find out where the triad had sourced the tiger that wiped out SafariWorld's feline population. For that reason, Knight had instructed the cab driver to follow Cobus when he left the triad warehouse at the port.

Knight got out of the taxi and loitered on the street for several minutes after Cobus went inside the Emperor Sauna. Then he decided to go inside and take a look for himself. Since Knight was not a man with a badge, his investigations often required him to develop a cover story to gain access. Coming up with a cover story for a forty-two-year-old American in an Asian brothel would not require much imagination.

Knight stepped into the neon glow of the "sauna," where he was immediately confronted by the lineup of young women in their monochrome dresses. The bar and the tables were filled with customers, but Knight didn't spot the mysterious Caucasian who had entered just moments ago. He then noticed the staircase in back, cordoned off with a velvet rope.

The madam approached. Her beauty caught Knight off guard. No doubt a former lady of the night herself, the forty-year-old woman's large brown eyes and high cheekbones were assets that would not depreciate over time. The neckline of her black dress plunged deeply beneath the rows of ribs between her breasts.

She approached. Her familiar smile generated sex appeal that even Knight was at a loss to quantify. The body language suggested that she understood what types of perversions might have brought him through the front door, and was happy to be his partner in crime without judgment.

"Can I interest you in a massage, sir?" For a brief moment, Knight stood dumbstruck at the possibility that she might be offering to administer it personally.

"We have many beautiful ladies from many places," she added.

"I'll have a drink and think about it."

"Would you like some companionship while you consider?"

"I'll take those two." Knight pointed to the two youngest prostitutes in the lineup. Both were barely coming out the other side of puberty, and he knew that the more depraved his request, the more it would reinforce his cover as an outsider seeking forbidden pleasures in this world. "And I'd like to be seated upstairs."

"I'm afraid the upstairs is for VIP customers only, sir."

Knight asked the madam if purchasing a bottle of champagne would elevate him into that social stratum, and she confirmed that it would.

The madam then opened the velvet rope, and the two young girls led Knight away, lurching awkwardly like giraffes on their absurdly high heels.

Knight slid onto the red vinyl seat of the booth, flanked by the two teenagers. Across the room, he located his target, sitting with a mixed group of prostitutes and hard-looking men. He immediately recognized the man sitting next to the big white guy as Wan Koi, the notorious kingpin Ben Willmore at Fish and Wildlife had told him was untouchable.

As the white guy took a pull of his beer, his eyes met Knight's. He seemed instantly suspicious of the other white face in the room.

Knight welcomed the man's interest in him. He wanted the guy to squirm, and for his mind to race through the possible sinister reasons for Knight observing him. At some point, Knight would try to blackmail him, and the more exposed the man felt coming into that negotiation, the more receptive he would be to Knight's proposals.

Knight suspected, based on the video he had seen, that this was the supplier, and he hoped to gather as much dirt on the supply side as possible so he could squeeze the white criminal.

"Mister, what would you like?" asked one of the two girls sandwiching Knight.

"I have problems making boom-boom," he lied. Though he had many problems, erectile dysfunction was one he had rarely encountered, and in those rare instances, excessive alcohol consumption was always the culprit.

"Do you have anything that can help? Tiger cake? Rhino horn?"

In his younger days, Knight had found that strippers were the most reliable sources of cocaine when traveling in the States. And he suspected that the women here might be running a similar side hustle selling illicit aphrodisiacs to horny miscreants. And their supply would undoubtedly be coming from the syndicate that ran their place of business.

The girl pulled a small gray chunk of what appeared to be wood out of her bag and handed it to Knight. "Rhino horn. Here, we say women are like locks and men are the key. This will make you the master key." The other girl added seductively, "You can open all the locks."

Knight took the chunk and placed his cell phone flashlight behind it. As the light bled through the horn, it turned a warm yellow. Knight also took note of the long, symmetrical lines of the fiber pattern visible in his makeshift X-ray.

He handed the horn back, unimpressed. "This is water buffalo." Just as oregano sometimes masqueraded as marijuana, and baking soda got sold as cocaine, water buffalo was commonly used to scam customers who thought they were buying genuine African rhino horn. It was an especially effective gambit because both products had exactly the same medical efficacy—namely, the placebo effect.

The girl with the water buffalo horn glanced at the other girl, who hesitated, wondering whether to give this outsider the real thing. Knight sensed her apprehension and flashed some more cash. The girl then pulled from her purse a baggie of powder with a dragon stamp. Her body language alone—as if she were holding something radioactive—told Knight he was being offered the real deal.

He rubbed a pinch of powder in his fingers and smelled it. It had the vague aroma of what could only vaguely be described as toenails.

In recent years, Knight had overseen the removal of horns at zoos his company insured. The increase in the demand and price for rhino horn had led to a rash of break-ins at zoos throughout the United States and Europe, where thieves would try to harvest the horns from zoo animals. To discourage the raiders, the zoos had begun sedating their rhinos and using chainsaws to remove the horns. Though the process looked savage, it did no damage to the rhino, beyond a minor hangover. The chainsaws would cast off a shower of shavings that looked and smelled identical to the powder in Knight's fingers.

Satisfied, he placed the bag of horn in his jacket pocket and peeled off a few bills to pay the women for the contraband. Then, to the confusion of the prostitutes, he rose and departed. He had his theory about how the Caucasian man fit into Wan's operation, and wanted to test it as soon as possible.

Knight departed and caught another taxi back to the Sands, where he checked into a room. The moment the business center in the casino opened the next morning, he stuck a Post-It note on the baggie with "PEI EXOTIC PETS" written in Sharpie and overnighted it to Lara Klesser's lab at the University of Pretoria for testing. He hoped she might be able to give him some information on the source of the horn the white man had smuggled into Macau—information that might be useful should Knight want to squeeze the man for information.

CHAPTER 23
THE MONEY

Cobus sipped a Heineken as the dealer swept the cards off the table and dealt a new hand. Wearing a faded T-shirt and jeans, Cobus looked out of place in this remote section of the casino, which was populated almost exclusively with Chinese in couture attire. The marble hallway, located far from the bustling baccarat tables and slot machines of the main floor, was lined with luxurious VIP gambling rooms that could be rented for private junkets. Because China allowed only $3,200 worth of yuan to be moved out of the mainland at a time (and $50,000 total annually), this sort of private backroom game had become a popular way for China's elite to move larger sums of money out of the country. Yuan would go in, and dollars would come out, deposited directly into foreign accounts. The practice was so prolific that in 2013, the Sands casino chain was fined $47 million for allowing a narco-trafficker to launder tens of millions of dollars through the Macau Venetian.

But this did little to deter the billion-dollar gray market that flourished in the labyrinthine back corridors of Macau's casinos.

The only other people at Cobus's table were the dealer and a young, slim Chinese gambler wearing Gucci sunglasses, and earbuds connected to a phone in his pocket. A tattoo of a tiger crawled up the gap in the neck of his shiny tailored shirt.

The game was Texas hold 'em, and Cobus glanced down to see he'd been dealt a two and a four. It was a proper dog-shit hand, made worse by the three cards the dealer laid down on the flop. Cobus took a pull of his beer, then pushed a tall stack of chips forward, raising. Without a moment's consideration, his young Chinese opponent folded, shoving his stack to Cobus's ever-growing pile.

To the untrained eye and the cameras monitoring the casino floor—and to any law enforcement—it looked like any ordinary poker bluff. But Cobus's opponent was no ordinary gambler. He was the money man for the triad, and his job was to stay perched at that table and drip away money to anyone the triad owed cash. The accounts payable came in on his earbuds, and once the debts were settled, the benefactors of his carefully calculated ineptitude cashed out. Money and contraband were never to be in the same place at the same time, and this system guaranteed that the money side of the business was completely obfuscated as it entered and exited the triad accounts.

"I'd like to change five thousand dollars," Cobus heard over his shoulder.

He turned to see a man slap a thick stack of bills on the table. Cobus recognized him as the white john who had been eye-fucking him at the Emperor Sauna.

The Chinese dealer waved off the interloper, muttering under his breath in annoyance.

"What! My money's no good here? I just got taken to the cleaners at the Venetian. Figured these tables might be warmer."

The skinny triad moneyman glanced up at him and hissed, "Private game."

The unwelcome gambler swept up his money in frustration, adding a bit of theatrical huff to sell his ruse. He turned to Cobus. "Screw it. I'll just grab some of that overpriced sushi down the hall."

Cobus returned to his beer, masking his concern as the dealer tossed him his next hand.

———

Knight sat at the bar of Mizumi Sushi, devouring tuna nigiri with one hand as he continued to make progress on his pinball video game with the other. A clean beer glass sat next to the one he had poured for himself.

The white hold 'em player suddenly appeared at his side, looming over him like a storm front. "We both know you didn't come here to gamble."

Knight set down his phone. Afrikaans accent, no question.

"Neither did you, based on the way you were playing those garbage hands. So that's how they pay you, huh? Launder it through some sucker who sits at the table all day long on the phone, with a pile of money to give away."

The man glared at Knight in silence, playing his hand much tighter than he had in the VIP room.

"Sit down. I figured I'd need two glasses."

Knight poured him a glass from his large bottle of Sapporo, then lifted his glass in a Japanese toast. "Kanpai."

The visitor didn't reciprocate. He didn't appreciate being toyed with.

Knight gestured to his large platter of sushi. "Have at it."

"I don't eat sentient beings."

"You can have my seaweed."

"Why are you following me?"

"I'm not following you."

"Could have fooled me."

"I was following your employer. You were a lucky accident."

"Who are you?"

Knight chewed as he talked, gesturing with his chopsticks. "Who I am isn't important. What matters is that I know you're supplying rhino horn to the triads. That's a serious offense here."

The trafficker didn't dance around the issue. "What agency do you work for?"

Sensing that he had the guy on his heels, Knight ignored his question. "What do you think would happen if I tested the DNA for the horn you're putting on the market?"

The stranger hesitated, then spoke under his breath. "You'd find it's genuine white rhino."

"I don't mean what species. I mean, what if I ran it against the database of poached rhino DNA in Pretoria?"

Knight could see the Afrikaner's poker face crack as he laid that ace on the table. Because so few rhinos remained at Kruger Park, every time an animal was poached, the rangers sent the DNA to Dr. Klesser's Veterinary Genetics Lab in Pretoria. If Kruger horn turned up on the black market, the lab could trace it to the exact animal it was taken from.

Knight answered his own question. "What I'd learn is that all those horns you're selling came from the confiscated stash at Kruger Park. Not a single horn you are selling required you or your suppliers to kill even a single rhino. Which either makes you a crafty thief, or you're running some game to save animals—which, based on your vegan dietary preferences, would be the logical conclusion."

When Knight sent the horn powder samples to Lara's lab, he had hoped to find out which rhinos the South African had been poaching and use it to blackmail him for info on Wan Koi's operation. Knight had assumed the rhinos were poached on one of South Africa's many private hunting reserves, but was instead shocked to learn that the horn was from animals that not only were killed at Kruger, but whose horns had been recovered by park rangers before ending up on the black market.

The Afrikaner scanned the room, as if half suspecting some sort of takedown to happen right here and now. He returned his attention to Knight, clearly having had enough of his smug demeanor.

"Cut the shit. Who are you?"

"Relax," Knight said. "Your business is your business. As long as you help me with my business, I'm happy to keep a secret."

"And what is your business?"

"Insurance. When animals die, I lose money."

The South African guffawed at the revelation. "A fucking insurance guy."

"We're both trying to save animals."

"You're cashing in on them just like the syndicates."

"You have no idea who I am," Knight said, resenting the comparison.

As Knight's words hung in the air, a waiter approached. Knight turned and said, "I'll have two more orders of bluefin."

The South African shook his head in disgust. "You know bluefin is endangered, right?"

"That's why I'm ordering it. To the Japanese, it's worth too much money to kill the last one. So either I eat it, or the Japanese are going to eat it, but there is no version of reality where our kids will live in a world with bluefin tuna."

The man glared at Knight. "So we might as well dance on their graves?"

"It's simple math. I take no joy in the fact that certain animals don't have a place in the world we're creating, but I also know not to pick fights that are already lost. A man should never draw a line he can't hold."

"How about rhinos? What does your math tell you about them?"

Knight shook his head. "Trust me, you don't want to hear my opinion on that."

"And what happens if we can't even save the flagship species like pandas and tigers?" the Afrikaner pressed. "What chance do the snakes and fish have when they're on the brink? You can only lose so many species before humans are next to go. At some point, a line has to be drawn."

Knight could sense the man's passion and sincerity and respected his commitment even though it was ill placed. Everything was numbers to Knight, and unlike people, numbers didn't lie.

"Whatever lines we draw don't matter," Knight countered. "The new middle class in China is larger than the US population, and they want the shit that we have: cars, luxury goods, tuna. We hunted and ate nearly every wild creature we had hundreds of years ago. Why do you think there is a lion on the coat of arms in England? Because there used to be lions before we killed them all. Europe, North America— they used to have more lions and rhinos than Africa. We just got to ours first. Africa's wild game happens to be the last stuff on the menu, and now we get all fucking righteous about saving the animals."

"This is about saving our *planet*. Our home. Don't you *see* that?"

The waiter returned, setting the fresh plate of bluefin in

front of Knight. Knight took a nonchalant bite as the other man watched, looking viscerally inclined to knock him out.

Knight spoke through his mouthful of endangered fish. "Earth won't last forever. On a long enough timeline, we're all gonna get smoked by an asteroid anyway."

The South African knocked back his beer, then seized Knight's bottle of Sapporo and emptied the rest into his glass. "Do you know all rhino horn really is?"

Knight had heard it a thousand times, and beat him to the punch line.

"Fingernail. And a diamond is just a rock, and a Rolex is just a watch," Knight recited dismissively. "Things are worth what people say they are, and people have decided that *your* rhinos are worth more dead than alive. I didn't invent the invisible hand of economics, but it can really bitch-slap you if you try and fight it." Knight registered the Afrikaner's anger building as he systematically dismantled his worldview.

"So we should all just give up and find another planet to start over?"

"Look, I'm not the bad guy here. I grew up in Saratoga, New York. My dad was a trainer at the tracks."

The man scoffed at Knight's attempt at rapport-building. "Horse racing is a dirty business. I guess the apple didn't fall far from the tree."

Knight took offense, suddenly feeling the need to justify himself to this bleeding-heart moral arbiter. "My dad was one of the good ones. The other trainers used to shoot up their horses with snake venom. The horses would run like hell for a couple years, then drop dead. My dad didn't win many races, but he never lost a horse. I know animals, and my business is making sure people don't mismanage them. So yeah, I make money off animals—a lot of fucking money. But don't lump me in with those bastards raping Mother Nature."

Though Knight was normally an expert at reading people, he couldn't tell if his dinner guest had bought a word he said.

The South African took a deep breath. "What do you want?"

"Your boss shipped a tiger cub to the States. It was sick and killed a lot of tigers that my company is responsible for. I need to know where it came from."

The South African hesitated, then spoke quietly. "They have farms."

Knight was surprised at the revelation. He had heard rumors of people trying to farm endangered animals but assumed they were just that—rumors. The farming of tigers was highly illegal and would be in direct violation of the Convention on International Trade in Endangered Species of Wild Fauna and Flora (CITES).

The man leaned in. "The syndicate is going to bribe delegates at the next CITES convention to push through legislation to legalize farming wild animals. Tigers, rhinos, God knows what else."

Knight was familiar with the pitch for farming endangered animals. "Save wildlife by making it commercially viable."

"Except it's all bullshit. In reality, it's the final nail in the coffin. The second there is a legal market, demand goes through the roof and there's nothing to stop you from passing off poached animals as farmed animals. Once you legalize trade in a species, you've given up on it completely and it's gone from the wild forever. Goodbye, tigers."

"But you're trying to *stop* them."

Knight's visitor fell silent. "Where are the farms?" he pressed.

"Laos, Vietnam, Thailand. They're breeding hundreds of them in anticipation of the new CITES regulations."

"Can you get me the exact locations?"

The South African shook his head. "The big boss keeps that information close hold. But I guarantee that's where your sick tiger came from. There have been others that were dead by the time they arrived here for transshipment."

Knight called to the waiter. "I'll take the bill." He then turned his attention to his visitor, curious to understand him.

"Tell me, with all the fucked-up stuff in the world, like wars and starving kids, why do you fight for animals? And don't give me the line you tell chicks at bars. What's the real reason?"

"Because they can't fight for themselves." Knight could see in his eyes that this man was a true believer who was willing to die for his cause, and someday soon, he probably would.

———

High on opportunity, Knight glided back through the casino, toward the hotel section. He had hit a dead end in his claim investigation, but in the process he had unearthed something of much greater financial consequence.

He dialed his cell phone as he passed the baccarat tables. As it rang, he covered his ears to block out the cacophony of slot machines.

"Neil, it's Randall."

"What's that dinging noise?" said Knight's boss.

"I'm in Macau."

"Jesus, Randall, you're calling me from a casino at three a.m.! Go get some rest and call me in the morning—*my* morning."

"Hear me out, Neil. This could be big. Not just big—fucking *Forbes* cover story big. I think that cub with the virus came from a farm in Southeast Asia."

"So what?" Perkins said. "As long as the client didn't have

knowledge of that, the claim is still legitimate." *Knowledge* was always the operable word in an investigation. If the client didn't have knowledge that the animal came through illicit channels, they were in the clear. This was also the reason zoos notoriously didn't ask too many questions about where animals came from when they were trying to get their hands on rare and desirable inventory.

Knight was normally extremely professional with the old Brit, but at the moment, his inhibitions were blunted by booze and excitement. "Screw the claim! That's peanuts. If these tiger farms are real, this could be our ticket into the Asian market."

"Tiger farming? I know you're the animal expert, but I didn't think that was legal."

"It will be. I can't tell you how, but this is our chance to get in on the ground floor. Do you have any idea how massive this thing could be? And not just tigers, but other endangered species as well. We're talking about a billion-dollar market emerging over-night, and we'll be the only players on the field."

"I'm just sitting down to dinner with my wife. We'll discuss this tomorrow."

Waiting wasn't Knight's strong suit. He could see the future, and he wanted it right now. Or at least, he wanted the 10 percent commission he would receive for brokering the new business, which in this situation would amount to millions, possibly tens of millions, in his pocket.

"A little more time to investigate the source of the Safari-World tiger is all I'm asking."

CHAPTER 24
THE HUNTERS

Driving through the gates of the Adamawa Ranch, Davis felt as if he were journeying back in time. It was all so Hemingway—*glamping* for great white hunters. There were a smattering of luxurious canvas tents, stone-ringed fire pits surrounded by cushioned outdoor furniture, and long hardwood dining tables set with cloth napkins and gleaming silverware.

At first glance, the place seemed empty. Davis was set to be paneled for promotion at the end of the month and was running out of time. He needed to find terrorists dealing in endangered animals, and he needed to do it quickly. He prayed Knight hadn't sent him here on a wild-goose chase.

As he approached the lodge, Davis was greeted by Niles Becker, a rugby-strong ranger from Zimbabwe (or Rhodesia, as it had been called at the time of his birth). He wore a safari shirt and cutoff jean shorts. Every inch of his skin was baked by the sun except his eyes, which bore the white outline of the camo tactical sunglasses now dangling off the top button of his olive shirt.

Becker offered Davis a coffee, and the two men retired to couches in the posh indoor-outdoor lodge. As he sipped from the fine china cup, Davis observed that the walls were decorated with photos of white men and women kneeling with their giant kills. In their hands were compound bows, rifles, severed elephant tails, or the horn of a dead rhino.

Davis could sense his host gauging his reaction to the photos, as if Becker knew there were two Americas, but couldn't tell which one Davis was from.

"Do you like to hunt?" Becker asked his frail guest.

Davis's eyes fell on a picture of a dead lion with a hunter lifting its lifeless head. He recognized the rifle, an Accuracy International Arctic Warfare Magnum. It was the same model that had been used to neutralize Taliban at over a mile in Afghanistan. It seemed like overkill, but what did he know.

"Hunting's not really my thing." Davis trod delicately.

"People judge what we do," said Becker, "but we're the best shot at keeping these animals alive. The bulls here are forest elephants, which means they are worth shit for ecotourism because they are hard as fuck to find. If you don't make them commercially viable through managed hunting, there's no way you are going to have the resources to protect them." Becker went on to explain that they typically allowed their clients to kill only the old tuskers who were past their prime reproductive years.

Glancing around the curiously empty ranch, Davis asked if all the other guests had gone hunting. Becker informed him that there were no more guests and wouldn't be any for the rest of the year.

According to Becker, a Russian billionaire had passed through the month before with a half-dozen Eastern European prostitutes. He had asked to see the list with the quota of animals the Adamawa trophy hunting concession was allowed to harvest each year. He then insisted he wouldn't leave the ranch until he had killed every animal on their list. It took a month to blast his way through the quota, stalling out when only one animal remained on the list—a lion. And as it turned out, there weren't any lions on the property, because a band of poachers had come through and wiped them all out. In a business where client satisfaction is everything, Becker's men had to come up with a creative solution.

At first, Becker was reluctant to divulge his method, but Davis's skills as an interrogator ultimately prevailed. Becker revealed that one of his men had gone to the edge of the reserve, which flanked a national park. There, the lodge employee had cut a hole in the chain-link fence and tied a donkey to a tree just inside the hunting concession's border. That night, a large male lion slipped through the hole in the fence, and as it devoured the donkey, Becker's men woke the Russian. Donning night-vision goggles and using an infrared laser scope on a military-grade sniper rifle, the Russian crossed the last animal off his list.

Davis made a point of praising their ingenuity. After all, to Becker's earlier point, that money would finance their conservation efforts for the remainder of the year, with minimal environmental impact. Becker was proud of the work, and Davis was happy to give him that ego win to build rapport.

"The lions won't be an issue anymore," Becker added. "We've got plenty on our property, thanks to Knight."

"What, exactly, is your relationship with Randall Knight?"

"When we asked around the hunting community about our lion predicament, we were referred to Knight. He initially helped us find the new inventory. Now he insures our entire stock."

"Knight said I should talk to you about Boko Haram. He thought I might be able to help."

"Who do you work for?"

"US State Department." Davis suspected that Becker would assume he was from the CIA, as soon as the words left his mouth. At least, Davis hoped he would.

Becker set down his cup of coffee. "Let's take a drive."

CHAPTER 25
CLOSED INVESTIGATION

HONG KONG

Inspector Lam waited outside Director Cheng's office. She would not resist her punishment. Her son had survived, and that was enough. In some perverse way, perhaps the professional flagellation she was about to receive would help expunge her guilt. She was calm and at peace, or so she kept telling herself as she tapped her foot and clenched her fists above her knees.

At last, Audrey was summoned to face the consequences. She seated herself opposite the graying chief of the Narcotics Bureau, unable to make eye contact with the man who had been her mentor for so many years. Director Cheng could see she was a wreck—everyone could.

"Inspector Lam, we were notified by the hospital that your son was poisoned and that you were named as a person of interest."

Audrey appreciated the ambiguity of his phrasing, but it pained her even more that her actions had forced her boss into this uncomfortable situation. She would end it immediately, for both their sakes. "Director Cheng, I accept full—"

Director Cheng cut her off. "Let me finish." Audrey was aghast. How rude she had been to cut off her superior while he was talking!

"I have worked with you for fifteen years, and your record has been flawless," the director continued. "I know you have been under immense pressure with your son's illness, and to be blunt, I am always reluctant to judge a man—or woman—for their personal beliefs. My father used to drink bear bile every day for his liver. As far as I'm concerned, there is no evidence indicating you had anything to do with your son's poisoning." His tone indicated that he preferred to maintain the narrative he was presenting.

Audrey couldn't believe it. He was letting her off the hook, as well as willfully abandoning the one actionable lead that might solve the mystery of Joshua's near-death experience: Audrey Lam herself. After all, she was the one person who could say where the poison had come from.

"Sir, someone tainted the rhino horn with strychnine. It is possible there is more poisoned horn out there. Shouldn't we investigate . . ."

Director Cheng was clearly growing frustrated at her eagerness to dig her own grave. "As I previously stated, there is no hard evidence connecting your son's poisoning to rhino horn. And as you know, Inspector, we can't investigate an incident that didn't happen. I suggest we all let this matter rest, and just be glad your son's condition has stabilized."

Audrey looked out the window, avoiding her mentor, unable to bear the guilt as she nodded in agreement.

––––––

Racked with shame, she headed off to the hospital, making a special stop along the way to pick up something she wouldn't have considered buying only days before.

As she entered the hospital, she could feel the eyes of the entire staff judging her. She knew that everyone suspected she had administered tainted rhino horn to her son. When the doctors initially confronted her the day of Joshua's poisoning, they said there had been other cases of strychnine poisoning attributed to rhino horn in recent weeks. Audrey had maintained her silence during the doctors' questioning, knowing that her son had stabilized and that the dirty truth of the deal she had made with the devil would help no one. The only thing she could do at this point was make some changes in how she lived her life.

Audrey entered Joshua's room and handed him a plastic shopping bag. The boy opened it, revealing DVDs for various Marvel superhero movies. He lit up. "I thought I wasn't allowed to watch these until I was older."

"They say they are for people over thirteen. You're close enough."

Audrey gave her son a bittersweet smile, wanting him to enjoy what little time he may have left on Earth now that all therapeutic options seemed to be dead ends. She would quit being so obsessed with his future and focus on making the most of the present. The choice to abandon the rigid lines she had drawn felt freeing, and Audrey sensed that it would lead to some broader changes in how she lived her life—even beyond just her relationship with her son.

Joshua lowered the bag of DVDs. "Do you think the police are going to catch the person who poisoned me?"

Audrey paused, unsure how to answer, then placed a hand on her son's shoulder. "Of course they are."

———

That evening, the euphoria of her personal breakthrough faded, replaced by something darker. Someone had poisoned the rhino horn in Hong Kong. They had nearly killed her son, and they would kill others. And no one was following up on it, because her incident technically never happened. It was clear to Audrey that the path to atonement led through vengeance. She would find the people responsible and she would bring them to justice, regardless of whatever personal fallout might land on her.

Audrey left her son engrossed in an Avengers film, which would buy him at least two hours of amusement while she stepped out. She drove across town and double-parked outside the office building at the end of Ko Shing Street. She then slapped a police parking permit on her dashboard so she wouldn't be towed, and holstered her SIG P250 in case the questions she intended to ask instigated violence. She would ask the old woman *who* poisoned the horn, and if the old woman didn't know, she would trace the horn she had purchased up the supply chain to whoever was responsible.

Audrey got out of the unmarked car and entered the building. She strode through the arcade toward the traditional Chinese medicine shop. She peered through the security cage on the door.

The store had been cleared out.

CHAPTER 26
THE MESSAGE

MACAU

Cobus didn't know what to expect when Wan Koi called him at midnight. He simply told him to come to the warehouse at the port, no questions asked. At every turn, Cobus had been careful to cover his tracks and backstop his cover story, so it seemed unlikely the triad knew he had tainted a small but meaningful percentage of his shipments with gopher poison. On the other hand, he could think of no other reason they would summon him at a time the triads would normally be pickling their livers and exploiting the women in Wan's brothels.

Cobus had been trained in counterinterrogation and knew he could handle being tortured if it came to that. His cover was that of a crooked South African moving poached horn, and he had learned long ago in survival school that your cover is blown only on one condition: *when you say it is*. As long as you maintained the lie, no matter how implausible or outrageous it was, your captors would always have at least 1 percent doubt. And that 1 percent would keep you alive. Cobus knew he could maintain the lie and stay in his circle if his life depended on it.

He went to the docks and entered the warehouse, where he was surprised to find the entire gang assembled. The jittery hum of Wan's foot soldiers awaiting orders gave Cobus the sense they were mustering for something big. Several of the men took note of the South African, trading comments in Chinese, which Cobus did not take to be flattery. Other triad soldiers began laying out rolls of duct tape and bricks on a table in the center of the room. Those would certainly submerge his body in the silt of the harbor, if that was the plan.

Then a triad placed a large meat cleaver on the table.

Cobus spotted Wan conferring with Broken Tooth. He wondered whether he still had a seat at Wan's table. Or was he now on the menu?

"What did you call me for?" Cobus asked Wan.

"There's a shipment coming in tonight from Hanoi. Pangolin scales, elephant skin . . . rhino horn." Wan's mention of rhino horn was concerning. Last time Cobus checked, *he* was their supplier.

"We don't get the next rhino shipment until the end of the month."

"Not our shipment," Wan replied. "The 14K triads are moving in on our territory." Cobus's eyes fell on the meat cleaver resting on the table. "Give me your right hand," Wan demanded.

Cobus reached out, fearing that Wan had uncovered his poisoning scheme and was about to collect on his right arm. Wan gripped Cobus's wrist tightly, then placed a brick in his open palm. Cobus stood frozen, uncertain what to make of the odd ritual. Wan then took a roll of duct tape and began wrapping it around Cobus's hand and the brick, binding them together.

All around him, the other triads were taping bricks to their right hands as well.

"What are the bricks for?"

"To send a message."

———

Before Cobus arrived in Macau, all he knew about Chinese organized crime was what he had seen in Hong Kong action films. The movies were filled with fetishistic, ultraviolent gun battles. But he had been surprised to discover that none of the triads ever carried guns, and it turned out there were virtually no guns or gunfights in Hong Kong or Macau, due to strict laws that provided a fourteen-year sentence for firearm possession. Instead, gangs tended to resort to more primitive weaponry, and most real Chinese gang fights were frenetic melees involving a hodgepodge of household items like knives and pipes.

———

The convoy of five triad vehicles moved west through the streets of Macau. Cobus sat beside Wan in the back seat of the second vehicle. It was the first time Wan had invited him to ride in his car. Cobus didn't know the details of their current mission, but he had lived this moment before in Iraq—men steeling themselves to go out and visit unspeakable violence on their adversaries.

"I didn't sign up for this," Cobus calmly but assertively informed the gang leader.

Wan glared disapprovingly at Cobus. "A white man comes to me offering rhino horn. He is either a cop or a businessman. A good businessman would want to eliminate the competition. A cop would want to keep his nose clean. Which did you sign up for?"

Now Cobus understood. This was a test.

Before he could answer, the BMW pulled up to a small, run-down concrete dock at the edge of the aging Wanzai Port, which flanked the murky Inner Harbor channel. Wan gripped his meat cleaver and cast a smirk at Cobus, then opened the door.

Cobus hesitated. Before arriving in Macau, all he knew about Chinese organized crime was what he had seen in Hong Kong action films. The movies were filled with fetishistic, ultraviolent gun battles. But he had been surprised to discover that none of the triads ever carried guns, and it turned out there were virtually no guns or gunfights in Hong Kong or Macau, due to strict laws that provided a fourteen-year sentence for firearm possession. Instead, gangs tended to resort to more primitive weaponry, and most real Chinese gang fights were frenetic melees involving a hodgepodge of household items like knives and pipes.

Cobus glanced down at the brick in his hand—*fuck*—and opened his door as well.

———

The small fishing vessel tied up at the dock was tended by a skeleton crew of the 14K triads, who tossed bags of pangolin scales and elephant skin over the railing to the porters standing by. The 14K triad had been in a death spiral since Macau was cleaned up, and were now scraping by on the fringes of the city they once ruled with an iron fist. What little influence they had clung to was now being stripped away by the new ultraviolent breed of Sun Yee On triads led by Wan Koi.

By the time the 14K triads saw the Sun Yee On men flooding out of their vehicles, it was too late. The attack was swift and chaotic, like Viking berserkers hitting the shores of an unsuspecting village.

The 14K triads scrambled to defend themselves with fists and pocketknives as their brick-wielding assailants overwhelmed them with brute force, windmilling the masonry bound to their fists and smashing through the 14K defenses.

Cobus was right behind the first wave. He saw teeth and blood bursting from the rival gang members. He shouldered through the melee, driving an elbow into the face of a worker who tried to intercept him, then a left fist into the gut of another, who doubled over in agony.

He then rushed up the stairs to the bridge. He knew that the bridge would house the communications, and if the 14K triads got on the radio, reinforcements would be here soon, and bodies on both sides would pile high.

Opening the door, Cobus walked into the blunt end of a fire extinguisher. He staggered back, seeing spots, his cracked nose seeping blood. He looked up to see the captain staring at him, fear in his eyes. The captain had delivered his best shot, yet hadn't been able to fell the reaper now standing before him.

Cobus felt the primal rage grip him once again. Operating on pure animal instinct, he lunged forward, swinging his brick at the captain. The captain tried to defend himself, but it was no use. Cobus could hear bones cracking as he lit into his prey.

———

Wan arrived at the bridge moments later. Cobus stood, his taped fist bloody as he heaved with adrenaline. Beneath him cowered the captain, badly savaged but alive.

Wan gripped his meat cleaver and approached the captain. "Give me his arm."

Two other Sun Yee On soldiers lifted the captain off the floor and bent him over a table with his arm extended.

Cobus watched, literally seeing red as blood streamed down from a deep gash above his eye. Sensing the savage direction things were headed, Cobus turned to go.

Wan blocked his path, pressing the flat tip of his cleaver into Cobus's chest. "Stay."

"I did what you asked," Cobus grunted through the pain as he glared at Wan in a manner that suggested any objection might elicit violence.

Cobus began tearing the bloody strips of tape off his hands, then departed, leaving Wan to wonder what type of beast he had unleashed.

As Cobus made his way down the stairs, he could hear the screams of the captain being separated from his hand. Cobus felt no remorse for the medieval punishment being inflicted. He felt nothing but the electric hum of adrenaline. He was in the jungle now, and there was no right and wrong in the jungle.

———

Cobus returned home to the sparse apartment he had been renting near St. Lazarus Church. This was the apartment the triads knew about. Cobus knew they were mistrustful of the *gwailou* (foreign devil) and had been tracking him since he first made contact. The other apartment, his safe house, was a half mile away but required a circuitous hour-long surveillance detection route before he could be absolutely certain that he was clean and the safe house would not be compromised.

Cobus showered, unnerved that his own open wounds were doused with the blood of his enemies. Hepatitis was rampant in China's black societies, and Cobus didn't want to add liver failure to his list of concerns. His right hand quivered in pain. With no adrenaline left to numb the nerves, it was clear he had broken two of his fingers, which had been crushed between brick and bone.

Once he was cleaned up, Cobus began tending to his injuries. As he sat in his towel, taping his broken fingers with the same packing tape he had used to bundle his shipments, he heard a knock at the door.

Cobus tried to deduce who it could possibly be at four o'clock in the morning. He replayed the night's events in his mind. Wan had tested him, and he had passed the test. But then he had unnecessarily flexed his muscles by refusing to participate in the carnage on the captain. Cobus had defied the boss in front of his men, and the Chinese, more than any culture in the world, were concerned with saving face. Disobeying Wan was a risky move, made purely on impulse. In the poker game of alpha male dominance, Wan had raised, and instead of just calling, Cobus had raised again.

Now Wan was left with no choice but to fold, raise, or call. Folding wasn't an option for a crime boss looking to maintain the respect of his pack. Raising, however, meant that death could be waiting for Cobus on the other side of the door.

He reached for the hilt of his military-issue fixed-blade knife, which protruded from the slit between his mattresses. He had stashed it there in case anyone decided to come for Cobus in his sleep. Clutching his pigsticker behind his back, he cracked open the door, wearing only his towel.

Standing in the doorway was a breathtaking young Chinese

woman in a silk dress. Cobus recognized her instantly as one of the pole dancers he had eyed when he first met with Wan. *One man's trash is another man's treasure*, Wan had said of her.

Upon seeing her, Cobus deduced that Wan had decided to bury the hatchet, and he had sent one of his prized assets as a peace offering.

The girl began to speak to him in Cantonese, but Cobus interrupted her. "I don't speak Chinese."

Ignoring his comment, she said something else he didn't understand, then entered his apartment and shut the door.

Inside, the young woman stood before Cobus. The two stared at each other in silence. Her slender fingers then moved to her clavicle and delicately tugged the straps of her dress until they slid off her shoulders. The sheer fabric clung to her breasts, and the girl peeled it down until it cleared her firm contours and fell to the floor, leaving her in nothing but her thin black panties. Cobus took in her beautiful, fragile form, wondering how she looked so unspoiled after what he could only imagine had been some hard years in the flesh trade. Everything about her was so . . . *delicate*.

If he had met her at a pub in Jo'burg, he would have killed to win her affection. But here, he was just another john. The young woman sensed his reluctance to accept Wan's gift. As he looked away so as not to leer at her, she placed a hand on his damaged face, drawing his eyes back to her body.

She had a job to do, and if she didn't do it, she would report back to Wan that Cobus had rejected his peace offering. Not only would she be punished, but Cobus's slight would be the end of his relationship with Wan—and the end of his mission. In short, Wan had made both him and the girl his prisoners in this moment, and each held the key to the other's escape.

The woman cupped Cobus's genitals through the towel. He was immediately aroused despite his misgivings. She led him to a chair, where she removed his towel and took him in her mouth.

As Cobus looked down at her head rising and falling, he felt shame. He instinctively lifted her head, stopping her. He wanted to give her all his money and tell her to run away from Macau and never come back. She looked into Cobus's eyes, sensing his deep current of pain, and seemed to want to relieve him of it, even if only for an instant.

As he sat frozen before her, she rose to her feet. Tucking her thumbs in her waistband, she tugged her lacy black underwear to the floor and stepped out of it.

She gently stroked Cobus's face to placate him as she mounted him, then began rhythmically rocking with him inside her. *It's okay,* her expression told him, as if forgiving him for participating her in exploitation. Cobus locked eyes with the young woman, holding her gaze in silent understanding.

———

As Cobus climaxed, he shivered uncontrollably for several seconds, as a kaleidoscope of emotions he had been holding in suddenly strobed through him and was released, leaving him breathless. So much pain . . . and so much evil, all in the name of what he had told himself over and over and over was good. The woman saw the tears well in his eyes.

She pulled his face to her small bare breasts in a tight embrace, letting his tears roll down her skin.

CHAPTER 27
ALLIES

Knight leaned on the railing around the man-made lake, smoking a cigarette as he soaked in the opera music booming from the speakers of the Wynn Macau Casino. Geysers of water, dyed all the colors of the rainbow by submerged stage lighting, swayed and spouted and twirled with the rising score. All around Performance Lake, Chinese tourists hugged each other and took selfies.

Knight scoffed at the trite banality of the whole schmaltzy affair. Eventually, his thoughts began to wander, as if the Italian composer's original intentions for the piece were somehow bleeding through all the soapiness of the performance. He reflected on the ugly world he found himself in, and the horrors he had seen people in his business visit on the creatures in their possession—all the snakes and apes and big cats and horses that had been drugged and beaten and mutilated. Immense suffering so callously inflicted. Though Knight was no savior, he still wanted to believe that he had helped create better conditions for the animals in human custody, just as his father had.

Cobus joined Knight at the railing. His left eye was black.

Knight had decided to summon him for another meeting after conferring with Perkins and the other senior partners at Carlyle Insurance about the possibility of penetrating the Asian market.

Knight noticed a fresh dragon tattoo on Cobus's forearm. He was careful not to stare, though he knew the significance. Whatever got Cobus that black eye last night had also gotten him accepted into the Sun Yee On triad.

"Why did you leave Kruger?"

The light from the fountain show flickered off Cobus's face. "Because I didn't want to draw a line I couldn't hold," he said, echoing Knight's words from the sushi restaurant.

"So instead you went to work for the other side?" Knight knew there was more to Cobus, but the South African was playing his cards close.

Cobus stretched and squeezed his scabbed hand. "What if the animals they're killing could kill *them*?" he muttered ominously.

Knight sensed the darkness in Cobus and thought better of pursuing the line of inquiry.

"Who in the syndicate is running the negotiations for the tiger-farming legislation?" Knight asked. "Wan Koi?"

"Why are you asking?"

Knight had reached out to him under the implied pretense of investigating the infected tiger cub that the triad had shipped to SafariWorld. Though Knight wasn't explicit in the lie, he led Cobus to believe that this meeting was about gathering intel on the syndicate, with the ultimate aim of taking them out. "I thought we were past the point of needing to explain ourselves," Knight replied.

"Wan's older brother is some businessman named Henry Lee. He handles the legal side of the operation. Big brother is the brains. Little brother is the claws."

"Can you get me a meeting with Lee?"

Cobus shook his head. "He's in Hong Kong. He tries to keep his distance."

"Tell him I have a proposal. He'll be interested in what I have to say."

Knight flicked his cigarette into the lake. "I'll be at the Peninsula Hotel. He can reach me there."

————

Knight spent the next few days under self-imposed incarceration, waiting by the phone in his room, afraid of missing the call should Lee choose to reach out. He hadn't passed along his cell number to Cobus, because he didn't want anything that could be subpoenaed down the road if Lee's tiger farming came to the attention of US law enforcement before it became legal. The phone records for a hotel room in China, on the other hand, would be nearly impossible to obtain.

Knight passed the time in his little cell by cleaning out his in-box, ordering room service, browsing for clothes online, and reviewing his well-curated collection of pornography videos. He eventually found himself pacing, and to burn off the nervous energy, he had turned to air squats and push-ups during the day and emptying out the minibar at night. It was a long time to be alone with his thoughts, which were increasingly like house guests who had overstayed their welcome.

On the fourth morning, the phone rang.

"Be outside at the corner of Nathan and Salisbury Road in

ten minutes. Leave your phone and briefcase in your room. Bring nothing. Make sure your pockets are empty."

Knight stepped into his brown calfskin Ferragamo loafers, then shrugged on his lightweight trench coat over his blue Zegna suit. He thought twice about the Omega Speedmaster he was wearing, then unbuckled the metal band. Knight had seen a blurb about Lee in *Forbes* Asia, and the bio suggested that every move Lee made was dedicated purely to the acquisition of wealth. But what made the biggest impression on Knight wasn't the bland text of the puff piece, but rather the young Turk's photo. His perfect grooming and attire painted a portrait of obsession—a man who wanted only the best. And men who wanted only the best wanted to work with only the best. For a man like that, it wasn't about quality control; it was about ego. Yes, Knight knew the type well, and he knew how to navigate their psychology to his advantage.

He withdrew the $40,000 Breguet watch he had stored in the hotel safe and fastened it on his wrist. A man of Lee's refined taste would recognize the rare watch's exposed mechanics instantly. It would serve not only as Knight's membership card in the new-money class, but also as the opening salvo in their negotiation before Knight ever opened his mouth.

Before heading out the door, he opened the curtains to heavy rain. *Shit.* He reached for his umbrella, then paused.

The instructions had been clear. *Bring nothing.*

———

Knight stood in the downpour, his socks wringing water into the bed of his god-awfully expensive shoes every time he shifted his weight. Christ, he must have been standing here for twenty minutes on this damn corner in the rain. He resisted the urge to check his watch, for fear that its minimal waterproofing wouldn't hold up in this steamy climate.

The whole cloak-and-dagger setup for the meeting reminded Knight of a call he once got in Texas. One of his clients in El Paso was considering buying three adult hyenas for his roadside menagerie, and Knight requested to meet with the seller, to make sure the hyenas had been properly cared for before he underwrote their longevity. Their caretaker allegedly worked for a wealthy Mexican seller, and the meeting had been arranged at the last minute. The location for the rendezvous was a restaurant the man had chosen without leaving room for negotiation. Shortly into the conversation, it became clear to Knight that the anxious so-called caretaker was nothing more than a cutout who knew next to nothing about the animals and likely had never even seen the hyenas they were discussing. Over the years, Knight had come across numerous animals rescued from narco zoos in Mexico and South America, where the carnivores had served as both decoration and garbage disposals.

The encounter in Mexico had shaken Knight, who told his client he would not be able to insure the hyenas. He then cautioned the Texan that it was possible the hyenas—one of the few mammals known to eat their prey bone and all—had developed a taste for human flesh that could prove particularly hazardous for anyone interacting with the creatures.

But Lee was not some criminal, Knight assured himself. Lee was no different from the celebrated marijuana moguls who had made millions from the newly emerging legal cannabis trade in the United States. He was an entrepreneur and an opportunist capitalizing on an evolving market landscape—just like Knight.

———

Knight felt a hand seize his shoulder as he stood in the down-pour.

"Don't move."

He swallowed, rock still. He looked down to see a metal detector wand tracing his body from behind. Moments later, a limo pulled up, and the man with the metal detector opened the door of the car, gesturing for him to get in.

Knight slid onto the seat, his drenched clothes streaking the leather with water. He tugged his sleeve up nonchalantly to make sure his watch was exposed for Lee's observation. Opposite him, Lee looked him in the eye coldly, taking the measure of the sales-man who had been so eager to pitch him his business.

"Speak."

Lee's severe tone caught him off guard. *Where to begin?* "My name is—"

"Randall Knight. You're a partner at Carlyle Insurance. I know; I did my research on you. You have five minutes."

Knight leaned forward, forcing a confident smile. "I did my research on you too. You're a businessman. So am I. My company insures animals—everything from exotic to livestock. And from what I gather, animals are a business that you're about to venture into for the first time."

He was uncertain how direct he could be with Lee about his not-yet-legal plans. Lee's face betrayed nothing.

"If your tiger-farming legislation gets pushed through next month, you'll be looking to start big-cat production on an industrial scale. People think animals are like any other widget, but they're not. Things can go south with animals real fast, and catastrophic inven-tory collapse is something I deal with every day. And it's something I can also help my clients avoid. That's why men like Sheikh Humaid and Sergei Kerimov count on me." He hoped the social proof of his two billionaire clients would increase his value in Lee's eyes.

Knight continued. "If you're looking to do what I think you are looking to do, you can't afford to have a volatile supply chain."

Lee looked out the window, lost in thought. Knight couldn't read whether he was processing Knight's pitch, or had already passed on it in his mind.

"Mr. Lee, I know animals. And I know how to keep them alive. If we partner up, we both stand to make a lot of money."

The driver suddenly cut off his pitch. "We are at your hotel, Mr. Knight."

Knight looked at Lee, hoping for a response. Lee continued to gaze contemplatively out the window.

Knight reached for the door handle, hoping he had gotten through to the sphinxlike entrepreneur. "I'll be here for two more days before I head home."

CHAPTER 28
EXTINCTION CITY

HONG KONG

Knight's dream of the Mongolian steppe had been evolving lately, and this time the big mare was taking him farther than he had ever ridden. From an escarpment high above the ocean of grass, he scanned the horizon.

His humming body suddenly pulled him from his slumber. He had gone a tad too deep with the whisky last night, and now the bounce back in his central nervous system woke him at 5:00 a.m. with the shakes. Accustomed to such alcohol-induced sleep interruptions, he popped a milligram of Xanax and fell back asleep.

As Knight returned to his dream, he spotted a towering medieval city on the horizon. It was the first sign of humanity he had ever encountered in the dreamscape. He nudged the horse's ribs with his heels and took off at a gallop toward the stone spires in the distance.

Then the goddamn pounding on the door snapped him back

to his darkened room, where he lay sweating in his sheets, with a down pillow clutched over his head.

"Come back later! I'm sleeping!"

Bang. Bang. Bang. The knocking felt like an ice pick. Assholes! Couldn't they see his door hanger telling them to fuck off?

Pissed off, Knight rolled over in his boxer shorts and T-shirt and pulled the pillow off his head, taking inventory of the dimly lit room. Light seeped around the edges of the giant blackout curtains. *Oh, right—still in Hong Kong.*

Knight sat upright and suddenly was keenly aware that none of his various depressants and benzos had worn off yet. "Christ," he muttered as he wobbled to his feet.

Knight padded across the carpet and cracked open the door to see Lee standing in his suit, flanked by two associates. Lee's muscle pushed past without a word, turned on the lights, and began rifling through Knight's belongings.

"Hey, what the hell are you doing!"

The men ignored Knight as they inspected his things. He suspected they were seeing whether he was secretly law enforcement. Knight turned to Lee and gave him an imploring look.

"The Sky Dragon wants to meet you," Lee revealed. "Put on your clothes and don't bring anything else."

———

Moments later, Lee and his men ushered Knight into an elevator. It felt more like being taken into custody than to a meeting.

To Knight's surprise, Lee pressed the up button.

"Is he here in the building?" Knight asked.

"No."

"Where is he?"

"Myanmar."

"Myanmar!" Knight guffawed. "I'll need my passport."

"No, you won't."

———

The sleek Sikorsky helicopter was idling on the roof when Knight and Lee emerged on the helipad. They loaded in, and the bird lifted into the sky, banking over Victoria Harbor.

Six hours later, Knight was sitting in the back of a silver Range Rover, rumbling down a dirt road alongside a rice paddy. It had been a long day between the helicopter and the private plane, then a two-hour drive into the middle of the jungle at the southern tip of China. Lee had been silent for most of it, and Knight was at a loss what to do with himself without his phone to fidget with. So he spent most of the journey looking out the window at the terraced rice paddies that gave the hills the appearance of overgrown ancient temples.

The sun was getting low in the sky, and Knight began to worry that this might be a one-way trip. He nervously wondered if proving himself useful might serve as a life insurance policy. "There's something you should know," he said to Lee. "When I was doing my research on your operation, I heard stories about people getting strychnine poisoning from your rhino supply."

Lee barely registered the comment, his thoughts clearly elsewhere. "We'll look into it."

The SUV slowed to a stop, and Lee gazed into the forest. "This is where you get out."

"Where are we?" Knight asked.

"The border."

As the Range Rover stopped, Knight looked out the window

to see a trail coming down the hill from a rubber-tree planta-tion in the jungle. At the bottom, a skinny Burmese man with an AK-47 stood guard beside a man on a motorbike.

The door of the Range Rover opened, and Knight stepped out, caught between the Chinese mob and some sort of Burmese mountain militia. Knight glanced back at Lee, concerned. Lee tugged the door shut, and the Range Rover rumbled away.

The man with the AK-47 signaled for Knight to mount the back of the motorcycle. He hesitated, fearing what might happen if he did, then weighing that against what might happen if he didn't.

Knight hugged the driver's hips as they rode up the hill through the rubber trees in Myanmar. At the top a shiny Audi A4 was wait-ing. Knight relaxed. It seemed an unlikely choice for a hearse.

Knight was even more surprised when the Audi ferried him down the other side of the mountain, where a city of brand-new high-rise buildings stood like a mirage in the middle of a remote emerald valley.

———

Knight's research would later reveal that as far as the international community was concerned, the city of Mong La didn't exist. During the 1980s, the area now known as Special Region 4 had been the top opium-producing region in the Golden Triangle, ruled by a Shan warlord named Sai Leun, who lived at the center of an eighteen-hole golf course he had carved out of the jungle. Sai Leun's army and the Burmese government had been at war for some time, and the two sides eventually arrived at a stalemate. To save face, the Burmese government agreed to let Sai Leun have his own autonomous region with its own police force and army, as long as he continued to fly a Burmese flag in his new de facto narco nation.

No longer in Myanmar's sovereign territory, Sai Leun faced increasing pressure from the United States to shut down his opium production, lest the DEA come in and give him the Pablo Escobar treatment. Conveniently for Sai Leun, Mong La, the capital of Special Region 4, also shared a border with China. So rather than fight Uncle Sam, Sai Leun burned the opium fields and turned his little geopolitical black hole into a playground for China's elites. Eight massive casinos were erected on the outskirts of Mong La virtually overnight, but because Sai Leun had no experience running casinos, he needed to bring in some outside help. And as fate would have it, the triads who had been running the gambling operations in Macau had just been pushed out and needed a new place to set up shop. That was where Sky Dragon came in.

Knight's driver took him past the ladyboy discos and the casinos and dropped him off right in the center of town. All the writing on the buildings was in Chinese, and everyone except the vendors who worked in the shops was Chinese as well.

The driver directed Knight to go to the end of the street, and before he could press for more specific instructions, the Audi was gone.

As Knight perused the luxury stores along the sidewalk, he was stunned to discover they were not selling Gucci and Cartier like the shops in Macau and Hong Kong. Everything in these shops was related to the trafficking of endangered species: ivory carvings, bear paws, leopard pelts, rhino-horn bead bracelets, swatches of elephant skin, lion teeth, tiger teeth and fur, jars of bear bile, and wine with every variety of exotic creature rotting in it.

Welcome to Extinction City.

Knight felt a splash as he stepped, and looked down to see his shoe resting in a rivulet of blood on the sidewalk. He traced the stream of blood to its source: a decapitated king cobra still writhing on a wet stump that served as a chopping block. A bony Burmese man in a stained T-shirt and flip-flops swept the cobra's head onto the pavement next to several others before swiftly gutting the snake and stuffing it in a plastic bag for a customer.

"Shit."

Knight checked his loafers, which stamped bloody footprints with every other step. He passed two barefoot young Buddhist boys walking the opposite direction, looking out of place in their orange monk robes.

Knight approached the front of a fine-dining restaurant that looked as if it belonged in Manhattan rather than in this remote jungle. Outside the restaurant, it seemed that every species of endangered animal was for sale: cages with komodo dragons, Asiatic black bear cubs, Burmese star tortoises, macaques, clouded leopards. Knight passed a Chinese customer inspecting a scaly pangolin curled up in his hands. The little armadillo-like creature was one of the most endangered animals in the world, and any number of zoos in the States would have paid thousands to add it to their collection. Given its present location, however, Knight suspected that the pangolin would not be in captivity much longer.

Knight anxiously entered the restaurant, which was filled with wealthy middle-aged Chinese men who had come to Mong La to gamble, fuck underage girls, and eat creatures on the brink of extinction. Everything in the restaurant gleamed, from the dark-red varnished tabletops to the chrome light fixtures, to the frosted-glass Chinese landscapes on the walls. The centerpiece of the restaurant, and the pièce de résistance, was a giant fish tank filled with brown liquid.

The customers suspiciously eyed the white patron—the first

gwailou ever to walk through the door of the establishment. Knight warily approached the fish tank. Inside, he could make out the faint shape of some giant creature, its skin slowly decaying and becoming part of the brown slurry. Knight followed the contours of the body to the skull, where he suddenly realized what he was staring at: a fermenting tiger carcass. *Jesus Christ!* Knight did his best to swallow his reaction.

"Tiger wine," a voice cracked.

Knight turned to see an old Chinese man in faded slacks and a collared shirt that was thin from many washings. Though his creased skin hung loose on his face, the old man's eyes had the twinkle of a young boy's. He poured two glasses of the tiger wine from a plastic spigot in the tank, then offered one to Knight with a pleasant smile.

Knight politely waved off the old man's hospitality. "No thanks."

"I believe your Abraham Lincoln said that men with few vices have few virtues." The old man nodded at the glass.

Knight recoiled. "Really, it's—"

"When my family's future is at stake, I need to know who I am dealing with."

Knight suddenly realized who was standing before him. "Sky Dragon . . ."

The old man smiled in acknowledgment.

Knight raised his glass to the old man before bringing it to his lips and forcing down a gulp of the murky brown liquid, which burned like battery acid.

"You will join me for dinner," the old man insisted.

———

As the waiter delivered the food to the table, Knight used his chopsticks to inspect the plate of sautéed meat before him, uncertain what species he was pushing closer to extinction. *Fuck it.* He took a bite. It reminded him of rabbits he had shot as a boy.

"My son speaks highly of you. He thinks you could be the missing piece of our operation."

There was something calming about the Sky Dragon's voice. It reminded him of afternoons with his grandfather at the track when he was a child.

Knight was careful to choose his words, oozing respect. "I believe I can help you build your business."

"What do you think of tiger?" Sky Dragon asked nonchalantly.

The question caught him off guard. "Um . . . what do I think of *tiger*?"

"Your meal. There are only a few restaurants in the world where you can eat tiger."

Knight resisted the urge to vomit as he forced the bolus of endangered wildlife down his throat. Now was not the time to show disgust or disdain.

"I eat McDonald's, so who am I to judge, right?"

The Sky Dragon laughed at the quip, his eyes twinkling. "Here, they say we eat everything with four legs except the table."

"And everything that flies that isn't a plane," Knight countered, familiar with the old joke about Chinese dietary habits.

"In the West, you decide that some animals are friends and some are food."

Knight saw his opening. "I believe that animals are a product, and there is good business and bad business. Dealing in products like heroin that kill your clients and land you in hiding in

Myanmar is bad business. Your son is trying to build an empire for your family that will take your operation out of the black market and into the global economy. In my opinion, that's good business, and the kind of business I want to help build. So if you want to know what I think of tiger meat, honestly, I think it tastes like cat urine, and that tiger wine just tastes like cheap sake. But we aren't here to discuss food. We are here to discuss the future of your family."

The seconds felt like hours as the Sky Dragon considered the words. Knight's brutal honesty had landed him in trouble before, and he began to wonder whether he was about to end up in a Burmese rubber-tree plantation with a bullet in his head for his impudence.

Finally, the Sky Dragon spoke. "So you will help us."

"I will deal only with Lee. I don't want any connection to the *other side* of your business. And I'll need to see the farms myself to do my diligence before we make any formal arrangements."

Knight pinched a piece of tiger meat in his chopsticks and held it up for the Sky Dragon. "I need to know what we're insuring."

CHAPTER 29
DEALER'S CHOICE

HONG KONG

"Hello, I am calling from the police department," Inspector Audrey Lam said to the receptionist who answered the phone. "I was wondering if you have seen any cases of strychnine poisoning in the past month." She waited as the woman reviewed the hospital's recent admissions records.

Early in her career—God, was it twenty years now?—Audrey had investigated a string of heroin overdoses in the slums of Sham Shui Po, on the outskirts of Kowloon. Toxicology reports on the victims revealed that the heroin had been spiked with fentanyl to increase its potency. The information about the addition of fentanyl, which was fifty times the strength of heroin, had not trickled down the supply chain to the end users, who proceeded to shoot their normal heroin dosage into their veins, with ghastly consequences.

One of the deceased young women Audrey had come across was on her knees with her face prostrate on the floor and her arms resting limply at her sides, as if frozen in some bizarre yoga pose. She had collapsed to her knees so quickly that she couldn't even control her arms to break her fall, instead smashing her face on the floor and cracking her cheekbone. Audrey and her colleagues managed to identify the source of the tainted shipment, which by that point had ended ten of the eleven lives it would ultimately claim. The eleventh was the dealer, who leaped from the thirtieth-floor balcony when Audrey and her colleagues came to arrest him for manslaughter.

Audrey suspected that her son's poisoning had followed a similar pattern, and was spending her day off work calling every hospital in the area to ask whether they had seen cases similar to Joshua's. The hospital receptionist on the other end of the line revealed that indeed there had been two cases of strychnine poisoning in the past week. Audrey scratched down the numeral "2" next to the name of the hospital. Each of the hospitals on her long list had a number written next to it: 2, 1, 0, 3 . . .

The receptionist revealed that one of their two poisoned patients had died, while the other, like Audrey's son, narrowly pulled through.

"Can you give me the name of the one who survived?" Audrey asked.

———

Inspector Lam knew the area in East Kowloon where the poisoning victim lived. It was a tenement block she had visited more than once in her years as a narcotics detective. While Hong Kong was generally a safe city, Kowloon still had some rough spots, and Audrey felt the need to press-check her pistol, making sure a round was chambered before getting out of her car.

Audrey entered a rickety elevator, noting the complete

absence of maintenance records. The car whined and lurched and chittered, and its fluorescent light flickered as it labored toward the fifteenth floor. Audrey suspected that the car would not be serviced until it eventually froze in place or fell to its ruin. Statistically, it was unlikely to happen during this ascent, but she breathed a sigh of relief as she alit on the fifteenth floor, making a mental note to take the stairs on the way down.

Audrey knocked on a door at the end of the hallway, which bore the address the hospital receptionist had given her. A middle-aged woman answered. Audrey held her badge up. "Mrs. Lo, I'd like to speak with your daughter."

The woman invited Audrey inside and offered her a cup of tea, which she politely accepted in an effort to build rapport, but which she didn't actually intend to drink. The woman's only child was her fifteen-year-old daughter, who looked closer to eighteen in her tight-fitting trendy clothes and thick makeup. Audrey questioned the girl for ten minutes in the living room, but the conversation revealed little about the source of the strychnine that nearly killed her.

Audrey asked whether the girl had ever taken any controlled substances of any kind, and the mother interjected, "She's never done anything like that. She is a good student. She never has any trouble."

Audrey pressed the daughter to answer on her own behalf, and the girl confirmed she had never taken any illegal substances of any kind. "What about any illegal traditional medicines?" The girl assured the inspector that she had never tried any traditional medicines beyond the herbal teas her mother forced on her when she was sick.

"So you don't have any idea how you got poisoned?" Audrey asked.

The girl offered that it could have been from the curry fish balls she bought at a food stall earlier on the day she was poisoned.

Audrey sensed that the girl was not being honest. There were numerous tells—she was limiting her movement, pausing before answering, and offering few details when she did speak. While these weren't damning behaviors in and of themselves, they sparked enough suspicion that Audrey asked the girl's mother for permission to search the girl's room. The woman, who was equally mystified by her daughter's poisoning, readily consented, and Audrey told the two of them to stay in the living room while she entered the bedroom.

She was struck by the juxtaposition of the attractive, mature-looking teen and her room with its toy-themed bedding, mountains of stuffed animals, and posters of boy bands on the walls. Puberty had fallen on this home like a thunderbolt, and both the girl's mother and the decor had yet to catch up.

Searching the girl's closet, she felt some foil packets hidden inside the toe of a high-top sneaker. Audrey withdrew the hidden contraband: a daisy chain of condoms. She returned the prophylactics to their hiding place, not wanting to shame the girl in front of her mother in a way that would only lead to higher-risk behavior down the line.

Audrey eventually made her way to the girl's dresser, squeezing each sock until she found a long, striped one that contained a marijuana pipe. Though Audrey had no reason to suspect that the girl had been poisoned by smoking cannabis, it offered two key insights. First, she had been lying about her innocence regarding illegal substances. Second, Audrey knew that people who trafficked in contraband typically didn't limit themselves to one variety.

Audrey returned to the living room and presented the pipe to the girl.

"What is that!" the mother interjected.

Audrey ignored the woman, keeping her laser focus on the girl, who trembled with fear. "Who do you get your marijuana from?" Audrey asked.

The girl required little coaxing before she gave up the name of an older boy at her school: Johnny Chu.

"Has Johnny ever given you rhino horn?" the inspector pressed.

The girl glanced at her mother in shame, then nodded.

———

Johnny Chu lived in the New Territories, as Kowloon West was commonly known. He was nineteen and had recently moved out of his parents' home with money he had made supplying party pills to his friends. He was new enough to the drug game, and a small enough player, that he had managed to stay off the Hong Kong Police Department's radar.

On this night, as on many others, Johnny's apartment was packed with sexy young Hong Kong hipsters who had come to his house party-cum-speakeasy. Dressed in gaudy designer threads, he popped a bottle of champagne, which was flypaper to the young girls dancing in his living room. As Johnny filled their champagne flutes, his eyes fell on one of the skinny teenage girls, whose body sparkled with sweat in the strobing lights he had set up to give his apartment a dance club atmosphere.

He set down the bottle of champagne and pulled a small plastic bag from his pocket. The girl noticed a dragon stamp on the packet as Johnny pinched out some white powder and sprinkled it in her glass.

———

Outside the apartment, Audrey approached Johnny's door. She could hear electronic dance music seeping out into the hallway. She knocked, but no one answered, probably because they couldn't hear the pounding on the door over the pounding of the music. Audrey turned the knob and slipped inside the glowing blue light of the apartment.

———

"Drink this," Johnny told the skinny young girl.

"What is it?" she asked with a mix of apprehension and curiosity.

Johnny leaned in, placing his hand on her waist. "No hangover." He slid his hand around to her ass. "And you can fuck for hours."

The girl met his eyes and lifted the champagne flute to her lips, surrendering to his intentions. The music suddenly stopped.

Confused, Johnny turned to see an unfamiliar face bearing down on him.

"Give me that!" Audrey shouted as she grabbed the champagne flute out of the girl's hand and tossed it across the room, shattering it on Johnny's TV and cracking the giant screen.

"Hey! What are you doing!" Johnny shouted at her.

Audrey pulled her badge, conspicuously resting her other hand on the SIG Sauer P250 service pistol holstered on her belt.

"Narcotics Police," Audrey informed the assembled crowd, who stood in silence. Audrey turned her attention to the girl whose drink she had intercepted, and told her to turn on the lights. As the partygoers shielded their eyes from the glare, Audrey's gaze fell on a coffee table, which was covered in various drugs and paraphernalia.

"That looks like about five grams of ice," she informed Johnny casually. "And I'm guessing this is two to three grams of ketamine."

"Somebody brought that," Johnny protested, buying time. "It's not mine."

Like many drug dealers, Johnny was an amateur legal scholar and knew he was facing hard time if Audrey uncovered the true scope of his business. Johnny cast a furtive glance to one of his friends, then flicked his gaze to an aluminum baseball bat in the corner.

Just at the edge of Audrey's peripheral vision, the thuggish teen snatched the bat and stepped toward her.

Audrey spun, whipping her SIG P250 up at his nose. The young man could see in her eyes that the detective would not hesitate to drop the hammer and paint the wall with his brains. He released the bat and raised his hands.

"I want to talk to my lawyer," Johnny demanded.

Audrey cast her gaze around the room, making sure the assembled captives were made aware of their legal liability. "All your friends here are looking at seven years for possession of DD," Audrey said, using the regionally known initialism for dangerous drugs. "What do you think your lawyer is going to be able to do when your friends decide they would rather drop those seven years in exchange for fingering you?"

Audrey picked up a bag of powder off the glass table. "Or we can forget about all the drugs, and you can tell me where you got this."

Johnny's eyes fell on the small packet of gray powder with the dragon stamp, dangling from her fingers.

CHAPTER 30
THE RABBIT

MACAU

Henry Lee's Louis Vuitton loafers clicked on the old aluminum bleachers as he made his way to the front row of the Macau Canidrome. His tailored suit looked out of place at this relic from Macau's seedier past, before the big international corporations took over the region's gambling and entertainment. Though most of the neon signs still worked, the Canidrome had the gritty feel of a third-world soccer venue.

The crowd on this particular weeknight was mostly down-on-their-luck inveterate local gamblers who had eschewed the glitz and glamour of Macau's new palaces. They mumbled among themselves as the trainers paraded their cadaverous, aerodynamic greyhounds whose mouths were muzzled in little metal cages to prevent them from attacking their competition. One of the dogs lowered its hind legs and shivered as it defecated.

Lee took his seat under the harsh glow of the stadium lights in the half-empty stands. Two seats down, a man studied the night's racing program. The man lowered his program, and for the first time in two years, Henry Lee looked into the eyes of the Red Pole of the Sun Yee On triad: Wan Koi.

"Nice of you to leave Hong Kong," Wan said to Lee.

Though the two men's lives were separated by only sixty-five kilometers of seawater, Wan saw them as creatures of two different worlds that represented the yin and yang of the new China. If Hong Kong was China's superego—a tightly controlled, sterile corporate biosphere—Macau was its id: a booming, unregulated frontier town.

Both men kept their eyes pinned on the track, not wanting to draw attention to the conversation.

"I heard about your incident on the boat. You need to tone down your operation."

Wan watched the track as a fresh batch of sinewy greyhounds were led to the starting gate.

"Did you know these dogs will live and die at the track?" Wan asked his older brother. "Most will be losers. A few will be winners. But none ever get out of this life."

A bell dinged, and the dogs took off at a dead sprint, their bodies reaching and stretching as they lunged desperately after the stuffed mechanical rabbit zipping ahead of them.

"It doesn't have to be that way for us," Lee replied. "I am trying to build something for our family, but I need you to cooperate."

"Power is never won. It is something you must fight for every day. Or did they not teach you that at Harvard?"

"The drugs, the murder—it has to stop," Lee replied.

"Someone has to carry on the family business," Wan snapped with a hint of resentment.

"The family business is distribution. And it will continue to be. I am going to need you by my side to handle all the sourcing and supply chain. We can be partners, Wan. But it won't happen if you are stupid and risk everything with your petty crimes."

Lee's tone rankled. Wan's arrogant older brother had believed he was better than Wan since the day Wan was born.

"Father always thought you would take over after him," Wan replied. "But you were too infatuated with the West to come home, so that burden fell on my shoulders." He cast a bitter look at Lee. "And now you come back and tell me how to run my business, because you took some classes and read some books?"

Lee could see that Wan was angry, and softened his tone. "Even Father knows it is time to change. He told me to speak with you. Please, work with me to find a new path."

As Wan considered his older brother's proposition, Lee's eyes fixed on the race. "Or you can keep running around in circles, chasing a stuffed rabbit until you finally get put down."

Lee stood, turning his back on Wan as he departed, leaving his younger brother to ponder the fate of dogs.

CHAPTER 31
PSYOPS

Cobus ate his vegetable curry in a hole-in-the-wall just off a small cobblestone alley. He was relieved to be away from the crucible of Macau's vice district. During his past two months in China's Vegas-by-the-sea, he had found himself drawn to the old colonial section of the city, and its handful of restaurants that still offered traditional Macanese cuisine on menus written in both Chinese and Portuguese. Part of the appeal was the escape from the materialistic pressure cooker of "new Macau," and part of the appeal was that the hybrid colonial/indigenous culture reminded Cobus of Johannesburg, where he had always enjoyed chowing down on flavorful African dishes against the backdrop of the city's refined Edwardian architecture.

As he rolled the food on his tongue, he withdrew a creased photo of Basani from his wallet. The memento felt like a keepsake from another life—a parallel universe where she hadn't died but was back home in Kruger, waiting for him to finish his operation.

Cobus had been on edge twenty-four hours a day since arriving in Macau. He was playing a dangerous game and could feel his cortisol levels elevated to where they had been in Iraq. The electricity of his situational awareness buzzed down the back of his neck as a man entered the restaurant . . . Wan Koi.

Cobus wasn't supposed to meet with Wan again until the new shipment—the last—arrived in three days. Moreover, Wan was a nocturnal beast, and his presence had the eerie feeling of a vampire stepping out into the midday sun.

Cobus slid the photo of Basani into his pocket as Wan sat down at his table. "I've heard reports of people in Hong Kong getting poisoned by rhino horn," Wan said.

Cobus slowly finished chewing the bite in his mouth, using every millisecond to cycle through his options. How much did Wan know? That would affect what type of lie Cobus could maintain, and whether one of them would need to die in the next thirty seconds.

"I know," Cobus replied, catching Wan off guard. "I heard about them too. But the reports are bullshit. It's a psyops tactic used by law enforcement. They're trying to scare your buyers to reduce demand."

"Then our product should be fine," Wan responded coolly, the matter apparently settled.

Wan reached in his pocket and produced a plastic pouch of gray powder with a dragon stamp on it. Cobus knew instantly it was from his powdered rhino horn supply. He watched in silence as Wan poured the powder into Cobus's half-empty cup of Coca-Cola, stirring it with Cobus's straw.

"To your health," he said, and slid the cup to Cobus.

Without a word, Cobus knocked back the Coke and placed the cup upside down on the table. He met Wan's gaze, annoyed. "No more games."

Satisfied, Wan withdrew a piece of paper from his jacket. As he did, Cobus surreptitiously checked the time on his watch.

"I have job for you," Wan said. "One of our dealers in Kowloon was busted by a cop. She never filed a report."

Cobus considered the odd request. The fact that the cop didn't file a report suggested she was not harassing Wan's dealer in a law enforcement capacity.

"You want me to find out if she works for the competition?"

"No, I want you to send her a message."

"Like the one you gave those 14K boys at the docks?"

"Whatever you must do to make her stay away from our operations."

Wan unfolded the square of paper on the table. It was the personal information of a woman Cobus had never heard of— some inspector in the Narcotics Bureau.

Cobus glanced at it and looked up. "I'll handle it."

As Wan finally turned his back to leave, Cobus again checked his watch. It felt like an eternity before the door finally shut behind Wan. The second it did, he exploded from his seat like a .338 Lapua Magnum round.

———

Cobus barged through the kitchen in the back of the restaurant, slamming into a cook and knocking over a boiling pot of noodles as he passed.

He'd had no choice but to drink the poisoned horn Wan presented him with. It was an all-or-nothing bet that he could outrun the poison snaking through his bloodstream toward his central nervous system.

Cobus calculated that he had ten minutes at most from the time he drank the strychnine until his muscles would start convulsing. Two minutes had already passed. Respiratory paralysis and death wouldn't follow for another couple of hours, but once he collapsed, he would be powerless to treat himself, and the journey toward death would be irreversible.

Cobus seized the chef by his stained apron. "Bathroom! Where's your bathroom!"

The bewildered chef shrugged and shook his head, having no idea what the crazy foreigner was jabbering about.

Seconds later, Cobus located the grubby little bathroom. Shoving aside a mop bucket, he knelt before the toilet. He pushed his second and third fingers down his throat and retched.

Cobus vomited everything in his guts until he had nothing left. He staggered to the sink, checking himself in the mirror. His face was clammy, and he was sweating profusely. He checked his watch. It had been five minutes. Too long. Some of the poison was already racing through his bloodstream, hunting for neurons to hijack.

"Fuck . . . Fuck!"

Cobus rushed out of the bathroom. Looking like some crazed addict, he tore through the cobblestone streets of the old town, hunting for a drugstore. His life was being measured in seconds, and it took thirty-seven more of them before he was rifling through the shelves of Watson's Pharmacy. An employee looked on, probably wondering whether she should call the police about the agitated ghost-white foreigner ransacking her store.

"Charcoal! I need charcoal!"

The woman nervously directed him to a bottle of activated char-coal. He snatched it and shoved a wad of cash into her hands, then sprinted off, grabbing a bottle of water on his way out the door.

———

Cobus sat on a bench in the Waterfront Park at the end of the block. The metronome of his breathing began to lose its calibration as the poison in his brain caused his diaphragm to misfire. *Shit.* Was he too late already? His trembling fingers frantically struggled to open the bottle of charcoal. His extremities felt as cold as ice, and the freezing sensation was migrating toward his core.

Panicking wouldn't help. Cobus paused to gather himself, remembering the mantra from his marksmanship training: slow is smooth, smooth is fast. He took a long breath, then opened the bottle with shaking hands and dumped the black charcoal powder into his water bottle, spilling much of it on the ground. Covering the mouth of the bottle with his palm, he shook it vigorously until the charcoal was suspended in a black cloud.

Cobus brought the bottle to his lips, and drank down the chalky black mixture in one long, painful go. He resisted the sudden urge to vomit again, knowing that if he expelled the medicine, it meant certain death.

Fighting to keep the liquid down, he checked his watch. Nine minutes had passed since he ingested the tainted rhino powder. He was standing at the precipice of death, but if the charcoal could sequester enough of the strychnine, he would likely pull through.

Cobus breathed a sigh of relief. He stared absently at the gulls soaring over the water, then at the trees beside him. He noticed a small yellow wildflower poking through a crack in the pavement nearby. Cobus had missed nature since he got to the city, and now he realized he'd been surrounded by it the entire time. He just hadn't been looking closely enough. He suddenly felt an over-whelming sense of calm, as if he were home. Before he could finish the thought, his body began to jerk violently.

Cobus collapsed, curling up on the bench as he flopped like a fish on a dock. His mind was suddenly flooded with one single primal emotion: terror. He was about to die in a very bad way.

Then all was blackness.

CHAPTER 32
THE PETTING ZOO

CHIANG MAI, THAILAND

Sun Tzu's first rule of the risk mitigation business: *know your client as you know yourself.*

While Knight saw an incredible windfall in his future if he partnered with the triads, he also didn't want to bet his career—and possibly his life—on a business that could be volatile and illegal. The tiger wine venture would work only if Lee and his father could deliver a steady supply of healthy tigers once the trade was made legal.

Chiang Mai was a half day's drive from Mong La, and as good a place as any to start his due diligence. The Sky Dragon had revealed to Knight that one of his suppliers was a chain of private zoos in Thailand, and had suggested that Knight visit the zoos to see the condition of the tigers they would soon be using to make health tonics. The patriarch of the triad was probably not being totally forthcoming with the scope of his operation, but Knight was a skilled investigator. He was confident he could pull a thread once he had one in his grip. He would start in Chiang Mai and see where that took him.

_____

The drive south through Myanmar was a front-row seat for the environmental apocalypse being wrought by globalization. The landscape oscillated between giant old-growth triple-canopy jungle and swaths of clear-cut agriculture. As in Africa and most of Southeast Asia, Chinese companies had fallen on the region like a biblical plague, buying up the jungle, stripping it of all the old wood, and replacing it with banana trees, nut palms, and other crops that thrived in tropical climes. The whole world was for sale, Knight observed, and no amount of shopping at Whole Foods, or clicktivists' retweeting statistics, or protests at liberal universities could stop the invisible iron fist of economics. Soon, Earth would be nothing more than a giant tennis ball covered with the green fuzz of billions of acres of farms. And perhaps someday, that green fuzz would be gone too.

As he crossed into northern Thailand, jungles once again sprang from the earth. The Thai government had not yet sold itself off to outside influences. But rather than give Knight hope, it only reminded him how much was yet to be lost—a sentiment reinforced on the way into Chiang Mai, when he passed several new coffee plantations that had been hacked out of the rain forest.

_____

Knight arrived at the Tiger Palace in the early afternoon. To make time on the road, he had held off on eating lunch, and he was relieved to see that the zoo carried a wide array of Western food options, such as club sandwiches and Johnnie Walker Red, both of which were needed after a long day bouncing down cratered roads that made him feel as if he were in a sweltering paint shaker.

After a quick meal and two fingers of Johnnie Red, he explored the popular tourist attraction, which was mostly populated by Caucasian visitors in tank tops and shorts. Though the zoo seemed like so many others he had insured in the United States, this one offered something extraordinary. For fifteen dollars, visitors could go into the cages and play with tiger cubs and even adolescents. Knight watched two teenage German girls flash the peace symbol as they snapped a photo with one of the larger cats, which was rapidly approaching adulthood. It was a striking image to take in and enough to make a risk assessor's hair stand on end.

Knight paid to enter one of the cages, where a baby white tiger was curled up half asleep. He had seen white tigers before. They were a rare albino breed of Bengal that were popular on the Las Vegas magic circuit or as exotic trophy pets. It was an important clue to the true nature of this place that billed itself as a tiger "conservation" facility. The fact that white tigers originated in India meant that either this place was committed to rescuing a broad, international array of highly rare and desirable cats, or it was actively breeding them for exploitation.

He knelt and rubbed the goose-down fur at the base of the cub's ears. The cub purred, impossibly docile.

He addressed the tiger like an old friend. "Those must be some good drugs they've got you on."

Knight knew that the main reason no zoos in America allowed tiger experiences like this was because the tigers would make a quick meal of the patrons. Any zoo offering petting experiences—particularly with adolescent tigers—would have to be drugging the tigers, which would never be tolerated back home in the States.

A young American girl knelt beside Knight as her parents stood off to the side. She beamed at the magic of seeing the little zebra-striped creature up close with its sparkling light eyes and its paws like mittens. She began rubbing the cub's belly vigorously.

"Do you have a dog at home?" Knight asked.

The girl nodded.

"Dogs love it when they get their bellies rubbed, don't they?"

"Yeah, my doggie wiggles his foot when I do this," the girl said as she scratched the cub's stomach. "Why isn't the tiger doing anything?"

"Cats are a little different," Knight told her. "They like it when you pet their chin and behind their whiskers."

The girl slid her hand under the cub's chin and coursed her fingers through its fur. Its jaw went slack, and it meowed like a house cat.

She turned to Knight, beaming a smile of pebbly baby teeth. He returned her infectious grin, for a moment putting out of his mind the dark theories he was formulating about the true nature of this zoo.

"Do you want to know how they say hello?" Knight asked as the girl's parents watched nearby.

The girl nodded eagerly.

"They touch foreheads."

The girl hesitated, uncertain whether Knight was pulling her leg. He nodded for her to give it a try. She leaned her head forward until the fur tickled her skin. The tiger returned the gesture, increasing the pressure between their skulls.

Knight noticed a handler cleaning tiger feces out of the adjacent pen and spoke to him through the wire mesh that separated them. "Hey, how many tigers do you have here?"

"We have pens for two hundred, but not all of them are full right now."

Right now. Those last two words were telling. Knight knew that unlike most wild animals, tigers were as easy to breed in captivity as rabbits. To have unused capacity at a tiger exhibit was almost unheard of, meaning that some of the cages must have been recently vacated, or they were newly constructed and Tiger Palace was scaling up its operation.

"They're all cubs," the girl observed as she scanned the zoo. Knight had noticed the same thing the moment he arrived. Not a single tiger on display had crossed the threshold into adulthood.

"What do you think they do when they get older?" she asked.

Knight looked at the young girl. Though he was normally a man who reveled in shattering illusions and exposing lies, he didn't have the heart—or lack thereof—to tell her the dark truth. Instead, he forced a smile. "They probably release them into the wild."

Knight rose, surreptitiously pulling a small clump of fur from the drugged tiger to send for analysis. He needed to find out whether it shared any DNA with the tiger that had wiped out the SafariWorld population. If the infected cub had indeed come from this supply chain, it would be only a matter of time until the feline leukemia virus spread wider. Not only would Lee's business ambitions be in serious jeopardy, but (and of more specific concern to Knight) Lee's cats would be uninsurable.

Knight placed the fur sample in his folded visitor map as he pressed through a door into the staff area in back, searching for any sign of mature tigers. He made his way down a hallway, emerging onto a loading dock where a large tiger was being ushered into a cage. It paused as it approached the confined space. A worker struck its haunches with a long bamboo cane.

The tiger snarled and lunged forward, and the cage slammed shut behind it.

Then, to Knight's surprise, a forklift transferred the cage to the back of a large green military truck. Knight angled for a view inside the truck and spotted other cages, stacked like small shipping containers.

A Thai worker suddenly got in Knight's face, shouting for him to leave.

Knight put his hands out and projected ignorance. "Relax, buddy. I'm just looking for the bathroom."

CHAPTER 33
THE VICTIM

MACAU

A shopkeeper called the police after the body in the park across the street hadn't stirred for five hours. The officer approached slowly, unable to spot any signs of life on the hulking Caucasian. The man's body was lying on its side, feet still resting on the ground, as if he had been sitting one moment, then fallen over. His right arm dangled off the bench, revealing a small dragon tattoo on his inner forearm. The policeman immediately recognized it as the mark of the Sun Yee On triad.

———

When Cobus was a boy, his father had taken him and his older brother to the beach in Plettenberg Bay on the Eastern Coast of South Africa's Cape. The section of coast extending from Plettenberg to Durban was notorious not only for its rugged beauty and perfect surf, but also for the large number of shark attacks that had left local surfers maimed or dead. One afternoon, as Cobus and his father straddled their boards, Cobus had asked his father what the chances were that a great white would come where they were surfing.

"They're here, boy," his father told him. "They're always here. This is their home. But it's a beautiful home, isn't it? If we want to experience life, we must accept the possibility of death." Cobus's father then spun on his board and kicked into a passing wave, leaving Cobus alone just beyond the breakers.

Cobus sat alone for several minutes on his board, the dark water beneath haunting him, his brain converting every oscillating shaft of light into a large silhouette spearing at him from the deep. Suddenly, a burst of seawater startled him, and he spun to see a bottlenose dolphin breaching several meters away. The dolphin was soon joined by several others, including a calf that was scarcely larger than a rugby ball. They weaved around Cobus, diving under his board for the fish that lived on the reef beneath. A wave finally came that could take him to shore, but the young man let it pass. He turned his eyes from the dark water skyward, to see the awesome tumult of gulls, terns, and other seabirds that had come to dine on fish with the dolphins. Though the sharks were down there, they didn't come for Cobus that day.

———

In the blackness of the abyss that had swallowed him, Cobus once again heard the seabirds calling out from above. He cracked his eyes open to see a gull banking gracefully, then pumping its wings to accelerate. At first, he thought it was some type of dream— perhaps his life flashing before his eyes. Then his gaze fell on children playing soccer and flying kites in the Waterfront Park. The shark had spared him once again.

The police officer jostled Cobus. It was only when he strained to get himself upright that he realized the immense pain he was in. Every joint ached from the spasms and lactic acidosis that had ravaged his body. He rubbed his cheek, which was still stiff from lockjaw induced by the poison. Cobus had ingested all manner of alcohol and drugs during his military days, but this was an apocalyptic hangover unlike anything he had ever experienced.

His brain foggy, Cobus absorbed the fact that he had escaped death. But instead of serving as some sort of resurrection that instilled new purpose and direction in him, the ordeal had the opposite effect. *Of all the people to spare*, he asked the universe, *why me?* He had seen so many good creatures who brought light into the world killed before his eyes, while he, a man who brought only darkness and death, somehow slipped between the raindrops. Ironic that even now, when any just god would have allowed him to be felled by his own hand, he somehow still endured.

As Cobus struggled to process his situation, the officer placed a rubber-gloved hand on his shoulder and asked whether he needed to see a doctor.

Annoyed, he waved the policeman off. "I'm fine. I'm fine."

As the cop departed, Cobus withdrew a folded piece of paper from his pocket. He squeezed his eyelids, then opened the paper to see the inspector's photo staring up at him. This woman, Cobus thought to himself, was unaware of the danger lurking in the blackness.

Cobus was now her shark.

CHAPTER 34
THE FARM

THAKHEK, LAOS

In the week since his meeting with the Sky Dragon, Knight had been on a whirlwind tour of Southeast Asia. The patriarch of the Sun Yee On triad wanted him to partner with his son to protect their supply chain, but first Knight needed to do his diligence on the illegal tiger trade, from farm to table.

What he discovered through his travels was a vast archipelago of places just like Mong La—little black holes scattered throughout Asia that were run by organized crime and existed outside any international oversight. There was the Kings Roman Casino in the Golden Triangle in Laos, where Knight had been offered a "wild tiger banquet" that his Russian hostess finally admitted had been sourced from the "tiger zoo" across the street. There was Boten, a former truck stop turned casino boomtown that sat in a two-mile seam between Laos and China, legally part of neither. In this disavowed pleasure island, Knight saw every variety of wild cat for sale on the main drag. He interviewed the staff in these regions, unearthing stories of tigers being transferred by an enterprising general via Laotian military helicopters. Everything, everyone, everywhere was for sale or, at least, rent.

Though it didn't pertain to tigers, Boten was also home to the most horrifying sight Knight encountered in his research. When he had announced his interest in traditional Chinese medicine, one local entrepreneur whose video shop featured a substantial collection of bestiality pornography informed Knight that Boten produced the finest bear bile in Laos—if you could call the de facto Chinese protectorate "Laos."

Curious about the source of the bile, Knight paid the shop owner to tell him where he might find the farm. The man directed him to a nearby road, where he ventured up a hill, passing an abandoned ladyboy disco featuring chipped murals of transgender dancers. He continued several hundred yards down an overgrown dirt path in the forest that eventually ended at a small, dilapidated warehouse.

Knight pressed inside the dark building and was immediately overwhelmed by the smell of ammonia. As his eyes adjusted to the darkness, what he saw inside was far beyond any inner circle of hell he could have imagined. Fully grown bears were splayed in "crush cages" with wooden slats inserted in the bars to prevent the bears from standing up. Catheters had been attached to their abdomens to drain them like maple trees, and the open wounds where the catheters piped directly into their gallbladders were dusted with antibiotics to prevent infection. As Knight later confirmed, the bear would live its entire life, which could be twenty years, in this position. Sick at his stomach, Knight turned to see a Laotian man trying to pin down a recently captured black bear cub that cried as it paced and lunged wildly against the bars its cage. The worker jammed a pole through the bars, hobbling the bear cub onto its belly as it screeched in fear. Knight felt tears welling up in his eyes, but his concern soon returned to his own well-being as the worker spotted him and proceeded to chase him out, swinging a rusty shovel at him as he fled outside.

At each stop along his journey, Knight gathered samples for DNA analysis, which he would send to Lara in South Africa. Though some of the samples turned out to be African lions that vendors were trying to pass off as tiger bones and teeth, most of the product he tested was genuine tiger. The portrait the genes painted was stunning, with individual farmed tigers whose lineage could be traced back to wild populations all over the Asian continent, many of which had been driven to extinction.

The Asian demand for all things tiger was striking. There was tiger bone jewelry, tiger skin rugs, tiger skulls, tiger meat, tiger teeth, and every manner of tiger wine. Knight even encountered rice wine with a severed tiger penis floating in it. The hooch tasted conspicuously like the other tiger-part wines he would get shit-faced on while building rapport with the locals.

During one of those research benders, a slurring local had regaled Knight's translator with a story about how he might be able to procure the most expensive type of tiger part that existed: pink tiger bones. It was the first time the animal expert had ever heard of pink tiger bones—or pink bones of any sort, for that matter. When Knight inquired further, the man described the process for making them pink, which involved sedating the tiger, then skinning and deboning it alive so that the heart still pumped blood as the bones were harvested. Knight declined the offer, doing his best to hide his disgust at the gruesome practice.

Though all these "special economic zones" that Knight visited on the border of China were ostensibly run by local business interests, he could see the triads' fingerprints everywhere. They had taken their expertise at gambling, prostitution, and smuggling contraband from China and set up shop just over the border, in countries where land and local officials could be leased on the cheap.

And throughout the journey, one place kept coming up: Thakhek, a name that could be uttered to Knight only while breaking eye contact and lowering one's voice. It was the spring from which all the tigers throughout the region seemed to flow. Knight suspected that Thakhek—whatever it was—would be essential to Lee's plan to deliver tigers to market on an industrial scale.

————

Even by Knight's thorough investigative standards, it was an extremely long thread he had tugged to arrive at this ramshackle thatch-roofed restaurant on the side of a dirt road in the middle of nowhere. The table where Knight sat overlooked a small brook that ran through the jungle ravine below. Though unable to understand a word of Lao, he was hungry, so he put his faith in the owner's hands when the man came to take his order. Knight immediately had second thoughts as his eyes fell on a skinny monkey, chained to a post in the corner of the restaurant as it ate a bag of Fritos. *Surely, the monkey was a pet and not a dish*, Knight tried to convince himself. They wouldn't waste a perfectly good bag of Fritos on a mere protein source.

Minutes later, the Laotian man brought a bowl of noodle soup as Knight spoke on the phone with Perkins. He gave the soup a stir and was relieved to find no mystery meat.

"The samples from the Tiger Palace weren't a match for the cub," he informed Perkins. "But I've got a lead on where it might have come from."

"I know you're looking into the farming business while you're over there," Perkins said, his frustration evident, "but you need to wrap up the SafariWorld claim, Randall. We're beginning to look bad. If their claim is legitimate and we lose a major zoo client over it, you're going to lose your job."

In the specialized insurance business, the last thing you wanted was a reputation for dragging your heels on claims. The rule was to pay fast or investigate fast. Any claim under $250,000 wasn't even worth investigating, but on a sizable claim such as this, Knight might be able to buy two months from the time of the incident.

He glanced in the back of the shop to see the owner's wife tending to their sick child. The owner, who had returned to the task of cooking, coughed violently into his hand. Knight knew he was closing in on the source of the cub and, with it, the source of the disease that had wiped out SafariWorld's tigers. Knight dropped his spoon in his soup, not wanting to roll the dice on whether their contagion had found its way into his meal.

"Just give me a week. The claim will be void, and we'll be in the tiger farming game."

Knight scanned the restaurant and found a rack of illegal tiger wine bottles for sale. There may not be any more wild tigers in Laos, but he had certainly found himself in tiger country. And he couldn't help but fear a connection between the store owner's illness and the locally produced beverage.

Perkins relented. "One week, Randall. You have one week."

"I'll keep you posted." Knight hung up, placed a wad of kip on the table, then went to meet his driver, who was waiting outside in an inconspicuous Hyundai.

————

The Hyundai weaved around potholes as it pressed deeper into the jungle. The sun was already retreating toward the mountains by the time they arrived at a long driveway. Knight signaled for his driver to stop. He then waved a large stack of money at the driver, indicating that it would be his upon Knight's return if the driver didn't abandon him. The driver nodded, and Knight headed off down the driveway on foot.

A quarter mile down the driveway, he reached a walled compound in the jungle, with razor wire atop the perimeter fence. He stepped carefully toward the guard post, prepared to launch into his scripted cover story. He would spin them a yarn about how he was an agriculture specialist who had just been hired by a Chinese company that was razing the old-growth forests in the region to plant rubber and banana trees. Any mention of the Chinese would open a lot of doors in Southeast Asia and Africa, for the Chinese had ingratiated themselves with local leaders throughout the developing world. Moreover, gift giving was popular in Chinese culture, and Knight would claim he wanted to impress his boss with some tiger wine or perhaps a tiger tooth necklace. The story had worked in Vietnam and Myanmar, and it would certainly work here. But Knight was surprised to find the guard post empty and the gate hanging open.

Curious about the security lapse, he checked his surroundings, then slipped inside the compound. He soon located the main office and pressed open the door.

"Hello?" Knight called out. He tried again in Lao. "*Sabaidi?*"

Wading in deeper, he found a man sprawled in a chair, his mouth agape. Flies circled the body, which had not yet begun to smell. As Knight slowly moved closer in breathless dread, he could see blood oozing from the eyes and nose—the same symptoms exhibited by the tigers that had died of feline leukemia at Safari-World. The insurance man immediately processed the distinct risk that he was standing at ground zero of the next global pandemic.

"Shit." Knight backed away, covering his mouth with his sleeve as he retreated from the room.

He left the offices and crossed toward a warehouse building. On the way, he passed a stack of empty cages like the ones he had seen being loaded onto the military trucks at the Tiger Palace in Thailand. Nearby, under a tin roof, he found a group of enormous earthenware vats covered in tarps, which were secured by ropes around the lip.

Next to the vats, he happened upon crates of empty new tiger wine bottles bearing the same label he had seen at the roadside shop an hour before. Through his travels, Knight had learned enough about tiger wine production to suspect that each earthenware vat contained dead tigers in various stages of decomposition.

He climbed up on a loading dock and moved inside the warehouse, where he found rows of cages like a giant prison block. There had to be hundreds, if not thousands. Through the bars, he could make out dead tigers, their forms obscured by shadows. Others were still in the process of giving up the ghost, stirring in their anemic agony.

Knight heard the loud snarl of a tiger in the distance. He searched for the source of the sound, tracing it to a room at the end of the hallway. Inside, he spotted a Laotian worker gripping a long metal rod as he cautiously approached a tiger.

Knight edged back into the shadows, then watched in shock as the worker jabbed the tiger with the rod, sending electricity crackling through its body. The tiger immediately crumpled, and the slaughterer continued to hit it with electricity as it convulsed on the ground.

"Wait!" Knight called out at the horror of it all. He hadn't intended to make a sound, but the word burst reflexively from within him.

The worker turned with the electrified rod in hand and waved it threateningly at the pale-faced intruder. Knight put out his palms as he inched backward. "Whoa, whoa, whoa, take it easy!"

The worker continued to advance on Knight, coughing violently in his direction.

Knight recoiled in fear and moved into the hallway as the worker pursued, screaming at him in Lao. Knight turned and sprinted, triggering the predatory instincts of the surviving tigers, who snarled in terrifying dissonance at the fleeing meal.

Another worker emerged to investigate the commotion, blocking his path. Knight collided with the man, knocking him back against the wall and barging past him. He raced toward a door.

Bursting through the exit, he checked over his shoulder to see the workers chasing him. Distracted, he didn't realize he had exited onto the loading dock.

Knight toppled off the ledge at full speed, landing horizontally on crates of recently filled tiger wine bottles, which shattered under his weight.

With no time to waste, Knight rolled off the crates of broken bottles and scrambled. As he staggered away, he checked his forearm to find blood dripping from a cut. "Shit!"

The workers yelled at Knight from the loading dock as he fled back down the driveway, leaving a trail of infected blood in the dirt as he fled back to the Hyundai, which he hoped was still waiting for him in the jungle.

CHAPTER 35
THE LONG JOURNEY

NKI NATIONAL PARK, CAMEROON

Unlike many elephants throughout Africa and Asia, the calf had never been named. None of the elephants in her herd had. Names were a human construct that did not exist in elephant culture, and these forty elephants had rarely crossed paths with humans. Occasionally, one of the older ones would wander off. The others would hear the crack of thunder in the distance, and the elephant would never be seen again, as if it had been reclaimed by the very gods who placed it on the Earth. This was the fate of the calf's father and, seemingly, all fathers in the herd once they passed their prime.

As the calf's mother drank from a shallow pond in a clearing, the calf approached and lifted her trunk, resting it against the warm, safe wall of her mother's belly as she began to suckle. The sensation of the milk leaving her body gave the mother a sense of primal relief and calm.

The crack of thunder startled the mother. She had never heard it so close. Suddenly, her baby's lips unlatched from her nipple, and the baby collapsed to the earth. The mother turned, horrified at the sight of blood pouring from the baby's belly. The mother shrieked, and all the elephants came rushing to her side to see the source of her daughter's anguish. That was when the thunderstorm started.

The booming came from the forest, accompanied by what seemed to be a swarm of invisible insects that loudly buzzed by, occasionally biting the elephants and leaving them with deep, searing wounds that gushed blood.

One by one, the elephants collapsed—first to their knees, then to the dirt—until the entire herd had been felled, their ten-million-year-old bloodline extinguished in a matter of minutes.

Something stung the mother's neck, and she dropped like a stone, unable to feel her body or legs. As she lay in the dirt, she looked into the eyes of her calf. She watched as a fly crawled across her daughter's brow and walked to the center of her open eyeball. With every ounce of strength remaining, the mother thrashed until she could use her trunk to snort the offending pest away. The mother collapsed her cheek back against the dirt, and she could then clearly see that whatever spark or animating force had always burned within the child's eyes had departed.

If there were gods in Africa, they did nothing to spare the mother's agony. The apes emerged from the trees and set upon the mother with their rusty saws, carving into the seam where her tusks met her snout. Unlike rhino horn, which was merely dead cells like hair or fingernails, elephant tusks evolved from teeth and bore all their characteristics, including nerves.

The apes dug through the enamel first, then the dentine layer. That was when the mother felt the most electrocuting physical pain she had ever endured. She bucked, knocking the ape back and leaving his hacksaw half buried in the tusk. Another ape unleashed a swarm of loud cracking insects that stung the mother's head, finally offering her the relief the gods had denied.

———

The mother's tusks were then removed and lashed to the backs of two of the apes, who carried them through the jungle, to a road where the tusks were eventually loaded into the back of a truck, to begin a long journey to Tanzania under the watchful eye of American spy satellites.

Along the way, this particular ivory would be sliced into disks, which (because the ivory was hollow) would make natural bracelets. These bracelets would then be painted brown and labeled as artisanal wooden bracelets "MADE IN AFRICA."

The boxes of bracelets would arrive in Macau days later, alongside a shipment of macadamia nuts inside a shipping container aboard the *Wan Hai 212*. The container would be taken off the deck by a large loader and placed on a container handler that looked like a giant forklift. The handler would in turn load the container on the back of a truck, and the truck would drive to the Sun Yee On triads' warehouse, where it would back into the loading docks.

Wan Koi's men would unload the bracelets and immediately begin chipping away at the veneer of brown paint that camouflaged the Boko Haram ivory. Nearby, hundreds of plastic packets of rhino horn powder with dragon stamps were awaiting distribution as well.

None of the contraband would remain long. Though only a small percentage of the Chinese population was in the market for illicit animal parts, in a nation of 1.4 billion people, that small percentage still amounted to a voracious appetite—one that Wan hoped to feed. Nearly half the sales would happen online, and Wan's men were soon busy photographing the contraband and uploading product listings—not just on the dark web but also on popular Chinese Internet marketplaces, where coded keywords let them easily evade the filters meant to prevent illegal sales. Most of the animal parts, however, would be sold in cities along the South China Sea, where the Sun Yee On had developed street-level distribution networks.

That evening, four go-fast boats skipped across the open water of the South China Sea. The choppy surf gave way to glass as they entered the calm Victoria channel, flanked by the twin cities of Kowloon and Hong Kong.

———

Inspector Audrey Lam had also been on a journey of her own. Johnny Chu had given up the name of his supplier, who, in turn, had revealed that a new shipment would be arriving in Tsim Sha Tsui tonight. The revelation that the contraband would be coming through the harbor in Southern Kowloon didn't surprise Audrey, for the area was known to be home to many gangs who dealt in illicit goods.

Audrey cased the waterfront and found an office building that overlooked the harbor. She entered and made her way up a stair-well to a fire door that opened onto the roof. Concealed by the shadows and the ledge, she photographed the go-fast boats as they arrived and were immediately offloaded by waiting porters. She zoomed in on what appeared to be gang tattoos on the arms of the men—one of the few clues that might help identify the smugglers.

———

The loads of animal parts were then transferred to motorcycles, which zoomed off into the night to be delivered to the street-level dealers. One load included a live and very rare pangolin (listed on CITES Appendix One), which would find its way to a traditional Chinese medicine shop whose walls were lined with dried shark fins.

Another TCM doctor, located inconspicuously in a second-floor office, received a shipment of paws severed from Asiatic black bears that had died on a bile farm in Laos.

Yet another shipment found its way to an upscale jewelry store in a hotel lobby in the financial district. A well-dressed woman working the store opened the box, revealing an array of beautiful ivory bracelets that had been carved from the nursing mother in Cameroon. These particular bracelets would stay in a safe in the back room until a handful of particularly wealthy and discreet customers the saleswomen had already lined up could come pick them up. Occasionally, a buyer would ask whether the elephants had been harmed, and the chipper saleswoman would assure them that the tusks grew back, which any five-second Internet search would have proved false.

The most valuable shipment, of course, was the rhino horn, which was delivered via motorcycle courier to a bouncer working outside a nightclub. Shortly thereafter, one of the packets would end up in a VIP booth, where a wealthy businessman was flanked by young women who had flocked to him for the free champagne he stocked at his table. The powder was sprinkled first into the man's scotch, then into the champagne flutes of the eager and titillated young women.

The horn then passed their lips, as did the strychnine that Cobus had added.

CHAPTER 36
THE ELEPHANT KILLERS

Davis fanned away the giant mosquitoes that orbited him as he followed Becker deeper into the forest. The shrubby open canopy of the whitewood trees offered little protection from the punishing equatorial sun, and the dense undergrowth forced them to high-step along a circuitous course. Davis's slacks and dress shirt were soaked through with sweat and mud from the river crossings, and his face was red from overheating in the heavy, damp air.

Though he was sunburned and exhausted, Davis felt alive. He had something he hadn't had in years: a mission. It was just like the Jack Ryan novels that had shaped his views of what a career in the agency might look like. And the more pain he endured as he ventured beyond his comfort zone into this malarial frontier, the more real his fantasy became.

———

The analyst and the hunter emerged from the woods into an overgrown clearing. As they trudged forward through knee-high grass, the droning of insects began to drown out the forest sounds. Ahead, Davis could see dozens of gray mounds dotting the field like boulders. As he advanced, he covered his mouth at the unspeakable tableau stretched out before him. There were at least forty elephant carcasses, looking like giant deflated balloons. The grass and dirt were painted a dark maroon, and large appendages littered the landscape. Upon closer inspection, Davis realized that the abandoned limbs were all severed trunks. He could barely force himself to breathe.

"It's different here," Becker said. "In South Africa, they use hit-and-run tactics. Here, they don't shoot and scoot. They dig in and slaughter every last animal in their area of operations."

"What happened here?" Davis managed to force out through a wave of nausea.

Becker walked him through the attack, explaining that over a dozen Boko Haram militia members had come for the herd. When they arrived, the oblivious elephants stood only yards from their position, feeling unthreatened by the humans. The animals didn't recognize the AK-47s and belt-fed .50-caliber machine guns the men were carrying.

Davis approached the body of a baby elephant whose tusks hadn't yet come in. Unlike the other animals, its body was completely intact, save for the bullet wound torn in its side. David knelt, touching its body.

"They hit the baby first," Becker informed him.

"Why?" Davis groaned. "It didn't even have any ivory?"

"Elephants have a strong social structure—stronger than humans. The poachers know that if you shoot the baby first, the herd will never abandon it." Becker went on to explain that they had intentionally shot the baby in the abdomen to wound it, to make the agony of its wailing so unbearable that the entire herd would gather around.

"I'm not a racist," Becker said in his thick Rhodesian accent. "But these people are fucking animals."

Davis turned to Becker, a renewed purpose in his eyes. He had wanted to make a difference since he joined the agency, and now he would finally have his chance.

"Do you know which way they went?"

"Their spoor headed north into the forest, but we didn't follow."

"Why not?" Davis asked with a tinge of indignation in his voice.

"These guys who did this aren't poachers—they are professional killers trained in bush warfare. We're not an army, bru. We're not equipped for that."

Davis considered the issue as an idea took shape. "I'll need to use your Wi-Fi back at the lodge."

———

They returned to the empty hunting lodge, where Becker made coffee as Davis got to work on his computer. The agency had resources no other country had access to, and Davis would use them for good.

Becker set a cup of coffee in front of him. "You said they were killed five days ago?" Davis pointed to satellite images of the forest he had pulled up on-screen. "These satellite images are from that day."

Becker could see a cluster of large dark spots in a clearing. "There's the herd."

Davis toggled the display to thermal imagery, noting a

constellation of white dots in the forest. "Looks like fourteen heat signatures coming from the northwest." He tapped a key, and the image jumped forward in time. With each additional tap, the human heat signatures jumped closer to the herd in a stop-motion video.

As the staccato imagery flickered past, Davis went speechless at the sight of white-hot lines—streams of lead from the .50-caliber machine guns—connecting the poachers and the elephants.

The matrix of white lines vanished, and the poachers swarmed the carcasses like insects, then finally retreated once the harvest was complete.

"Can you find out where they went?" Becker asked.

Davis turned his attention to Becker, already a step ahead of the professional hunter. "We're going to need another pot of coffee."

The two men worked through the night as Davis pored through classified spy-satellite feeds, tracking the movement of the ivory from the kill site across sub-Saharan Africa. Zooming in on the photos, Davis could see images of the Boko Haram poachers returning to an encampment where the ivory was aggregated with other contraband and loaded into a pickup truck. The truck then delivered the shipment to an airfield, where Davis managed to cross-reference the plane's transponder and track it as it flew east to a dirt landing strip in Tanzania. A US satellite that had been pushed over eastern Africa to aid with the hunt for the Lord's Resistance Army showed a box truck waiting for the plane when it landed, as two thermal signatures stood by to receive the cargo. Tracking the truck as it made its way east beyond the vigilant eye of American spy satellites was the most challenging aspect of Davis's hunt, but thanks to the hundreds of small commercial satellites that now photographed the entire landmass of Earth every day, he could leapfrog open-source images without ever losing sight of the Boko Haram contraband.

———

Less than twenty-four hours after the kill, the box truck drove down Mandela Road in Dar es Salaam and turned off at the entrance for the container port. It approached a checkpoint with an armed guard. The driver passed a thick envelope out his window, which the guard took before waving the truck through.

The truck then wended its way through the Dar es Salaam container port, stopping at the *Wan Hai 212*, a large, rusting container ship. The ship was already being loaded with a shipment of illegal timber and other African exports bound for Asia.

———

A week later, Davis was back in the conference room at the CIA's Counterterrorism Center, presenting his findings to the group. The room was mostly empty as he made his case to Ron Nelson and Director Wilkes, who had requested the progress report. Time-lapse satellite imagery tracked the shipment of ivory.

"The cargo is then loaded onto container ships bound for Macau," Davis informed them. "This is hard evidence that Boko Haram is financing its operations with illegal blood ivory. What's more, after they transferred the ivory, we were able to track the militia members back to a compound in Northern Nigeria, which I believe is where their command element is based."

Nelson cut him off. "Boko Haram?"

Davis volleyed back with smug confidence. "The Islamic

African terror group currently holding two Nigerian politicians and twenty schoolgirls hostage."

"We know who Boko Haram is," Wilkes interjected somberly, still processing Davis's findings.

"Until now, we didn't know the location of the hostages," Davis proclaimed. Through his research, he had managed to get a fix on the twenty schoolgirls who had been missing for months and were presumably now child brides of the militia members—if they were lucky.

"So what?" Nelson said. "You want us to send in Seal Team Six and smoke a bunch of skinnies in the jungle?"

"I want you to understand that the only way we were able to locate this violent extremist organization was by tracking a primary source of their financing: the trafficking of endangered animal parts."

Nelson brushed him off. "I didn't realize we're in the business of hunting all of the, what, thousand militias running around Africa?"

"Boko Haram is officially designated a foreign terror group by *our* government!"

"Come on, Davis, this is a regional issue," Nelson countered. "These guys are just a bunch of thugs in mud huts."

"Twenty Nigerian girls are being held hostage!" Davis erupted, standing in disbelief at the front of the room. "If we sit by and do nothing, whatever happens to them is on us." He had found terrorists on our watch list holding children hostage. *Wasn't that enough?*

After a long silence, Director Wilkes weighed in. "We'll notify local authorities, but Nelson is right. This is not a US national security concern, and unfortunately, we can't save every poor kid in Africa. That said, your point about terror financing and its *potential* value tracking our enemies is well taken. What about that Sumatra terror link with Jemaah Islamiyah? Tigers, right? Now, that was interesting."

Before Davis had a chance to formulate a response, Nelson piled on. "Yeah, that's why we agreed to this whole boondoggle of yours in the first place. Did that fall through?"

To say it had fallen through would be an understatement. Davis had effectively proved that it was impossible to link tigers to terrorism, because there were no tigers in the region of Sumatra where they operated. Davis paused, unsure whether the CIA mantra that "The truth shall make you free" applied in this instance.

CHAPTER 37
THE GANGSTER SQUAD

HONG KONG

Audrey got off the elevator and stepped into the bullpen of the Organized Crime & Triad Bureau. Because narcotics cases often intersected with organized crime, she had been to this floor dozens of times before, but this time felt different. She was self-conscious of every movement. Looking as if she wasn't doing something wrong was more stressful than she had anticipated, and she could now appreciate the sense of relief that criminals frequently experienced when they were apprehended. Audrey had never paid much thought to how she moved or how she greeted people, so she had no baseline against which to gauge the normality of her present behavior. She was hypervigilant of every glance from the detectives working in the bullpen as she moved swiftly toward the corner office, hoping to limit her human interactions.

Inspector Tsao rose to greet her as she entered his office. They had met when they were both in the academy, and he seemed barely to have aged in the ensuing two decades. He still had the same athletic physique, the same thick hair without a hint of gray. His movie-star looks seemed only fitting since the Chow Yun-Fat movies Tsao watched in his teens had inspired him to pursue the Triad Bureau. Even the immaculate office of this perennial bachelor seemed like a movie set. Audrey had been attracted to him when they were in their early twenties, but she was too principled to reciprocate a work colleague's romantic interest. Now he was probably still dating beautiful women in their twenties, while she felt like a worn boot. She had married, had a child, divorced, and was now entering his office on two hours of sleep, in yesterday's clothes.

Tsao pulled out a chair facing his desk. "Please, have a seat." He circled around the desk, then paused at the sight of her. "You look exhausted. Have you been getting any sleep?"

"I'm fine. I was wondering if you had any intel on this crew moving product down in Tsim Sha Tsui." Audrey was careful to speak in vague terms, not wanting to burden Tsao with the truth of her off-the-books investigation.

She showed him one of her surveillance photos of a man in a tank top offloading a crate. "Does this tattoo mean anything to you?"

Tsao studied the photo. "Dragon with phoenix wings. That's the Sun Yee On triad. Was this narcotics?"

Audrey paused, then replied, "Rhino horn."

Tsao seemed surprised at the revelation. "I guess you go where the money is," he reasoned aloud.

"Someone is poisoning the rhino supply. I think it's them, or someone in their organization."

"Seems like that would be bad for business . . ." He looked puzzled. "*Your* unit is investigating this?"

Uncertain how much to give up, Audrey said, "No. Just me."

Tsao nodded silently. He had to know that her son had been poisoned with horn at the hospital and that this visit might be related. But Tsao was also savvy enough not to ask questions he didn't want answered.

"What can you tell me about them?" she asked.

"They were run by an old Kowloon gangster named Sky Dragon. Since we drove him out of Hong Kong, he's been living in exile in Mong La."

She had never heard of the place. "Where's that?"

"A warlord-controlled casino town in Myanmar. A lot of triads go there if there's too much heat on them in China."

"Who is running the Sun Yee On triad now?"

"We believe the new *dai lo* is his younger son, Wan, who moved their base of operations to Macau."

Tsao logged on to his computer and pulled up a dossier, pointing to Wan's photo. "That's him."

Tsao explained that over the previous year, Wan's phone number had been connected to numerous investigations, and a portrait was coming into focus of a powerful young kingpin who was staking his claim through spectacular acts of ultraviolence against his rivals. He was the kind of villain tailor-made for a hero like Tsao.

"You said he is the *younger* brother?" Audrey knew that the triads were patriarchal and that the eldest son would inherit the clan.

"The older brother studied in the US—Harvard Business School," Tsao said. "We see him around Hong Kong occasionally. He seems to have cut ties with the family." Tsao turned his attention to Wan's photo, venom on his breath. "If this crook sets foot in Hong Kong, I'll gladly run him down, but even Wan Koi is not dumb enough to take that risk."

"Do you have any known addresses or phone numbers for him in Macau?" Audrey asked as she scanned the information on Tsao's screen.

"Yeah. I'm not sure how current they are, but I'll print you out what we've got."

———

That evening, Audrey went to visit her son in the hospital. They talked about how, when he eventually got released, she would take him to whatever movie he wanted to see—"within reason, of course," she added with a smile and a squeeze on his arm. She stayed by his bedside and watched over the next twenty minutes as his breathing grew more metronomic and he gradually drifted off to sleep.

She always said *when* he got out of the hospital, never *if.* But as she stared at his innocent face, thoughts of *if* assailed her, and feelings of anger, impotence, and desperation whirled. She wanted justice for the boy's suffering. And those thoughts began to funnel toward a single enemy. Someone in the Sun Yee On triad had nearly killed her son, and their poison would certainly kill many more. And while she might not have the power to save Joshua from cancer, she could control what happened to the person who had hurt him.

Audrey knew what she needed to do. She would locate the triads, she would follow them, she would find out who poisoned the horn, and when the moment was right, she would deliver the man who poisoned her son to justice.

CHAPTER 38
THE VISITOR

Cobus perused the selection of stuffed animals surrounded by balloons and get well cards in the gift shop. He noted how, regardless of the species, all the dolls were proportioned like juveniles—oversize heads and paws, small round bellies, exaggerated eyeballs, and down-like fur. Affection for youth was one of the few things humans across all cultures seemed to share—a universal genetically coded survival strategy for the species.

It was the same reason Wan had been shipping baby wildlife to every continent except Antarctica. But when those same animals came into adulthood, the buyers would discover that a mature leopard or tiger or lion could be hazardous, labor intensive, and expensive to feed. Consequently, euthanizing adolescent cats had become a cottage industry in the Middle East, where there was no shortage of money or appetite for exotic pets.

Cobus settled on a stuffed teddy bear, then purchased a get

well balloon and exited from the gift shop into the sterile linoleum corridor.

Cobus had been following the detective all evening, but he
hadn't seen her since she entered the hospital two hours ago.
Knowing he would look out of place tailing her through the
quiet corridors, he had been reluctant to go in. The balloon and
the bear would soften his presence. He prowled the halls of the
hospital, expecting to find the detective interviewing a witness or
perhaps visiting some old relative who was nearing Saint Peter's
gates. Though he didn't know which room she was in, the building's linear layout guaranteed he would locate her eventually if he
kept moving down the spine of the building.

As he proceeded, peering cautiously into each room, he
passed a frail child with a bald head, being wheeled in the opposite direction. He knew that rhino horn had been touted as a cure
for cancer, and was glad to see this child surrounded by so much
modern medical technology. China was modernizing, and endangered wildlife had been abolished from official traditional Chinese
medicine. Though some still clung to the old ways, the use of rhino
for purely medicinal purposes was in its death throes. This meant
that the cartels had to develop a new sales pitch for the product,
so they rebranded horn as a status-displaying luxury good for the
new rich. This led to a boom in rhino-horn jewelry and the use of
horn as a party drug (albeit a completely ineffectual one).

Passing a room in the cancer ward, Cobus saw a boy watching
a Transformers movie in bed. Beside the boy, he saw the inspector
curled up in a chair, sleeping with her head on her balled-up jacket.

The boy looked over to see Cobus standing in the doorway.
Though he didn't know the big Westerner, he lit up at the sight
of the gifts in Cobus's hands. Cobus put a finger to his lips, then

pointed to the sleeping mother. The boy complied, and Cobus placed the balloon and the teddy bear on the table as he watched the boy's mother sleeping. He noted the service pistol holstered on her hip.

Moments later, Cobus stepped out. Seeing no one in the corridor, he picked up the boy's medical chart from its sleeve on the wall and photographed the pages of Chinese text with his smartphone.

———

That night, Cobus returned to the safe house he had rented. He imported the photos from his phone onto his laptop and ran the images through translation software with optical character recognition. Scanning the patchy translation of the boy's medical chart, he was horrified to discover that the weakened child had nearly perished from strychnine poisoning. The revelation kicked Cobus in the stomach. Though he had done plenty of evil in his life, he had always been able to justify it with his simple moral code: *You're either in the game or not, and if you're in the game, you accept that you're playing for the ultimate stakes.* Whether a poacher pulled the trigger or not, if he wandered into Kruger with a rifle, he was in the game. Same with the gun-toting sixteen-year-old Iraqi Cobus had dropped from five hundred yards on a ridge-line, or the Vietnamese diplomat who formed an alliance with a Mozambican kingpin. And by Cobus's math, anyone who know-ingly purchased the horn of a dead rhino was also in the game. But the young Chinese boy fighting the ultimate fight against a horrible disease was no more in the game than the animals in Kruger that Cobus had sworn to protect. It violated everything he stood for, and no amount of moral gymnastics could justify the suffering he had inflicted on the innocent creature. In the name of the greater good, *he had become nothing more than a human poacher.*

He rose and aggressively paced the tiny cage of an apartment, trapped in his own horrible sins, huffing about in an infinite loop. Just like an animal in captivity, he was suffering from *zoochosis* as the prolonged stress of being trapped caused him to exhibit repetitive stereotypic behavior. He marched back and forth, rubbing his face and scratching at the top of his head.

Finally, Cobus exploded, driving his fist into the wall, rebreaking the bones in his right hand that had been crushed in the brick-slinging mayhem at the docks. The pain sent a wave of electricity from his skull to his feet, forcing him to slump against the wall just to support his own weight.

———

Knight parked outside a run-down apartment block in the Taipa district of Macau. Nearly every balcony of the thirty stories that towered over him was strung with laundry—the flags of the tenements. Though the evening was cool, he was drenched in sweat and his hands shook.

He searched for the elevator, only to find its door crisscrossed with red masking tape. Clammy and feverish, he struggled up the stairwell, hauling himself by the bannister. By the time he reached the landing on the eleventh floor, his shaky legs could barely carry him. Ever since he returned from Thakhek, Knight had been running a temperature of 103 degrees and couldn't keep food down. The sleeve of his white dress shirt was stained rust-colored from the pus and blood that oozed through the dressings. He had recently replaced the bandage he got at a Laotian roadside clinic, where a young nurse had stitched up his cut. The fever was likely just from the infection in his arm, and he tried to push the worst-case scenario out of his mind.

Knight approached a door and knocked. It cracked open an inch, and Cobus's eye appeared above the security chain. Cobus unlocked the door and let Knight inside his spartan apartment, sealing both of them inside.

"You look like shit, bru," Cobus told him.

"Truth in advertising," Knight replied as he beelined for the sink. He took a glass from Cobus's drying rack and filled it with murky tap water.

Cobus kept a safe distance from his sick guest. "What was that disease your tiger cub died of in Miami?" he asked, making no effort to hide his assumption about Knight's illness.

Desperately thirsty, Knight chugged the water, then answered. "Feline leukemia."

"You said it doesn't jump to humans."

"I just have a bacterial infection in my arm," Knight said, though unconvinced of it himself.

Glancing around the apartment, he noticed a bucket of gopher poison on a shelf, confirming his suspicions about Cobus's dark gambit. "I gather that the triads don't know you live here."

"I keep a nicer place across town that they know about. This is just where I work. Why did you want to see me?"

Knight had reached out to Cobus after investigating the tiger farms. He had grown concerned about the business venture he was about to enter into, but not to the point that he was willing to walk away from an eight-figure opportunity. Knight needed to know the depth of the depravity he was wading into, and what kind of moral backflips would be required to justify his participation. "How much do you know about their operation?" he asked the South African.

"Everything."

"Show me."

Cobus withdrew a stack of folders from his desk. One of them brimmed with maps. "These are the locations of all the farms."

Knight flipped through the maps, recognizing the locations of the farms in Laos, Thailand, and Myanmar, many of which were buried in the jungle, like illegal narcotics-growing operations.

Cobus withdrew more documents. "Shipping manifests," he said. He then handed Knight several folders. Knight opened the top one to find a photo of Lee. "These are dossiers on all their major players."

He was shocked at how much Cobus knew about Lee, given how deliberately the business mogul had walled himself off from the Sun Yee On's operation. Knight dug deeper through photos of Wan and Broken Tooth and other triads he had been lucky never to cross paths with. He suddenly felt very exposed by the extent of Cobus's investigation.

"Do you have anything on me?" Knight asked.

"Why would I have anything on you? You said we're on the same side."

Knight turned to Cobus, hoping he was telling the truth, then went back to studying the documents.

"Are you going to help me stop them?" Cobus asked.

CHAPTER 39
BUSINESS

Knight's hands shook as he buttoned his shirt. He needed to look polished for his three o'clock meeting, and physically and mentally he felt trampled. His fever still hadn't dropped, and he was having trouble thinking, his mind pinballing from one half-formed thought to the next. The only upshot to his ailment was that he had already shed five pounds of the bourbon and rib eyes that had accumulated at his waistline.

As he dressed, he watched a breaking news story on television with the headline "OUTBREAK IN LAOS." He had first seen the news alert pop on his phone and had immediately surfed the channels in his hotel room until he found live coverage on Al Jazeera. Knight wasn't surprised to see that the authorities had stumbled across the facility in Thakhek, since he was the one who called in the anonymous tip about the outbreak as soon as he had gotten the hell out of Laos.

Knight had reported the outbreak less out of a sense of duty than out of self-preservation. It was under similar circumstances, in similar regions, that swine and bird flus had mutated and jumped to humans before spreading like wildfire through airports around the globe. These were the same international airports Knight frequented almost daily.

On screen, aid workers in biohazard suits could be seen hauling out the wrapped carcasses of tigers and humans. "The World Health Organization is currently responding to an outbreak of feline leukemia virus in Thakhek, Laos," the reporter announced. "The virus, previously occurring only in cats, made the jump to humans at what authorities say was a captive tiger breeding program."

Captive breeding program—that was one way of putting it.

As Knight pounded the Ciprofloxacin he always carried with him in case he contracted traveler's diarrhea, he was suddenly keenly aware of moisture gathering at the base of his nostrils. He took a tissue and dabbed his upper lip, afraid to look at it. If it was blood, it meant his ailment was not a bacterial infection from his wounded arm, which could be treated with antibiotics. It would mean he had contracted the feline leukemia virus and would likely be dead within twenty-four hours. Knight took a deep breath and closed his eyes before mustering the courage to look. Clear—just a sniffle.

Knight checked his watch as he finished buckling his pants. He couldn't be late for the meeting he was no longer certain he wanted to attend.

———

Knight emerged from the subway at Admiralty Station, a lone white face bobbing in a sea of Chinese commuters. As he walked downtown past the vaulting tower of the Bank of China, he conferred on the phone with his mentor, who was just having his morning toast in his London solarium.

"How'd it go at the farms?" Perkins asked as he chewed.

"They're worse than anything I've ever seen," Knight replied, instinctively checking over his shoulder for triad eyes and ears.

"Are they insurable?"

Ever since Knight gave him the hard sell on insuring farmed wildlife, Perkins had been sold. Now he seemed to sense it was Knight who needed to be resold.

"We'll cut you in on ten percent of everything you bring in," he added.

Knight considered, his heart hurting more than his wounded arm. The deal with the devil was turning out to be uglier than expected. And he was walking quite a tightrope legally. Although the special economic zones in the Golden Triangle, where the farms were located, operated effectively beyond the reach of international law, on paper they were still part of nations where tiger farming would be legal once Lee got his new legislation pushed through. So in that regard, they were technically insurable. But the conditions of the farms were another, more troubling matter, from both a moral and an underwriting perspective.

"I'm about to meet with the prospect. I'll get back to you later today."

Knight boarded the funicular tram at the base of Victoria Peak. As he swayed in his seat, climbing up the mountain, he was filled with anger at the abuses he had seen in Laos, Myanmar, and Thailand. He began litigating his arguments against Lee's business in his head, working himself up and growing more incensed as he approached the terminus atop the peak.

He stepped out onto the observation deck, where he found Lee standing at the glass railing, looking out over the harbor as if surveying his dominion. Knight joined him, taking in the sight of Kowloon and Hong Kong stretched out before them, divided by the harbor.

"So are we partners, then?" Lee asked.

Knight lit into Lee, the raw emotions from his ordeal lending venom to his argument. "I've seen your operation in Laos. They're electrocuting tigers!"

Lee was unmoved by Knight's outburst, having grown accustomed to righteous Western indignation. "It's either that or starving them," he replied matter-of-factly. "We don't want to damage the furs. I thought we were meeting to discuss business."

"Business!" Knight nearly burst out laughing at the absurdity. "You want to talk *business*? Your product is never going to make it to market. Between disease, inbreeding, and malnutrition, your supply is beyond salvage. Christ, that virus at the farm in Thakhek could have wiped out half of Asia if the World Health Organization hadn't come in and contained it." *That is,* Knight thought to himself, *assuming I'm not the lone human host who escaped and is now wandering about in one of the most densely populated cities in the world.*

Lee was a portrait of equanimity. "I only need to secure two more votes to get the farming legislation passed through CITES, and I already have a hundred-million-dollar commitment from a pharmaceutical company to start production on day one."

"Lee, you have no product!"

But in this moment, Lee seemed to know Knight better than Knight knew himself. "You wouldn't be standing here if you didn't have a solution to propose. That's why you came here, isn't it?"

Knight hesitated, torn between the money and his soul. Lee could sense his reluctance.

"Well, Randall Knight," he said, "you are the man who knows how to keep animals alive. What do we do?"

Knight considered, unable to believe what he was about to suggest. There was only one honest answer to the question. "You'd have to wipe out your inventory and start over." *Wipe out your inventory.* It sounded better than telling Lee he must slaughter hundreds of majestic endangered animals by electrocution, starvation, flaying alive, or whatever other ghastly method he might use.

"Done. Then what?"

Lee's willingness to destroy several million dollars' worth of cats caught Knight off guard. The man was ruthlessly forward-looking, and now he left Knight with no off-ramp from the conversation besides continuing with his proposal.

Knight felt the strange sensation of being outside his body, listening to someone else say the words. "I can connect you with breeders in the US with clean gene pools, and drug companies that can supply livestock antibiotics. You'd want to take the same approach as a zoo. Run each individual tiger's DNA through software to determine the best genetic matches. Use computer models to calculate optimal couplings. That way you can avoid inbreeding and genetic degradation of your stock." Knight paused, barely believing the words coming out of his own mouth.

"How soon could we be producing new tigers?"

"Four to sixth months. It would push you back, but you'd still be first to market."

"Then we have an agreement?"

Knight avoided eye contact with Lee, hoping he might still be able to talk them both out of it. "It's going to cost you. A lot."

Lee nodded, pleased to have Knight behind him. "Get back to me with a price."

As Lee departed, Knight clutched the railing to hold himself upright, still processing the bargain he had just made, as the fever ravaged his body.

CHAPTER 40
DEATH OF A SALESMAN

Davis sat stiffly in a chair in the hallway, reflecting on the depth of the hole he had dug for himself. He had lied to his daughter's private school when he told them that the check he had sent was lost in the mail. He had lied to his wife that everything was fine at work. The more desperate he became, the more lies he had told to paper everything over. He *needed* a promotion, or his little house of lies would come crashing down.

Davis could feel his breath growing shallow, as if his lungs couldn't expand to bring in enough air. He'd had a full-blown panic attack two years ago, which landed him in the hospital and then tethered him to a Xanax prescription that he had only recently managed to wean himself from. However, when a wave of anxiety hit him—as had occurred in Sumatra and was happening again right now—he would still have to force himself to breathe through it, to avoid it snowballing into a fit of hypoxia and hyperventilation. He cursed himself for throwing out the last bottle of Xanax and not heeding his doctor's advice to keep one in his wallet just in case this very situation arose.

If there was ever a time Davis didn't want to look like a man coming apart at the seams, it was now. Today, he would find out whether he was getting the bump to GS-14, and though he hadn't gotten his investigation over the goal line, he had gathered compelling data on poaching networks in Africa and had drawn concrete connections to genuine terrorists on the CTC's shit list.

Davis paused, holding his breath with his eyes closed as he waited in the hallway.

"Director Wilkes will see you now," a woman's voice announced.

Davis opened his eyes and stepped into the director's office, where he was flanked by Wilkes's second in command, Ron Nelson. Davis sat down, still holding his breath, praying the symptoms would go away before he had to speak.

Director Wilkes interlaced his fingers as he rocked back in his chair. "First off," he said, "I want to let you know that everyone at the agency really appreciates the work you've been doing here. Your passion and entrepreneurial spirit are commendable." Davis could feel the oxygen level in his brain dropping as he continued to hold his breath. It was a narrow tightrope he had to walk between passing out from hypoxia and having a breathing-induced panic attack. "Unfortunately, the panel met, and we can only promote three GS-13s this cycle under current budget exigencies."

The punch to the gut literally knocked the wind out of Davis. "This is my third cycle at GS-13 pay grade!"

Nelson chimed in, piling on with his contempt for the damaged goods in the chair beside him. "We need to put the money where the action is. You know how it goes, Kev."

"I was really hoping you could deliver on that Sumatra connection," Wilkes added. "I assume that's dead?"

Davis had no choice but to bluff. "It's still developing."

Nelson cornered him, taking great pleasure in it. "Developing, is it? Developing how?"

Davis retreated from Nelson's interrogation, turning his attention back to Director Wilkes. He knew he was against the ropes, but he needed to know how dire his predicament at the agency was. "I've heard there's going to be a round of cuts coming up. Is that true?"

Wilkes lowered his eyes. "No, it's just talk." The old man leaned forward and forced an encouraging smile. "You just focus on your work and you should be fine."

"*Should* be?" Davis asked.

Wilkes hardened, responding with a dose of tough love. "If you're asking me to make you any promises, I can't do that. At the end of the day, this place is a bureaucracy like any other. Everyone has to justify their job, including me."

Davis nodded, his situation sinking in. A fourth cycle at his current pay grade suddenly looked better than lining up at the unemployment office with his hat in hand.

"That will be all," Wilkes added, inviting the GS-13 bagman to depart.

———

Davis marched back down the hall, his body aquiver with anxiety. He had been living the past several years in fight-or-flight mode, but this was an escalation. He had gone into the meeting hoping for a promotion—no doubt a long shot, but he had made legitimate progress connecting animal trafficking to terrorism. Now, however, his back was against the wall. If he couldn't prove the Sumatra connection he had already written off in the early days of his investigation—before pivoting from Asia to focus on African terror groups—his days at the agency would be numbered.

Davis entered his office to see his giant map with a link-analysis chart staring back at him, yarn stretching between various note cards: Tanzania, Vietnam, Laos, Thailand, Myanmar, Cameroon. Everything was connected. Or was it? It didn't matter either way, because only one connection would carry any weight for Director Wilkes. Only one connection could save Davis's career.

He reached for a card over Sumatra, Indonesia, that read "Jemaah Islamiyah." J.I. was a legitimate national security concern ever since the 2002 Bali bombing killed seven Americans, and it was all the agency was interested in. The J.I. card had a piece of red yarn connecting it to Macau, demonstrating the Sumatra connection Davis had sold them on. And it was bullshit. The tiger couldn't have come from anywhere near Sumatra.

Davis suddenly began ripping all the yarn and photos off the wall. "Fuck you! And fuck you! And fuck you!" he shouted as he tore the photos into pieces and flung them angrily about the room, then swept all the papers off his desk onto the floor.

He glimpsed his secretary outside his office. She couldn't hear anything through the glass, but she could see the skinny officer tearing apart the room as he yelled hysterically, letting every shred of pent-up rage loose like a wild animal. He picked up his trash can and hurled it against the wall.

CHAPTER 41
THE FEVER

HONG KONG

The dream was always the same: a flowing ocean of grass for a thousand miles. But Knight's black horse would carry him the distance. It would nourish him with its blood and milk as he traversed infinity on its back. But this time there was no horse, and not a single sign of sentient life.

Knight was now all alone, wading in the sharp, knee-high grass that fought him for each labored step he took. He spun, finding nothing but cold, endless prairie that spanned the horizon in every direction. A sense of panic overwhelmed him. It began in his mouth and crept through his whole body, robbing him of breath as he wandered the empty Mongolian steppe, staggering through the void in terror, toward his inevitable doom.

———

He awoke from the dream around noon to find himself drenched in sweat except for his mouth, which was chalk dry. He raced to the bathroom, cupping water into his mouth and letting it run down his cheeks like the blood of the horse that had left him to die in his subconscious.

Knight placed a thermometer under his tongue, then gingerly peeled the bandage off his forearm. The gauze resisted, leaving wisps of fiber clinging to his grisly patchwork of stitches.

He pulled the thermometer and checked it. He had been well above a hundred degrees for the past week. Finally, he was back down to ninety-nine. He breathed a sigh of relief as he swept his pharmacy shopping bag and all its contents into the wastebasket.

———

Cobus sat in the bar area of the ornate hotel lobby, scanning the room as he spoke on the phone with his old friend. "Lawrence, this is the last shipment." Lawrence was curious whether something had gone wrong with Cobus's plan, but Cobus didn't want to burden him with the specific moral consequences of their actions. They intended to punish the sponsors of death in their homeland, not poison innocent children.

"Things have gone too far," was all Cobus would say.

"Are you coming back home?" Lawrence asked. Cobus could hear the concern in his voice.

"I don't think so."

Cobus hung up, left alone with his thoughts of the young boy he had nearly killed with his gopher poison. He took a sip of beer to calm his nerves, then went back to his surveillance. Across the lobby, he spotted his prey.

———

As Knight headed for the front door to get some fresh air, Cobus intercepted him, blocking his path.

"Have you no conscience?" The South African fumed. "I thought you were going to stop them. Instead, you're cashing in on extinction."

"What are you talking about?" Knight had never told Cobus his true intentions for his relationship with Lee, and the sudden accusation caught him off guard.

"Don't bullshit me, you bastard."

"I'm not bullshitting you," Knight protested. "I don't know what you're talking about."

"I know what you're doing with Lee. I know all of it."

"You don't get it, Cobus. *I'm* not doing anything," Knight said, trying to convince them both. "This deal is happening with or without me."

Cobus towered over Knight, looking as if he might maul him. He formed his words with measured rage. "Listen to me, Knight, because like it or not, it's time to draw a line."

Not in the mood for the environmentalist's naive pleas, Knight tried to push past him. "Spare me the sermon."

Cobus gripped the front of Knight's shirt and twisted, pulling him close, violence in his eyes. "Shut up and hear me out before I put your teeth through the back of your head."

Knight stopped in his tracks, taken aback by the threat.

"You think you're some spider crawling on top of the web," Cobus continued. "But you're *part of* the web. Everything in this world is connected, Knight. If this endangered-species farming legislation goes through, you will personally be responsible for killing the last wild tiger. The last rhino. When our children ask us why we live in a world with no wild animals, you'll know you were responsible."

Knight raised his open palms in supplication. "They are already dead. It's simple math—the numbers don't lie."

Cobus took the measure of the man whose shirt was still bunched in his fist. "How much money do you think your dad could have made if he doped his horses like everyone else?" Cobus's words hung in the air. "Imagine if he saw what you've become."

Knight leaned back, but Cobus had him. "I'm not the bad guy!" he spluttered.

Cobus released Knight's shirt, and Knight stumbled back, regaining his balance.

"Fuck you, Knight. If you're not the bad guy, who is?"

For once, Knight was at a loss for words. Cobus lowered his voice. "I'm going to the cops and I am telling them everything. About the farms, about how you've been advising the triads on their supply chain. I'll give you one last chance, Knight. If you walk away now, I'll leave your name out of it."

"I can't just walk away now!"

"You're a weak little shit, Knight."

Knight tried to talk some sense into the South African. "You think the triads are just going to let you roll on them? You need to calm down and start thinking rationally for once in your goddamn life."

"I'm the only one stopping you people from killing the animals," Cobus growled.

"You're on the losing side! Don't get caught in the crossfire on this."

"If you want to kill the animals, then you will have to kill me too," Cobus said without hyperbole.

He then turned his back on Knight, leaving the horse trainer's son alone as the doubt and shame took hold.

CHAPTER 42
POISON

MACAU

Broken Tooth pushed his way along the crowded sidewalk, jostled by the flow of foot traffic coming at him. Saturday night was always mayhem at the bars and "saunas" that lined Macau's vice district. He approached the Emperor Sauna, threading between the young women beckoning potential customers inside.

Upstairs, he found Wan holding court with several of his top foot soldiers—49s, as the triads called them—who were draped with prostitutes the boss had provided to reward their loyalty. Broken Tooth was referred to as the Straw Sandal—the top messenger in the organization—and tonight he came bearing news that he was certain would lead to violence.

The 49s watched as Broken Tooth leaned in and whispered something in Wan's ear. Wan set down his drink as he listened, his features hardening.

———

Ten minutes later, Broken Tooth was hurrying to keep up as Wan marched into their warehouse at the docks. Earlier that night, three people in Macau had nearly died from strychnine poisoning after consuming rhino horn powder. Broken Tooth had investigated the poisonings after one of Wan's dealers was arrested (having been identified to the police by a friend of one of the victims).

"Are you sure the product wasn't poisoned by the dealer on the street?" the Red Pole asked his Straw Sandal.

"That's what I thought at first," Broken Tooth replied. "But the people who were poisoned bought the horn from three separate dealers. The only thing they all had in common is that the horn came from us."

Wan approached a stack of packages of ground rhino horn on a table. Somewhere along the supply chain was a snake, and he needed to trace it to wherever in the chain it was hiding. "Did any of our men touch these packages yet?"

"They just came in last night," Broken Tooth said. "The only person who has touched them is the South African."

Wan carried one of the packages to the wall of caged exotic animals awaiting distribution. Most of them were diurnal and were sleeping. Snapping open his knife, he cut into the package. He stepped over to a small cage containing a live pangolin, then dropped a pinch of rhino horn powder in its water dish, mixing the powder and water together with his knife. "We will know the truth soon enough."

The men waited and watched over the next hour as the slow-moving little ball of scales stuck out its long, slithering tongue and lapped from its water bowl. As its body processed the liquid, the creature began to spasm and curled up into a ball, quivering with each convulsion. Within minutes, it lay sprawled on its side, little toothless mouth agape, its long tongue dangling on the floor of the cage.

Wan stared at the carcass, boiling with rage at the revelation that Cobus had delivered him poisoned product.

Broken Tooth turned to him. "What do you want to do?"

CHAPTER 43
THE ACCOMPLICE

KOWLOON

Knight scrolled through the e-mails on his laptop as he worked the phone in his suite at the Peninsula Hotel. "Knock off a hundred grand, and I could take the whole lot off your hands," he told the man from Houston on the other end of the line.

The man knew Knight and knew that he always delivered. Knight hung up and added the inventory to a growing list of tigers on his notepad: Sumatrans, Amurs, Bengals, Malayans, Indochinese. He noted whether the cats were male or female, breeding age or cubs.

If his business venture with Lee was to succeed, he needed to procure dozens of tigers within the month. It was dusk in Hong Kong, which meant the breeders stateside would all be starting their days. Knight had carpet-bombed the breeding community with inquiries, and now the e-mails were pouring in: "Pet Tigers for Sale."

Knight had a reputation for operating in moneyed circles, and all the breeders were chasing him with their best product. He clicked through photos of cubs with heads and paws too big for their tiny bodies. The photos were meant to tug at a buyer's heartstrings: a cub hiding in a laundry bin, nursing on a bottle, playing with a bulldog, licking its owner's face . . .

Knight would gladly take all the cubs off their hands, but what he really needed were fully grown breeding cats he could launder into Lee's big-cat "sanctuaries" in Southeast Asia. He clicked deeper down his in-box, stopping at an e-mail featuring a mature purebred Sumatran with a stunning iridescent burnt-orange pelt. The price was $100,000—fair market value for such a specimen. Knight raised his phone to call the owner, then paused, entranced by the tiger's fiery eyes peering back at him with their raw, primal intensity. A few seconds passed. Knight realized he had stopped breathing. All he could think about was the fact that any tiger he bought would end up in a vat of rice wine. He forced himself to take a breath and shut his computer.

Knight crossed to the window, feeling unmoored and adrift as he looked out into the dying light of the city. He thought about pouring himself a Johnnie Walker from the minibar, but he couldn't move.

For the past several years, his mind had been orbiting an idea. It was like the sun: always there, just out of sight, never to be examined directly. But ever since he saw the farm in Thakhek, he had felt the urge to stare into it, though knowing that if he did, it would be blinding. That thought was the ghastly possibility that Knight had built his life profiting off the suffering of animals.

His phone buzzed in his pocket. He answered, gathering himself.

"How are my tigers coming?" Lee asked.

"I'm working on it."

"Good. I also owe you some gratitude. We investigated the rhino poisoning you mentioned, and discovered the source. It was one of our suppliers—a South African."

Knight's stomach sank. He remembered that in his frightened state in Myanmar, he'd tried to prove his indispensability by revealing to Lee that his supply chain was being poisoned. He hadn't mentioned Cobus by name, but it wouldn't have taken long for Lee's people to connect those dots. Knight had written the conservationist's death warrant. The only remaining question was whether it had already been carried out. He swallowed, his throat dry.

"A South African?" Knight played dumb. "Where is he now?"

"Macau. We're handling it."

———

Knight called down for the valet to fetch his rental car, then raced out the door. Within minutes, he was pulling onto the newly constructed Hong Kong–Macau Bridge. The cars formed a uniform stream of electrons traversing the circuit over the inky void of the Pearl River Delta.

Knight mashed the gas pedal, swerving chaotically around traffic as he dialed his phone. He had already tried Cobus twice and hadn't gotten through. "Come on, you dumb tree-hugging son of a bitch! Answer your phone!" The call went to a generic voicemail, and Knight hung up.

The cars ahead slowed as a road worker waved for them to stop. Knight gripped the wheel in frustration.

"Fuck . . ." Knight paused, taking inventory of just how far off track he had gotten. He had told himself that the tigers were going to be farmed whether he liked it or not—at least, if he participated, he could help them harvest the animals humanely and safely. But this was different. A man was going to be murdered.

Knight tried to convince himself that Cobus's imminent death was Cobus's fault alone. *He chose to go to war with the syndicate. He had signed his own death warrant when he poisoned the supply.* But Knight was an expert bullshit detector, and he knew that the voice in his head was full of it.

He fished through his jacket pocket and found Kevin Davis's business card. He studied the card, considering what he was about to do. The cars behind him honked, and Knight looked up to see that the vehicles ahead of him had moved forward.

———

Back at Langley, Davis sat on the floor of his demolished office, catching his breath. He knew that gossip of his little meltdown would travel fast, adding more insult to more injury. He was a dead man walking at the agency. He had also missed his window for a career on Wall Street—no private equity firm or hedge fund wanted a forty-three-year-old who hadn't worked in finance in eighteen years.

Fuck it. Fuck all of them. He sank back against the wall and cracked open a can of soda. For the first time since he could remember, Davis suddenly felt like a free man.

As he let the high-fructose corn syrup run down his throat, the phone rang. He rose to his desk, which had two phones and two computers (one for internal comms and one for external). He answered the external phone. "This is Davis."

"It's Knight. I need your help." Knight rushed to get the words out. "If I give you a cell phone number, can you locate it for me?"

Still basking in the catharsis of his outburst, Davis responded to the absurd request with oddly polite detachment. "Sorry, Knight. I'd love to help out, but it doesn't work that way."

"Trust me, I'll make it worth your while." Sun Tzu. The battle was always over before Knight set foot on the field.

"I can't use agency resources to do personal favors," Davis explained.

"What if I told you I could get you your connection between trafficking and terrorism?" Knight had a strong hunch Davis was like the mammal curator he'd met at SafariWorld. People in need were generally willing to turn a blind eye to provenance.

"It only matters if it's connected to Sumatra, and I'm guessing that's not what you're calling about."

"And what if I could deliver your Sumatra connection?" Knight countered enigmatically.

Davis lowered his voice. "If you're talking about falsifying evidence, that's a federal offense . . ."

"Not to be a dick, Davis, but we both know you're circling the drain at the agency. I'm offering you a chance to prove to everyone that you were right."

Whatever fantasies Davis had of telling everyone he worked with to go screw themselves suddenly evaporated.

"This thing your offering—is it real?"

"It will be," Knight assured him.

Despite his best instincts, Davis could feel Knight reeling him in. Knight was slippery, but was he any slipperier than other sources the CIA relied on?

"Which terror group?"

"Whichever one you want."

Davis could sense that the deal was Faustian in nature, but he was desperate. "When would I get it?"

"How soon can you be in Hong Kong?"

Though Davis didn't know what deal the devil was offering, he proceeded to log on to his internal CIA computer, looking out the window to make sure no one was watching.

"What's that phone number you need located?"

CHAPTER 44
THE FATE OF DOGS

MACAU

As slot machines dinged all around him, Cobus approached the money cage on the floor of the Wynn Casino. He presented a large stack of chips he had just collected from the triad's accounts-payable department in the private poker room. The casino offered the option of paying out in Macanese patacas, the yuan of mainland China, or Hong Kong dollars. Like most international gamblers, Cobus preferred the Hong Kong dollar because it was the most fungible. In fact, many Chinese gamblers came to Macau with their yuan purely because it was one of the most efficient and untraceable ways to move their newly gotten wealth out of mainland China.

The teller handed Cobus a brick of Hong Kong dollars, which he stuffed in his jacket before leaving the casino. He made his way across the street, checking his six as he passed beneath the giant glowing pineapple tower of the Grand Lisboa Casino. The casino was a former triad haunt from the time when men like the Sky Dragon ran the city, before they were forced into exile and their gambling rackets were taken over by men like Sheldon Adelson and Steve Wynn.

Cobus knew that the area around the Grand Lisboa was still a popular hangout for the vestiges of the triad clans. This posed a particular risk to Cobus, who was already constantly on edge since both Wan and Wan's rivals had cause to put him down.

He proceeded quickly and inconspicuously toward his primary apartment—the one the triads knew about. During his time in Macau, he had deliberately established a pattern of life for the benefit of the triads surveilling him. His scripted routine was to take his earnings home via an indirect route and place a portion of them in the freezer for safekeeping. The rest he would store in the drop ceiling of his safe house when he wasn't being tailed. It was all just obvious enough to lull his observers into a false sense of confidence. Cobus had occasionally found their spoor in his apartment and knew that they had repeatedly searched every inch of the space. By now they would be confident they had developed a complete picture of the corrupt South African merchant's life.

Just beyond the reach of the neon lights, Cobus strode through the tangled narrow streets that were home to the tenements of St. Lawrence Parish. He had chosen this particular neighborhood to live in because it was a good place to lose a tail if circumstances required it, and tonight, he sensed that they might. He had noted several pairs of eyes tracking him since he left the casino. It was likely standard security procedure for the triads, but Wan was closing in on the truth—if he hadn't already—and Cobus couldn't afford to make any assumptions about his pursuers' intentions.

As Cobus redoubled his pace, a motorcycle approached from

behind. In the side-view mirror of a parked car, he could see that the bike was carrying two riders. He maneuvered to put the parked car between himself and the riders, who were bearing down on him quickly, their bodies obscured by the glaring headlight.

Cobus knelt low behind the cover of the car, pretending to tie his shoelace as the motorcycle passed without incident. Yes, he was being paranoid, but in the jungle, paranoia was a valuable survivable skill.

He walked deeper into the city. A Mercedes behind him slowed as it threaded the narrow street. Cobus spun just in time to see the barrel of a submachine gun emerge from the darkened interior of the Mercedes. He dived behind a parked car. The windows beside him exploded. Cobus clutched his right biceps. One of the Uzi's nine-millimeter rounds had hit him. If it nicked the brachial artery, Cobus would have a fast-ticking clock as blood jetted from his body. Mercifully, the bullet had found only the small vessels near the surface.

It was an amateur hit by men who never had proper firearms training. They had blown through an entire thirty-two-round magazine in three seconds of inaccurate fire, giving their prey a brief window while they had to reload.

Weighing his options for escape, Cobus took off in the direction the Mercedes had come from. Unable to turn around in the narrow alley, the big sedan had to chase him in reverse, wobbling and scraping against parked cars on both sides.

Cobus sprinted toward the historic center of Macau, a UNESCO heritage site clustered with Portuguese colonial architecture. One of the first things he had done when he arrived in Macau was to plan out numerous escape-and-evasion contingency routes in case he ever found himself in the crosshairs of either law enforcement or the gang he was betraying. The Portuguese colonial section had been developed three centuries before the advent of the automobile. Its tight walkways and stone staircases would buy him time, and time on the run equaled distance from the threat. But first, he had to make it down three blocks of the main road, where he would be completely exposed before entering the Old Quarter.

Cobus gasped for air as the Mercedes screeched onto the main road behind him and turned so it was once again facing forward. It closed in quickly. Guns came out the windows, and shots rang out. Bright sparks chipped the stone all around Cobus as he turned a corner onto a walking street and bolted up a staircase.

The Mercedes stopped. Wan and three other triads got out and gave chase through the Old Quarter.

Cobus sprinted for his life through the crowded maze of the old city, his boots pounding over the uneven cobblestones. He raced up snaking staircases and down narrow walkways between buildings crowded onto the hillside at every possible angle.

Caroming around a tight corner, he emerged into a brightly lit courtyard, where he had to swim through a shoal of tourists gathered outside the large yellow St. Dominic's Church. Across the square, Cobus spotted Wan's men hemming him in, forcing him to veer from his planned escape route.

As he headed farther north, Cobus found himself in unfamiliar territory—that is, assuming he was still even going north, which was impossible to divine in this labyrinth. Where he was going now didn't matter. All that mattered was putting distance between himself and the pack of predators racing through the jungle in search of him.

Cobus emerged from the crush of buildings onto a large avenue. For a moment, he considered carjacking a passing driver.

Then, improbably, across the avenue he spotted a forest stretched out before him—Mong Ha Park.

Darting across the street, Cobus looked back as Wan and the three other triads emerged from a narrow alleyway. A second later, he disappeared into the wooded park.

The dense thicket clawed at Cobus as he fled. He could hear the voices of the men behind him, closing in. If they were good, they would spread out and funnel him to a location where their colleagues would lie in wait and make the kill. Cobus needed to change his vector before it was too late. He veered down a hillside, hoping to slip around the front of the enemy line unnoticed.

As he ran through a thicket of sharp, spiky palm fronds, Cobus saw a shape in the darkness. His only hope was to close the distance and pounce before his attacker could get off a shot at his charging silhouette.

The attacker lifted his gun as the big South African tackled him to the ground. Cobus found a familiar face glowering up at him.

Broken Tooth tried to fend off his attacker, but his arms were pinned under more weight than he could move. Straddling the triad, Cobus grabbed a large, flattish rock and hoisted it above his head. The scream cut off abruptly as the rock came down.

Cobus felt Broken Tooth's head implode, then felt the body go slack. The other triads must have heard their comrade's scream as Cobus culled him from the pack, because they were already running to Cobus's position. He needed to keep moving.

He scrambled down the hill, sliding on loose dirt and leaves and shoving branches out of his way until he fetched up at the bottom. Stepping out of the dense foliage, he emerged in a remote section of the city.

He heard the calls and the crashing of the triads coming down the hill behind him, so he raced toward the only cover he could find: a small stadium on the outskirts of the city—the Macau Canidrome.

―――

Neon greyhounds flickered above the locked gate. Cobus jumped as high as he could and grabbed the fence. Rolling over the top, he dropped to the other side and sprinted away from the gates, past the betting booths, moving deeper into the complex.

Cobus's shoes clacked on the pavement as he ran down a dark corridor in a back area of the Canidrome. With footsteps closing fast behind him, he paused at a locked door.

Cobus kicked in the door and entered a dark hallway. He about jumped out of his skin as a dozen sinewy greyhounds barked wildly, lunging at him from their cages. He hurried past them and out the other end of the hallway, emerging onto the dog track, which was cloaked in darkness.

The stadium lights suddenly snapped on, exposing Cobus with their brutal white glare. He spun, a hunted animal searching for threats. He saw a tunnel opening in the stands across the track. For a moment, it looked like his best shot at escape. Then he saw the shadow of a man in the tunnel, coming for him. Cobus scrambled for the only cover he could find in the open arena.

―――

Wan emerged from the tunnel, Glock pistol in hand as he searched for Cobus. He scanned the stadium. There was only one place Cobus could be hiding: the metal starting gate for the dogs. Wan moved warily down the track, toward the starting gate. Drawing near, he raised his gun.

Just as he rounded the corner of the gate structure, Wan

turned and was momentarily distracted by the sight of the stuffed mechanical rabbit staring back at him.

Capitalizing on the distraction, Cobus leaped over the metal gate, tackling Wan and sending his pistol flying. Wan tried to dive for the gun, but Cobus was on his back before he could reach it.

The two men savaged each other as they wrestled in the dirt—both trained martial artists accustomed to violence. As Cobus got the upper hand, Wan drew a stiletto blade and spiked it into Cobus's shoulder.

Cobus tried to yank the knife out, but it was planted in bone, and his hand was too slick with blood to maintain a grip. As he tugged at the knife, Wan snaked around his back and got him in a choke hold.

Bees swarmed in Cobus's vision, and he could feel himself fading as his brain starved for oxygen. He reached back with the arm that hadn't been stabbed, clawing for Wan's face, trying to gouge the eyes. Instead, he found an ear. He would have to take what he could get before he passed out in the next two seconds. He yanked with all his remaining strength, and Wan's ear came free with a *pop*. The grip on Cobus's neck relaxed at once.

Badly wounded, both men rose to their feet to regroup. Wan touched the wet, bare section of scalp where his left ear had been. He looked up to see Cobus clutching the severed ear in his fist. He tossed the bloody flesh in the dirt, and both men turned back to the business of killing each other.

BAM!

———

Cobus and Wan ducked instinctively, then turned. Ten yards away, Inspector Audrey Lam stared down the barrel of her SIG

Sauer P250 handgun at the boss of the Sun Yee On triad. She had been stalking Wan Koi through Macau all night, waiting for him to be alone. She had lost him briefly in the park, but now she finally had her chance to punish him—in a place where no one would witness his death.

"Don't move."

The men complied. Blood trickled down the side of Wan's face from the hole where his ear had been uprooted. "What do you want?" he asked Audrey. "Money?"

Though Audrey had never seen the burly South African before, he seemed to recognize her. "Her son was poisoned," he informed Wan.

Audrey twitched the gun onto Cobus. "Who did it?"

Wan nodded toward Cobus. "It was him."

Audrey studied Cobus, who said nothing. "Is that true?"

As Audrey's gun quivered unsteadily in her hands, he looked in her eyes, and for a brief moment she saw what looked like a hint of remorse.

"Yes," he said.

Audrey's finger tensed on the trigger.

Exploiting Audrey's focus on Cobus, Wan dived for his handgun in the dirt. Cobus went for it too.

Audrey hesitated, unable to pull the trigger on either man. Wan snatched his gun off the ground, but his adversary was on him before he could fire off a shot. As the two men wrestled for control, Cobus managed to turn the gun on Wan.

Audrey startled as the gun discharged point-blank into Wan's heart. His body toppled backward and lay motionless on the track.

Cobus turned toward Audrey with Wan's pistol in his hand.

Though he didn't put her in his sights, the gun swept toward the detective as he turned.

Audrey saw the muzzle heading in her direction and instinctively squeezed the trigger.

The bullet from her SIG P250 struck Cobus in the chest, dropping him to the earth like a newborn rhino.

Cobus struggled to sit up, the loaded pistol still dangling in his hand. He looked up at Audrey, his shocked eyes meeting the muzzle of her pistol, which was aimed at his face. Rather than engage the mother, he tossed Wan's Glock in the dirt, then collapsed on the track.

Audrey rushed to the man she had shot, pleading. "Why?" she cried. "Why did you poison them?"

As his face began to lose color, Cobus reached in his shirt pocket and withdrew two crumpled, bloodstained photos—one of a male African ranger and one of a smiling young African woman who wore a matching green uniform.

"They died for your horn," the man wheezed. "I just wanted it to stop." The photos slipped from his fingers and fell in the dirt.

Cobus stared silently at the sky. Audrey could see the blood hemorrhaging from the bullet hole in his chest. She stripped off her jacket and began applying pressure, desperate to keep him alive, as if her soul hung in the balance. He gagged and coughed, blood erupting up from his lungs and out his mouth and nose, staining the earth.

As Cobus began to drift off, Audrey heard sirens in the distance. She looked into his wide, empty eyes.

"Stay with me."

CHAPTER 45
THE DOSSIER

Knight swerved in and out of traffic on the snarled, narrow streets. Shortly after he hung up with Davis, Davis had uploaded a pin with the last known location of Cobus's phone. Knight looked down at the map to check Cobus's location, nearly rear-ending the car in front of him. He had already narrowly avoided collisions outside a McDonald's and a sixteenth-century temple as he made his way into Macau. Now he couldn't be more than a hundred yards away from the pin's location. The fact that Cobus hadn't moved in the past ten minutes made him easier to track but was also a cause for concern.

Ahead, Knight saw the flashing lights of ambulances and police cars gathered outside the dog track. His stomach sank as he parked his car and stepped out.

Knight approached an ambulance, trying not to draw attention to himself as he scanned the scene. A police officer intercepted him.

"I'm looking for a friend," Knight told the officer. The officer said to stand back. "Official police business."

Angling for a view over the cop's shoulder, he spotted paramedics moving without urgency as they transported a covered body out of the stadium.

No, it can't be.

Knight spun about and saw a second body already loaded into the open back of the ambulance. A paramedic had a resuscitator mask pressed to the patient's face as another paramedic performed chest compressions. Though he couldn't see the man's face, Knight recognized the tattoos on the tan, muscular arm dangling off the stretcher.

The sight of Cobus clinging to life tore through his heart like a bullet. Knight felt the blood draining to his feet and buckled over, sensing he was about to throw up. *Oh my God*, he thought, *what have I done?*

———

Thirty minutes later, the lock on Cobus's safe house shattered and the door burst inward. Knight was the only one besides Cobus who knew about the apartment, but soon others—both triads and law enforcement—would connect the dots of the South African's double life and come turn the place inside out.

Buzzing with cortisol and adrenaline from his fight-or-flight response, Knight rifled through the drawers in Cobus's desk. As he examined their contents, he was shocked at how comprehensive the man's intelligence gathering had been. Cobus had a complete organizational chart for the Sun Yee On triad featuring Sky Dragon, Henry Lee, and Wan Koi, as well as other soldiers with odd titles like Straw Sandal, White Paper Fan, and the lower-ranking Blue Lanterns. There were also reams of shipping manifests, photos, and copious notes he had taken on every aspect of the triad's operation. Knight was generally uncharitable with praise, but he was impressed by the professional nature of the investigation.

As he yanked out the files, he stopped at one labeled *Randall Knight*. He opened it to reveal a surveillance photo of himself and Lee meeting at Victoria Peak. The sneaky bastard had stalked Knight just as Knight had stalked him after stumbling across him at Wan's warehouse. Beneath the photo was a detailed log of Knight's activities in Hong Kong, as well as notes from conversations Cobus had had with Wan about Knight's plans to help the triad traffic endangered animals for Knight's own financial gain. The accounts of his criminal conspiracy were meticulous and irrefutable. Cobus had realized Knight was full of shit, and was secretly planning to hang him along with the rest of the criminals.

Knight picked up a trash bin and swept all the documents into it, then removed the plastic liner and wrapped it all into a bundle.

He then rushed out the door with the incriminating evidence tucked under his arm.

CHAPTER 46
THE SINNER

Audrey fled when she heard the sirens. She knew that if she was at the scene of the shooting when the police arrived, she would have a lot of explaining to do. *Why was a Hong Kong police officer delivering medical aid to a gunshot victim at the greyhound track? And why was her bullet lodged in his chest?* And she knew that if she answered those questions, she would never see her son again.

So she stopped applying pressure to Cobus's chest wound and slipped off into the darkness, leaving him to die.

———

A tropical storm began to pour down hard as she walked the two kilometers to the ferry terminal. Left alone with her thoughts, she was overcome with shame and guilt. She shivered uncontrollably as the rain streamed down her hair and seeped through her coat.

Soaked to the bone, Audrey stepped into the punishing light

of the terminal. She kept her hands in the pockets of her dark jacket, avoiding the eyes of the tourists lining up for the last ferry home to Hong Kong after a night of gambling and revelry. As she crossed the antiseptic linoleum floor, she saw splotches of pink liquid forming a trail behind her. The water continued to wick down the sleeves of her jacket, mixing with Cobus's blood contained in the fibers and trickling down to form a damning pool at her feet.

Audrey rushed into the bathroom. She vigorously scrubbed the congealed blood from her trembling hands. The door opened, and an elderly woman dripping with jewelry entered. Audrey froze as the woman crossed to a bathroom stall, oblivious to the bloodstained sink.

Audrey returned to her scrubbing, and when her hands were finally just stained a light shade of pink, she removed her jacket and stuffed it in the trash, covering it with wads of paper towels. Taking one last look in the mirror to make sure she had washed away the stranger's DNA, she barely recognized the damp, haggard woman with dark circles under her eyes staring back at her.

———

It was after midnight by the time Audrey made it to the hospital in Hong Kong. The janitor was buffing the floor as she moved down the corridor that had become her second home over the past six months. She entered her son's room to find him sleeping peacefully. Cartoons yammered quietly on the television. Audrey grabbed the remote control and switched it off.

She lowered herself to her knees by her son's bed. Clasping her hands together, she pressed them tightly against her forehead as she prayed. She begged God for salvation—not for her, but for the boy. *Please don't punish him for my sins*, she pleaded. As long as the boy survived, she would accept whatever tribulations her Maker felt appropriate to saddle her with. She was willing to burn in hell if only her son could rise from her ashes.

Audrey's body began to heave with grief as the emotions overwhelmed her. Tears rolled down her face.

The boy woke at the sound of his mother's inconsolable sobbing. Though he did not know exactly what she had been through, he clearly knew she had been through a lot and hadn't been sleeping. He placed his hand on her head, caressing her hair.

"It's okay, Mom. It's going to be okay."

Audrey nodded, desperately wanting to believe him, then leaned in close and kissed the boy on the head as she embraced him.

CHAPTER 47
EVERYONE HAS A PRICE

KOWLOON

Knight drunkenly swirled his glass of scotch, then knocked it back as he sat alone at the hotel bar at the Peninsula. The high-rises twinkled just across Victoria Harbor. The lights blurred together, just as they always did.

Knight was drained both physically and emotionally, and he could feel gravity pulling him into the stool as if he were on the surface of Jupiter. In his younger years, this was when he would have slipped off to the men's room for a bump of cocaine to get back in the game. But he had quit the drug a few years back, after learning that it typically spent a lot of time up someone's ass and possibly had led to a few deaths on its journey to New York. It was one of the few moral lines he had ever drawn in his life.

Knight waved to the bartender. "Another Johnnie Blue." The blended scotch was sixty dollars a pour at the hotel bar, but

Knight had no qualms about letting Carlyle Insurance underwrite his bender, given the money he would soon be bringing in.

A slender Chinese woman in a backless designer cocktail dress sat down next to him, casting him a seductive look. Knight suspected she may have a boyfriend back home somewhere, but she was a wealthy young player like him, and they were the type that never truly belonged to anyone.

"What brings you to Hong Kong?" she asked, rotating her stool ever so slightly toward him.

Knight's drink arrived. "Business." He gave the scotch a swirl to melt the ice, then took a sip. His eyes fell on the lights outside, which were getting blurrier with each drink.

"What kind of business?"

Knight had successfully conducted the seduction so many times that the act of reciting it was beginning to bore him. He launched into it on autopilot, his thoughts still elsewhere.

"I can put a dollar value on anything," he told her.

The woman leaned in, as they all did. "Even me?"

The Johnnie Blue hadn't offered the escape he sought. Perhaps the soft embrace of a beautiful stranger would. It would be easy enough to get her back to his room—or hers. Soon, he would assign a dwindling dollar value to her. She would try to convince him she was worth more, and he would have her under his control. "Even you."

"So can I," she told him.

Knight smirked into his drink. *That was a new one.* "Oh, yeah?"

The woman leaned in close, whispering in his ear. "Two hundred for my hands. Five hundred for my lips. One thousand for everything."

Knight laughed under his breath. Though he couldn't argue

with the specifics of her appraisal, paying for sex would deny him its true satisfaction—the conquest.

"How about I just buy you a drink?" he offered.

The woman forced a smile and walked away, leaving him alone again with his drunken toxic thoughts.

As one drink led to another, the bar began to empty out, but he kept his perch.

"I'll have what he's having."

Knight recognized the voice and turned to find a familiar face.

"Well, look who it is! Secret Squirrel himself." Knight was glad to see Kevin Davis. He didn't know why; he just knew that he was.

"How'd you know I'd be at the bar?" Knight asked sarcastically.

"I checked your credit card purchases," Davis replied without irony.

The bartender set a glass in front of Davis and filled it with scotch. Davis took a pained sniff and then forced down a sip of the burning brown liquid.

"What's driving you to drink all of a sudden?" Knight asked.

"You were right. I bet my career on connecting tiger trafficking to terrorism, but I'm chasing a ghost. I've got to be the unluckiest son of a bitch in history."

Bullshit, Knight thought to himself. "In my experience, unlucky people don't end up righting their ship. You know why?"

Davis forced down another painful sip. "Why's that?"

"Because they were never unlucky in the first place. They made their own bad luck. You doubled down on a bet everyone told you was dog shit from the start. That's not luck; that's hubris."

Knight paused, considering the predicaments both men found themselves in. "That's how mankind got into this whole mess."

"Did you find what you needed?" Davis asked, keeping it vague.

"I suppose so."

"And did you find what *I* need?" Davis added.

"That cub in Florida that killed all the cats at SafariWorld—it came from a tiger farm in Laos. The guys running the farms are some bad motherfuckers. If they aren't stopped, they are going to push through legislation that will be the end of wildlife as we know it."

Davis seemed to sense the rare note of sincerity in Knight's voice. "Look, Knight, I know it's typically your place to be the cynical one, but at this point I couldn't give a shit about animals."

Knight was taken aback by his tone. Davis continued, "I need a terror connection, or my career is over, and I flew eleven goddamn time zones because you promised me one. Can you deliver a link between traffickers and terrorists, or not?"

Knight gave him a conspiratorial look. "You said your job at the agency was tracking money, right?"

———

Two hours and four Johnnie Walkers later, Knight rubbed his red, tired eyes. He fished another bottle out of the minibar in his hotel room and poured it, mustering the courage to place the phone call. As he dialed, he thought about hanging up. There would be no way to unfuck this once it was done.

"I hope you have good news," Lee said in greeting.

"I found a supplier in the States who can deliver thirty mature purebred Sumatrans. It's all going to be off the books, so you're going to have to pay a premium for their silence. The cost will be three million US."

"How much is your cut?" Lee asked.

"This one's on the house," Knight told him. "As long as you

guarantee my company gets the insurance contracts when the legislation goes through and this all becomes legal."

"Where do I deliver payment?"

"I've got an account number." Knight nodded to Davis, who sat beside him, listening to a headset plugged into a recording box that was, in turn, tethered to the hotel landline. Davis handed Knight a printout of bank accounts known to belong to the Jemaah Islamiyah terrorist organization. One of the account numbers was highlighted. Knight dictated the digits to Lee.

"The money will be transferred in the morning," Lee replied, pleased.

Knight hung up, taking a deep breath as he absorbed what he had just done. Once the money was transferred, the triads would have unwittingly financed a high-profile Islamic terror group, placing them in the crosshairs of every major intelligence agency worldwide.

"How much did that call cost you, if you don't mind my asking?"

"Ten or twenty million spread over the next five years."

Knight unceremoniously tossed the plastic trash bag containing the evidence from Cobus's apartment to Davis. As Davis glanced in the bag, Knight added, "That's everything you need on their operation. Just leave me out of it."

Davis closed the bag. "Why are you doing this?"

"Because I'm an idiot."

Davis kept his eyes on Knight. "*Really*. Why?"

"I got into this job to protect animals, not kill them." Knight finished his drink as he considered, suddenly feeling a sense of camaraderie with the earnest son of a bitch sitting beside him. "Same reason you left your Wall Street job to join the CIA. I guess we all have to draw a line somewhere."

"That was just bullshit," Davis replied. Knight looked up, caught off guard. "I was laid off when the tech bubble burst. I needed any job I could get, and the agency needed folks with finance experience."

Knight laughed in spite of himself at having been conned.

Davis smiled as he recharged their glasses from a fresh mini bottle of scotch. "Like I said, I have bad luck."

CHAPTER 48
THE KINGPIN

"I need to know I can count on your vote," Lee told the two Afro-Caribbean men seated opposite him in his limousine. The men wore loose-fitting linen suits, and their faces were creased with concern over the potential political fallout of accepting Lee's proposal.

The CITES convention was only ten days away, and Lee still needed four more votes to ensure that the legislation allowing the regulated farming of endangered wildlife would be approved. Lee had arranged a dozen of these cloak-and-dagger meetings in the months leading up to the convention. CITES was like FIFA: every country got a vote, and those votes could be a valuable commodity for the entrepreneurial and unscrupulous. And like FIFA, the Caribbean proved to be a target-rich environment for those looking to buy votes. Today, Lee needed to lock in the Bahamas.

"It is going to look bad when an island nation with no tigers or rhinos votes for legal trade," one of the two delegates said.

"Half your island neighbors will be voting with you, and the money I am offering should offset any discomfort."

The moment was interrupted as two sedans raced up alongside them in traffic. They pulled to a stop diagonally in front of the limo, hemming it in. Lee looked back to see two more sedans pulled in behind them.

Outside, a man wearing a suit approached. He held a badge up to the window. Lee rolled down the window and addressed the officer in Chinese, inquiring about the nature of the stop. He hoped this would be a routine traffic stop and the men could continue their business in short order.

But this was no routine stop.

———

Two weeks earlier, the US Central Intelligence Agency had contacted the Hong Kong Triad Bureau. As part of an ongoing investigation, the United States had uncovered a complex and coordinated animal-trafficking operation involving Hong Kong and Macau. Rather than push for an extradition—which they would never get—the Americans had decided just to pass along the info to the Chinese so they could handle the matter internally. Inspector Tsao was put in charge of corroborating the American dossier, which proved to be a treasure trove of information about the Sun Yee On's activities and all the key players in the syndicate. Today, Tsao would collect his scalp.

"So you are the new *dai lo* now that your little brother is dead," Tsao told Lee. "I never thought the top triad would be stupid enough to set foot in Hong Kong."

The Bahamians inside the limo watched in shock as Tsao's men yanked Lee from the car and slammed him on the hood. Tsao twisted Lee's arms behind his back and cuffed him as Lee continued to protest his innocence. "I've done nothing!" he insisted.

Though Tsao would normally ignore such protestations, Lee was unlike the other scalps he had taken. Lee fancied himself a mastermind who could not only break the law but also *bend* it to his will. And Tsao wanted Lee to know he would suffer. "Our friends tell us you've been in the market for endangered tigers. Last time I checked, that's still very, very illegal."

CHAPTER 49
THE FINDINGS

Kevin Davis stood before the Counterterrorism Center's ranking brass as he delivered his findings. Projected behind him was a map of the world, with lines tracking the flow of global wildlife from their sources ("Production," as it was labeled) in the developing regions of Asia and Africa, through smuggling routes in Southeast Asia ("Distribution"), and on to the end users in the industrialized world ("Consumption"). It was a tangled web of warlords, cartels, corrupt politicians, and private zoos spanning dozens of countries. The eyes in the room were all drawn to names they had grown familiar with over the course of the Global War on Terrorism: Boko Haram in Nigeria, the Lord's Resistance Army in Uganda, and Jemaah Islamiyah in Indonesia.

"... In exchange for the endangered tigers, the triads deposited three million in a known Jemaah Islamiyah bank account," Davis revealed with rehearsed confidence. "We can therefore determine that animal trafficking syndicates are like any other type of trans-national criminal organization, with dollars spent on illegal wildlife not only financing terrorist acts, but also directly supporting murders, human trafficking, drug smuggling, arms dealing, and governmental corruption, making these organizations an imminent threat to global security." Though all these conclusions were true, the particular case study Davis had presented was itself a fabrication. But no one needed to know about that little detail.

Ron Nelson, Davis's nemesis, reliably jumped in to discredit his work. "Forget global security. Are they a threat to *national* security?"

Before Davis could respond, Director Wilkes chimed in. "Ease off, Nelson. I think the Sumatra link has that covered."

Director Wilkes then turned his undivided attention to Davis. "What about other players on the field? How many more trafficking syndicates are out there?"

Davis wanted to get a sense of Wilkes's body language to judge how hard he still needed to sell, but he could barely make out the director's silhouette through the blinding light of the projector. "To be honest, sir, we're in uncharted waters. No one knows how many players there are. But what we do know from Chinese law enforcement is that since the triads were apprehended, the street value of rhino horn hasn't gone up a penny. I would have assumed the reduction in supply would drive up the price, but this data indicates there are still plenty of other suppliers keeping a steady flow of product on the street. We've only begun to scratch the surface here."

Davis finished, his words hanging in the air as Wilkes considered his fate. Davis switched off the projector to gauge the director's reaction, but all he could see was a man who was generally exasperated from fighting an asymmetric global war on infinite fronts.

Wilkes finally spoke. "Phenomenal work, Davis."

Davis didn't have a chance to breathe a sigh of relief before Wilkes continued. "Unfortunately, resources are always tight."

Davis suddenly felt naked in front of the room—again. Soon, the meeting would adjourn and they would begin mocking him the second they rose from their seats. The jerks wouldn't even pay him the courtesy of waiting until he was out of earshot.

"But I would like to put four agents under you," Wilkes continued, to Davis's surprise. "Would that be enough to get your Animal Trafficking Section up and running?"

Davis lit up with a smile so big, he felt that his face might crack. His luck had finally turned.

CHAPTER 50
THE CAGE

MIAMI, FLORIDA

Knight wore a tan linen suit as he pressed through the crowd of tourists glistening with sweat and sunscreen in the muggy midday sun. The tail end of SafariWorld's summer season was back in full swing, and things had returned to normal, thanks in large part to the fact the guests had no idea how grave the outbreak at the zoo had been. Or that the tiger deaths were connected to the deadly outbreak in Laos that had claimed thirty-seven human lives in the previous weeks. Those links were never made, nor could they be if Knight and Davis's gambit was going to hold water. As far as the world was concerned, the infected cub had come from a national park in Sumatra, via Macau.

The insurance man found his way to the railing of the tiger exhibit. Beside him, scores of tourists observed the adult cats in their pens. They all had been procured through reputable suppliers and rescue shelters Knight could personally vouch for. They seemed as happy as they could be, given that they were wild animals that had evolved to roam thousands of miles in a natural habitat they would never see.

"Mr. Knight."

He turned as Kate Henley, the mammal curator, joined him at the railing. Knight had been expecting her. The investigation was over, and he had come to SafariWorld today to close it out. But at the moment of Ms. Henley's arrival, Knight wasn't thinking about the insurance claim at all. He was focused on the pen that once held the infected tiger cub, which was now empty.

"Where's the cub?" he asked.

"We put it down."

The news hit him hard. His eyes lingered on the large toy ball the cub had left behind.

"You could have kept it isolated."

Kate shrugged off the cold reality. "It wasn't worth the money. At the end of the day, this place is a business. It's all about the bottom line," she lamented.

Knight struggled to process the death of the innocent young creature. He sensed that in some cosmic way, he was complicit in its annihilation.

"What did your investigation turn up?" she asked.

Knight wanted to accuse her of the irrefutable fact that she had bought the tiger with the full knowledge that it had been illegally trafficked. He wanted to tell her that the people who sold it to her had also sold young girls and narcotics—that she was personally supporting murderers. But Knight and Davis had built a house of lies to take down the Sun Yee On triad, and none of the lies could be walked back or the whole thing would collapse.

"The cub was a genuine Sumatran."

Kate Henley's look of surprise at the cub's authenticity

confirmed Knight's theory that she, like everyone, was full of shit. "The distributor had links to an Indonesian terror group," he added. Knight let the revelation sit long enough to make her uncomfortable. "But there's no way you could have known that."

Knight took an envelope from his jacket. "This should cover everything." Kate opened the envelope and glimpsed the "10" followed by six more zeros.

"That information about the distributor—can we keep it between us?" Kate asked. "It would be bad for business."

Knight did his best to mask his disdain. "Just make sure any new tigers come through legitimate AZA suppliers."

Knight turned his back and walked away. As he made his way to the exit, he passed dozens of exhibits—a veritable Noah's Ark representing all the charismatic megafauna the world had to offer. The human families maneuvered to see the majestic animals, each of the *Homo sapiens* falling in love with a natural world that neither they nor the animals had ever experienced.

It was a paradoxical desire: wanting to possess something wild.

CHAPTER 51
DUSK

Oupa plodded toward the water's edge, the mud slurping with each step of his stumpy feet. Since his mother died, one of the tall primates who roamed the park had taken over for her, feeding him milk from a shiny clear gourd. But as the young rhino matured, his diet had switched to the soft grasses that carpeted his home.

The little bump on Oupa's nose had now grown into the shape of a small thorn, and the boy found the thorn useful for unearthing the delicious roots that lay hidden in the red earth. Though he occasionally crossed paths with the giant rhinos who shared the land, Oupa tended to keep his distance. He had been charged once by a dominant male protecting his territorial claim, and though the adult had ceased his pursuit as soon as Oupa squealed and fled, it had left the youngster with a healthy fear of conflict. And besides, there was enough food at Kruger for everyone without having to compete with the big boys.

The sun dipped behind the trees, and after a long day of foraging, Oupa was now feeling dehydrated. As he lowered his mouth to the water, he scanned the pond curiously. Normally, at this time of day he would be joined by a least a few impala or wildebeests who not only were thirsty but also liked the security of having a large herbivore with a sharp horn to protect them from carnivores like lions and cheetahs. But this evening, Oupa noticed, he was all alone.

———

The pair of legs moved swiftly through the miombo woodland near the Mozambique border. A second pair of legs followed. The men had come across the damp, grassy rhino droppings earlier in the day and been following the footprints of their source ever since.

As they approached the water hole, the men slowed, suspecting they would soon encounter their quarry. The young rhino spotted them through the brush. It turned, meeting the larger man's eyes.

"He remembers you," Lawrence said, standing behind Cobus.

Wearing a T-shirt and jeans, Cobus approached Oupa cautiously to avoid causing any fear. As he stood before the young rhino, he extended his hand, gently caressing the coarse skin on his cheek. Oupa tilted his head, nuzzling Cobus's hand.

"Are you sure you want to take the job in Kenya?" Lawrence asked. "You could stay."

Though South Africa had always been home, Cobus had corrupted it with his darkness, and he would need to atone for his sins in exile.

He had hoped to use the money he had made selling horn to the triads to start his own private reserve, but those plans had fallen through when the Chinese police searched his safe house and discovered not only the $2 million in cash hidden in the ceiling, but a large amount of strychnine and rhino-horn residue. There was nothing connecting Cobus's true identity to the apartment, but the money was inexorably linked to his crime, and he'd had to leave it unclaimed at the police station.

Cobus had since taken on a contract to do anti-poaching operations near the Ugandan border in western Kenya, where a warlord's army had been decimating the animal population. If war was going to follow Cobus, he would take it to a place where a war was needed.

"Keep him safe," he told Lawrence as he looked in the youngster's dark, soulful eyes. "If not the others, at least this one."

Lawrence nodded in silent promise.

Cobus's fingers retreated from the boy's face, and he stood a moment longer in silent communion with Oupa. As the sky began to shift from orange to purple, Oupa turned and lumbered away from the water hole. Cobus knelt, placing his hand on the earth as the boy disappeared in the dying light of the miombo.

ACKNOWLEDGMENTS

Many thanks to my friends at Appian Way and Warner Bros. who supported the research and writing of this book, and to Leonardo DiCaprio, whose desire to tell an animal trafficking story set this whole journey in motion.

I am deeply grateful to my good friend Damien Mander, founder of the International Anti-Poaching Foundation. He took me to the front lines and beyond in South Africa and Mozambique. And to Sean Willmore (Thin Green Line Foundation) for helping me understand so much. The passion both these men have for protecting wildlife and rangers has been an inspiration throughout.

Huge thanks to Karl Ammann for taking me along on his undercover investigations in Southeast Asia and for connecting me with his local fixers, who must remain anonymous for security reasons.

Thanks to my agent Mel Berger, my editor Michael Carr, and the good folks at Blackstone Publishing for believing in this book.

Big salute to author Josh Conviser for all the encouragement and advice.

Warm thanks to all those who took the time to educate me: Dr. Jane Goodall, Dr. Matthew Frieman, Dr. Cindy Harper, Dr. Andrew Rassweiler, Crawford Allan, Peter Lodge, and Chris Shepherd. To the many officers from CIA, Homeland Security, and US Fish and Wildlife who helped me get it right, I can't thank you enough. To all those I have left unnamed, please know that you are appreciated more than you can know.

Thank you to my mother, Dr. Lila Thorsen, for the notes and encouragement early in the process.

Finally, I owe my greatest debt of gratitude to my wife, Stacey, for all the support and for doing double-duty with our two young children while I was on the road researching this book.